Joyce Stranger's readers will be fascinated by this sympathetic yet gripping novel. She draws a picture of the English countryside—its animals and people—with the clarity and sensitivity that are her hallmark.

The story tells of a Collie man who is blinded but must learn to live again through the eyes of a Labrador Retriever. Steve, used to training dogs, should handle a guide dog with ease. He couldn't have been more wrong...

Also by Joyce Stranger

and published by Corgi Books

A Walk in the Dark

Joyce Stranger

CORGI BOOKS

A DIVISION OF TRANSWORLD PUBLISHERS LTD

A WALK IN THE DARK

A CORGI BOOK 0 552 11210 0

Originally published in Great Britain
by Michael Joseph Ltd.

PRINTING HISTORY
Michael Joseph edition published 1978
Corgi edition published 1979

Corgi Books are published by
Transworld Publishers Ltd.,
Century House, 61–63 Uxbridge Road,
Ealing, London W5 5SA

Set, printed and bound in Great Britain by
Cox & Wyman Ltd., Reading

Dedicated to
Herta Ryder
with love

This book is fiction. None of the people or the places exist; the Guide Dog Centre is also invented; and the general background to the training, though the bulk of the dog training is based on fact. I owe thanks to those at Bolton Centre for Guide Dogs who showed me round and helped with information as well as to my brother David who provided medical information that I used. I also owe thanks to all those friends in the dog world who have taught me about training my own dogs and given me a deeper insight into the skills required to make a good dog.

Chapter 1

Steve Drake whistled as he climbed the hill.

He was on top of the world, and would not have changed places with any man. Lig, his Collie dog, turned his head to see if he were wanted, but Steve was off duty, playing truant, relaxing from his busy life. Lig raced on, a speeding black and white figure, dark against the grey rocks and sparse grass, intent on a fox trail that twisted up the mountain.

Steve grinned as he watched the dog. Lig was the best Collie he had ever had, a wise, steady, sensible fellow, now six years old. He knew his dog well, and the dog knew his master, and constantly checked on him, watchful, making sure that Steve was never out of sight.

Steve sat on a rounded boulder to eat his midday snack. He was a tall man, well built, his skin weathered by the constant wind on the hill. His grey eyes held more expression than his face, often betraying his feelings, though his words rarely revealed them. His thick curly hair grew in sidewhiskers down his cheeks, but was well styled and lay neat against his head.

1

He glanced below him, satisfaction in his eyes. The biggest field on his farm was busy with ewes and their lambs. There were several with triplets, and a record number of twins. Moreover there was no sign of the mysterious twin lamb disease that was plaguing some of his neighbours and that saw off both lambs and ewes. Not one of his ewes had lost a lamb this year.

He looked down to the home field, where his cottage snuggled into the edge of the hill. It had once been a tied cottage, on his father's land, but Andrew had given it to his son, along with half his holding. Andrew needed to take life more easily now, but he would never give up entirely. He had been a farmer all his life, born on a farm, bred on a farm, and he would die in the cowshed, he sometimes said, with the big boisterous laugh that Steve still regarded as his father's hallmark.

It was a good life.

Dark trees ranged the mountain and swept down to the loch. The sand glittered silver in the sunlight, and, on the far island, shadowed by cloud, the ruins of an old castle reared against the sky. The island had a history of dire deeds; of men who raped and pillaged and killed, sweeping out of the night in their boats to raid the mainland, leaving behind them legends of disaster, and tales of ghosts that keened and cried through the night.

The clouds fled on, chased by a boisterous wind that ruffled the loch. There was no hint of the murk of history on the bright stones now. Steve wished he could paint, could record the changing colours and the breathtaking lines of the land, to look at when winter nights came swift and dark, and he was penned by four walls, longing for the wide open spaces.

He looked down again to his own fields. The lambs were romping, small, muscular bodies rock hard with health. They chased, and leaped, played tag, and then remembered with abrupt suddenness that they were babies, and Mum was nowhere near.

They raced in circles, bleating.

The shrill baas of the lambs were echoed by the deeper notes of the ewes. Steve grinned. He never tired of watching

2

the reunions, seeing each mother recognize her own lamb, some of them parting their legs to facilitate feeding, as each lamb tugged at the full udders, small tails wagging busily.

The sheep were thriving. Spring was total satisfaction. He could never do a paper job at a desk, or work in an office, or take part in any occupation that did not show a new life as part of its fulfilment.

Lig had exhausted himself.

He came back to lie at Steve's feet, tongue lolling, panting. Steve put down a hand, and the dog lifted his head, ears back in submission, asking for a caress. Steve stroked the hard little head. The Collie was in the peak of condition, his coat new-grown after moulting, the black gleaming, the white as clean as the fleece of any newborn lamb, the prick ears alert and watchful, the eyes dark and brilliant with eagerness.

Only recently Steve had been thrilled to be invited by the BBC to appear in the television programme 'One Man and His Dog' which would be filmed in September. Steve reckoned he and Lig had more than a fair chance of winning the Television Trophy. The dog was already a champion in his own right. What was more, he was wise and sensible beyond any dog that Steve knew.

It would be a year to remember. He stretched himself, admiring the may blossom in the hedges. In the autumn Mara, his fiancée, would return from America. Plans were already well ahead for the wedding. The hotel was booked; the church was booked; the guests were chosen and his mother was busy making a wedding dress fit for a princess. There was only one small flaw. His mother was not really well, though no one seemed able to find out exactly what was wrong. Plans for the wedding kept her excited, and helped her to forget her ill health.

Mara was small and slim and elegant, dark hair a dusky cloud around her face, dark eyes always laughing. She was a farmer's daughter, but she taught in a school, and this year she had been offered an exchange visit with a school in Texas. They should have married in the spring, but it was too good an opportunity to miss. Steve had insisted that she go and the wedding was postponed for several months to give her the chance of a lifetime.

Her last letter to him was in his pocket now. It was filled with entertaining little details of her life, and of the children in her classes. She had visited the most splendid ranch, where the cattle were counted in thousands and the acreage was unbelievable. She had visited another home where they bred Morgans, the sturdy horses beloved by Americans, and kept sheep; and she came to grief with language, with words like sidewalk and pocketbook; and for breakfast she ate English muffins that no one in England would ever recognize.

There were white clouds on the blue peaks that towered into the sky. An eagle was soaring, high overhead. His shadow swept across the ground, and Lig roused himself and barked defiance, warning the bird that he was on guard and would fight to defend his sheep.

Steve hoped it would not try for one of his lambs. There were hares and rabbits in plenty to feed its maw and those of its mate and the young one that must now have hatched, in the eyrie above the cliff on the Dragon Mountain. Once Steve had climbed the cliff, and heard the young one screaming for food, and then been forced to climb down, faster than he had wished, as the parents swooped with angry wings and stabbing beaks, raking towards his eyes. He had no desire to risk blindness. He could not imagine a worse fate.

The ground around him was starred with tiny white flowers.

Lig chased a bright butterfly.

It would soon be time to move, but Steve had a few minutes longer, and idleness was a rare luxury. He re-read Mara's letter. It brought her vividly to mind. The cottage, known by the unlikely name of The Nunneries, was almost ready for her. Steve had been working on it all year, with his father's help and that of any of the men who had time to spare and a desire to try his hand at building.

They had added two rooms to the original two up and two down of the old building. It had not been easy. The walls were over two feet thick, the stone uneven and pitted, and the old plaster rotten. Tiny windows were recessed deep.

4

Now there was a new bathroom, with a spare bedroom above it. He had built a staircase, that twisted out of the little useless room that had once been used as a feed room. Beyond the morning-room he had made an archway into the big dairy, and turned that into a kitchen. He had added a utility room for the deep-freeze and the washing machine and drier that was a wedding present from Tom Hastings, Mara's father.

The old barn had been replaced by a long low sitting-room, its windows overlooking the hills. They would be able to sit in the evening and watch the sun westering and revel in the sunsets, in the cloud on the mountain, bronze-burnished, or scarlet-edged, the sun dying each night in streamers of brilliant colour. There was nothing like the sunsets over the Western Isles.

When dusk came they would see the eerie mist that hid the castle, and hear the owls crying.

Steve's wedding present to Mara was to be a garden. She loved flowers. He had enclosed part of the field, building a warm brick wall to hold the sun; making a rockery outside the window of the new sitting-room; blending conifers to form a windbreak, the foliage multi-coloured; gold, blue-green, bright green, grey-green, a satisfying mixture that held the eye now, although the trees were tiny. Later, it would be a splendid sight.

He had always had an eye for colour, for shape and for the lie of the land. It was fun to plan. It was rewarding to build. It was a tremendous sense of achievement to see the outline forming. By the time Mara came home he would have a garden ready for her. He had paved a space against the wall, and planted clematis behind it.

He planted for scent, banking roses that would grow into splendid bushes, bearing vivid flowers. He chose carefully, avoiding those likely to be plagued by mildew or rust or to spoil in the rain. He had only the best; those with long buds, bringing fragrance to the garden.

He had painted the cottage white; with white walls that were a foil for climbers. He found an old knocker, a horse's head inside a horseshoe, clinging to an abandoned door in a junkyard. Now, polished until it shone, he could see the

5

bright wink as the sun caught it, even from here. There was nothing wrong with his sight.

Mara had chosen the curtain material before she left for Texas. His mother had made them; and his sister, visiting one day, had hung them for him and, for her wedding gift, had made matching cushions for the chairs.

The field beyond the house was bright with cowslips. A bee buzzed companionably in the heather. Lig, suddenly impatient, stood, his tail waving, knowing it was time to return to the farm. Steve reluctantly pocketed the remains of his lunch, and stood too, aware that he had lingered too long.

He whistled the dog to heel and walked down the mountainside, aware that the future held even more than this, and knowing that life was good.

The phone was ringing as he walked into the house.

He lifted the receiver.

He heard his mother's voice.

'Steve? I'm sorry, love, I don't feel too good. I promised Dad I'd pick up the freezer meat, but I don't think I ought to drive. It's all cut up, waiting at the shop. Some of it's yours. Have you time to fetch it for me? Dad changed his mind and went to the Beast Sale after all.'

Steve laughed.

Yesterday his father had definitely not been going to the market. Today it was obviously a different story. Andrew Drake was as changeable as any woman at times. Steve hadn't time but he would make it. His mother prepared his meals and did his laundry and she was busy with sewing that Mara would have done if she had stayed at home.

He could look over the lambs later.

One needed attention to a cut on its leg. Some fool had left a bottle in the field and one of the little beasts had trodden on it and smashed it, and cut itself badly just above the hoof. There were always youngsters with thorn twigs and bramble ends tangled in their fleeces. They tried to crawl through the hedge or jump over it, and ended in trouble. He seemed to breed miniature Houdinis. He needed eyes at the back of his head, but Lig made up for the lack of those.

He stopped at the gate for a word with Jack Farthing from the garage. Jack had a new young bitch with him, a Golden Retriever. She was friendly with puppyhood, and tried to eat Lig's tail. Lig, dignified, retreated out of reach, and she pulled on her leash.

'What do you think of her?' Jack asked, eager for praise for his new acquisition, even though he knew very well what Steve would say.

Steve patted her and laughed.

'You ought to get yourself a dog,' he said. 'There's only one breed. You know me. I'm a Collie man, through and through. I wouldn't have anything else as a present. Nothing in the world can touch them. She doesn't look bad, though,' he added, aware that he was being thoroughly tactless.

'A Collie's not much use for the gun,' Jack said. 'Every man to his taste. It's no use trying to convert you. You always were pigheaded, knowing better than everyone else, even at school.'

Jack whistled at Lig and patted him.

'I'd buy him off you, mind, at any price you cared to name.'

Lig returned to Steve.

'There isn't a man in the world who could give me enough for him,' Steve said. He signalled to the dog and Lig, knowing he was to stay and guard the yard, went to lie on the doorstep, watching as Steve climbed into the heavy old estate car that did duty as a runabout and was almost a vintage model.

'So you don't like my bitch,' Jack said, persistent, and trying to annoy.

Steve leaned out and grinned.

'Wrong colour; wrong shape; though if you like goldies I reckon she's probably a good one,' he said, relenting. He had always teased Jack.

'None so blind as those that won't see,' Jack said, and lifted a hand and went off, the pup dancing beside him.

Steve watched and shook his head. Jack never could handle a dog. His always rioted. He drove off, down the hill, changing gear for the corner, aware of Lig's eyes watching as he went. The dog hated being left behind, but he didn't want the Collie in the car when he had a load of fresh meat. Not even Lig could refrain from stealing under such circumstances.

Steve drove expertly and well, watching for trouble, ready to anticipate the actions of others at all times. He kept his mind on the job. He pulled in only once, to look at the new lambs in the field behind Jack Farthing's garage. The ewes here were later than his own. Some had not yet given birth. He assessed them expertly. There were signs of a neglected flock. The lambs were curious, and stopped grazing to look at the big man who leaned on the five-barred gate, unable to take his eyes off any new stock, rating its virtues, weighing its faults, and watching all the time for a promising ram to upgrade his own flock.

The freezer meat was ready for him.

The butcher, who, like most of the village, farmed, himself, in a small way, keeping store cattle, helped Steve pack the boxes into the back of the estate car.

'Almost forgot,' he said, as they stood by the shop door, while Steve foraged in his wallet for the money. 'They need a sheep judge at the Agricultural show in the autumn. Alec McGregor was due to judge but he's had a slight heart attack and been told to take it easy. I promised to ask if you would step in for us. It's more than three weeks after your wedding. You aren't planning a month's honeymoon, are you?'

'I'm planning a longer one than that,' Steve said, grinning. 'But not away from home. I'd be pleased to judge. Never can resist the sheep, and I'd be there anyway. This way gives me an excuse to go over them. I might find the ram I want that day. Mara will steward for me. Time I began to teach her about sheep.'

'Fine,' the butcher said. He watched Steve climb into the estate car. 'It's done you proud, hasn't it? Must be almost a veteran.'

'It is,' Steve said. 'All the same, it's time I turned it in. I had a spot of brake bother the other day, but Jack had it in and says there's nothing much wrong. It's just a feeling, that's all. Be seeing you.'

He slipped into gear. The children were coming out of

8

school, running gaily along the village street. He changed down for the sharp bend and the steep slope past the school. A car drove out of the school yard, and he jabbed his brakes.

Nothing happened.

He grabbed the handbrake and rammed it on, but the hill was too steep for that to hold. He saw the children's faces in the window of the tiny mini. He saw the woman's terrified face as she put on speed, but he knew it would not take her out of his way.

He swung the wheel.

The car skidded, brakeless, out of control, to hit the wall with a crash that echoed right along the village street. The young mother hid her face, shuddering, unable to bring herself to get out of the car and look.

The last sound Steve heard was the scream of a child.

And then there was only darkness.

Chapter 2

Life changed, all the time.

Anna Leigh stood at the door of her farmhouse, looking out over the fields. Time had put weight on her, and the once blueblack hair was shadowed with grey.

Winter had almost gone. There were catkins on the hazel, yellow, holding sunshine in their swaying stems. Monster, the biggest of the ducks, had eggs beneath her; she was one of Dan's promised Muscovies. Anna thought back, remembering.

It was fifteen years since the Leigh farm had vanished under the bulldozers that carved the motorway. Compton Hall was a memory, though there generations of her husband's family had spent their lives. She looked at the home that had grown from two derelict cottages. They had rebuilt, had extended, had changed it to a comfortable farmhouse residence; had acquired more land.

She had hated it so much at first. Had hated life without animals. Then somehow, they had acquired the nucleus of their present stock. She had missed the children, fast growing away from her, first at boarding school, and then at college, now branched out on their own.

Philip was married; a veterinary surgeon working as assistant in a busy suburban practice. Lisetta had renamed herself Lisa, and was researching one of the rarer crippling diseases in a hospital in Hampstead. Philip's life was dominated by the problems of small animals; Lisa's by a complex private life, keeping at a distance the men who wanted to marry her and take her away from the job she loved, to imprison her by their firesides in a small suburban home, where her life would be dominated by the problems of the neighbours and perhaps of her own small children. She did not enjoy babies.

Anna turned to look at the house, shaded by the trees beyond it. Setter's Dene. It was a name now famous for dogs. Not only the lovely Annally Alsatians that she had bred on from Zelie and Amba and Panther, but for the litters of Guide Dogs that were destined for the Centre, only five miles away in the adjacent town. Dave Masterson, the Head Trainer, had given her the first bitch when she had volunteered to help, as there was no one at the Centre with time to look after a whelping bitch and a new litter.

She walked over to throw a ball for Marcus, the big stud dog, great-grandson of her first Marcus, who had two championship certificates and needed a third to make him a full Champion. She did not know if she would ever have the heart to show him again. Life had no savour now.

It took all her time to keep Setter's Dene going. Six months before, Dan had come in from exercising a new mare; had come in wearily saying he was getting old; the ride had knocked all the stuffing out of him and he was exhausted and going to lie down. She made him a cup of tea, thinking nothing of it. He often complained that he was tired, and he was nearing sixty, and farming was a tough job.

When she went into the bedroom, she found him dead.

One moment, and everything ended, just like that. Somehow she survived the weeks that followed, complicated by the unnerving need for the police and for an inquest as Dan had never thought to see a doctor. She lived each day on its own, getting through it as best she could; writing routine letters; doing routine jobs. Philip came home for the first two weeks, and Gina told her she would be a grandmother soon. Dan would have loved a grandchild. Just as he would have taken pride in Marcus if he became a Champion.

Never count apples, Dan always said. Anna had always counted apples; making plans all the time, and her plans had been for the two of them. Now, she had to learn how to survive on her own.

Sam, her Golden Retriever, came to her, and rubbed against her, asking to be remembered. He hated to be ignored. He brought her gloves to her. Asking her to take him for a walk, somewhere, anywhere, to break the monotony. Perhaps if she walked in the woods some of the despair would vanish. There might be primroses.

A voice called over the fence.

Susan, the blind girl from down the road, was having a few days' holiday. She opened the gate, her Guide Dog Zanta pulling ahead of her, eager to greet Anna, who had bred the bitch in her kennels. One of the first of the litters for Dave, the Head Trainer in the Guide Dog Centre, who had been a great friend of Dan's. Sue released Zanta, who raced to romp with Sam and steal his quoit from him. The two dogs stood nose to nose, tugging at it, neither willing to let go.

'I've come to tea,' Susan said. 'Is there any cherry cake?'

'No cherry cake.' Anna's voice was affectionate. She had known Susan for fifteen years and still found it hard to believe that Sue was twenty-seven. In spite of her blindness, caused by an accident at birth, Sue was one of the prettiest girls Anna had ever seen. It was hard too to believe the vivid blue eyes were sightless. Being blind had never affected Susan. She found pleasure in so many tiny things. She adored visiting Anna, playing with the pups and the kittens, walking round the farm, eager to handle new young stock, to kneel to catch the scent of a flower, to finger the fragile petals.

'Come and see Dave's new litter,' Anna said. She led the way to the stable block, where, in the end stall, Mellie, a pretty little bitch, great-granddaughter of Anna's first brood

12

bitch, was nursing a litter fathered by Sam. Dave was sure a first generation cross would be hardy and intelligent. The litter was an experiment.

The pups were three weeks old. Old enough to come into the house. Old enough to begin handling and socializing so that they learned to trust humans from the start. Soon they would go to the puppy walkers, all except one, which was destined for a man newly blinded, a Scottish farmer. Dave had told Anna about him some days before.

There was a glint of light in the water trough. Anna bent down. Her new spectacles lay under the water. Sam, seeing her look at him, decided it would be wiser to disappear. Anna never knew what she would find next in the yard. Sam retrieved everything he could carry, in spite of his six years of age.

'One of these pups is gorgeous,' Anna said, leaning down to stroke the soft little head. 'The one I'm keeping. I've named her Gemma. She's far ahead of the rest of the litter and can stand already. Her eyes opened first too, and she's always the first at the milk bar. The only trouble will be that I won't want to part with her when the time comes for her to go away and be trained.'

She lifted the pup and put her in Susan's arms. Susan held the small animal against her.

'Darling Anna,' she said, her voice eager. 'Don't ever leave here, will you? I couldn't bear to think of someone else in the cottage; and I couldn't bear to lose contact with your pups. People who don't like animals just don't know what they're missing.'

'I doubt if we could change them,' Anna said. Susan's face was always more alive when she handled small creatures, whether they were kittens or pups. 'It was always hard to make people understand how much I missed Compton Hall when we first came here. "You'll get used to being without animals," they said. "Fancy being tied every day by cattle; and milking. You'll be able to rest."'

She laughed.

'Who wants to rest? I want to die on my feet, not sitting in a chair for thirty years, slowly rotting.'

'Don't die yet. I can't get used to Dan being dead. I expec

13

to hear his voice every time I come.'

Mellie was whining for her pup, sure it had been removed from the nest for far too long. Susan squatted and felt for the other pups, and laid the little one gently among them. Satisfied, the bitch returned to nurse them.

'I can't get used to being without Dan either,' Anna said. 'You don't realize, till you're left alone, how much the other partner did. There are so many things I can't do.'

She didn't add that the evenings alone were desolate. She had no desire to burden Susan with her own cares. Sue had enough to do, with her job, and with her mother, who had taken refuge, now her daughter was grown, in constant illness, using a heart murmur as a weapon to keep Susan at home.

Zanta, back in harness and knowing that Anna would give her a piece of cheese, was pulling towards the house.

'She's a slave driver,' Susan said, obeying the tug on the harness. 'And she's greedy. She knows what's waiting. I oughtn't to let her get away with it, but it's the only time she does pull. Can you manage to keep Setter's Dene going without Dan?'

Nobody but Sue ever spoke of Dan. Most of Anna's friends seemed to have rubbed him out of their minds, and if she spoke of him, anxiously changed the subject, not realizing her need to talk of the past, and prevent grief from destroying her. Susan seemed to understand, but then those blind from birth often had an extra sense about people. Anna had met others through Sue. Perhaps living with a permanent disability enabled them to recognize instinctive needs. Most people were over-civilized, and tried to pretend that death did not happen. On a farm, it happened all the time; and was taken for granted, a part of an inevitable cycle.

Anna found Zanta's cheese, and busied herself making coffee. Susan, sitting on the window seat, revelling in the warmth of the sun shining on her face, sat patient, used to waiting.

'I haven't worked it out yet,' Anna said. 'There isn't such a demand now for big dogs; I will have to breed smaller ones; perhaps Shelties and Westies. They don't eat much more

14

than a cat. Oddly, they sell at about the same price as the Alsatians. I'll have to find some way of adding to my income. Scott's asked me to have a tiny hospital ward here for any sick animals he treats whose owners can't cope. That will bring in a little, and most of it will be profit. It's mostly time that I need with them. I'm only just coming up for air. I've been coasting for the past few months. You don't seem to register what's happened. I keep expecting Dan to walk in, too. As if he'd been away on a long trip.'

Susan took her coffee cup, feeling for the table at her side, ensuring that it was safely away from the edge and that she couldn't knock it over. Anna, watching, admired the deft movements, born of a lifetime's practice.

'You've been baking,' Susan said. 'I can smell new bread. And something else. Is it hyacinths?'

'Blue hyacinths in a white bowl,' Anna said. 'And I bought new blue curtains, and I've redecorated the kitchen. It's brightened the place up. Dan always did the decorating, but I haven't made too bad a job of it.'

'Can the pups come in?' Susan asked. The pups would distract Anna and make her laugh. Sorrow was too constant a companion.

Anna went out with the big dog basket, and carried it back, with the squeaking pups inside. Mellie, anxious, followed close at heel, and carefully checked each head as if she were counting, when Anna put them on the newspaper-covered rug, beside the newly turned on electric fire. They had an infra-red lamp in the kennel still.

Susan knelt on the floor, to handle and stroke the puppies. Her desire was not entirely selfish. Most of these, they hoped, would become Guide Dogs, and as such they needed far more handling than most, being made, from the start, into happy sociable animals, able to go anywhere, used to all humans. Anna always handled her puppies every day, for some hours, before selling them, and this had made her an ideal breeder for Dave's purposes. He came over as often as he could to assess the litter. Often the duds could be weeded out at the start, and sold as pets to someone who did not need such perfect behaviour from their dog.

'There are lambs in the field beside our cottage,' Susan

said. 'I love listening to them.'

'Black faces and black knees this year; Tom must have bought a new ram,' Anna said. 'I've one of his orphans in the shed outside, needing a bottle soon.'

'I'll do it,' Susan said. 'Zanta needs a romp.'

She removed the harness, and Anna let her out of the kitchen door, to race with Sam, and chase Smoke up a tree. All her plush grey cats had the same name, one after another. Smoke never learned, though sometimes Anna wondered if he enticed the bitch. It was an unfailing game. Zanta left the tree, where she had been barking happily, and raced in circles after Sam, who was holding his quoit in his mouth. Presently he enticed her again to pull on it, and the two played an endless tug of war, round and round the yard.

Susan had picked the best pup out of the litter, and was holding her close.

'Is this Gemma? Scott told me about her when I took Zanta for her checks. He reckons it's one of the most intelligent pups he's ever seen.'

'He's right,' Anna said. 'She's a funny mite, even at this age, just beginning to look like a dog. She has a little old maid face, very wise looking, with two wrinkles across her forehead. She stares up at me, as if trying to work out what I'm thinking. She's always first at the milk, and she's fascinated by Sam. She crawls across to him and settles between his paws and stares up at him as if he's the most wonderful thing she's ever seen. I don't know if he's aware he's her father, but he's sweet with her. He looks so embarrassed if she tries to suck his paw.'

Anna leaned back in the big armchair. There were memories of Dan everywhere. He would have been assessing these pups, laughing with her over Gemma's quaintness, discussing the possible homes they would go to for walking, as there was always a long list to choose from, and it was essential that they should be handled carefully, and not spoiled for their future owners. Also they had to go to homes that would not agonize when they lost their pups. It was impossible not to become attached, and young children fretted too much when the dog that they had thought was theirs had to go away.

16

The sun had shifted, and was shining on the far field, though the big compound where the dogs were kept was now in shadow. She noticed for the first time that there was a hint of colour in the hedges; the white heather that Dan had planted for her was coming into flower, and bulbs were thrusting through the cold dark earth. She would have to dig her own vegetable patch this year. She couldn't make ends meet without the kitchen garden. It was time too to set the tomato seeds in the greenhouse.

It had rained for too long and the earth was sticky and would be impossible yet to dig. The pond was overfull; the little river was swollen to the top of its banks. During the past years she had learned that though it flooded the lower field, it never menaced the house. She had worried at first.

There was a lone magpie on the lawn.

One for sorrow. Anna often wished she were less superstitious. Dan had laughed at her. She knew the magpies were nesting now and there was often one alone. The other was probably already incubating eggs. She loved their bold colours and hated their predatory habits. More than one little bird had died in her garden, thrust through by that vicious stabbing beak. She only put food out under wire mesh, for the little birds to sample in peace.

Susan was a restful companion; making no demands, asking for little but the opportunity to play with the pups. Anna glanced out of the window. Sam and Zanta were exhausted, lying side by side in a patch of sunlight, panting. Her brood bitches were lying quiet, watching. Marcus was busily engaged with an enormous marrow bone, while Orry, his twelve-week-old son, in the compound beyond him, was dragging the kennel broom across the concrete. It was an awkward mouthful, off balance, and he struggled with it, making Anna laugh as she described the scene to Sue.

Gemma had left the rest of the litter and was sitting at Anna's foot, looking up at her, a quizzical expression on her face. The puppy was very forward for her age. Maybe cross-bred pups were. It was hard as yet to see whether she would favour Sam, and look like a Retriever, or show more of Mellie's Labrador traits. Mellie was a beautiful bitch, with an elegant little body, and an extremely pretty face. Her coat

17

was smooth and sleek, where Sam's was longer and waved, and her tail was smooth and otterlike, while Sam's was plumed.

Mellie, thoughtful, came forward, lifted Gemma in her mouth, and marched outside.

'Mellie says they've been in long enough,' Anna said. 'She's on her way back to the kennel with Gemma. She rations me. How many days have you off, Sue? They'll be ready for a lot of handling soon and I'm pushed to the limit here. I could do with some help.'

'I'm free for the rest of the week. Where's Racket's bottle? It is Racket, isn't it? Scott keeps me well informed!'

Scott Lewis, the vet, had formed a habit of dropping in on Susan and her mother, to ensure that all was well with Zanta. Susan couldn't see a thorn in a pad, or a tiny ulcer on a lip, and she would be lost if Zanta were too lame to walk, or became ill. They both lived in the same lane. Susan's mother was too preoccupied with her own ailments to notice the dog.

Susan took the bottle and went outside. She didn't need Zanta to show her round here. She had known Anna for a long time before she had a Guide Dog; and could find her way round the cottage and yard and the field beyond it without hesitation. She opened the shed door, to be greeted by a butting head and a noisy bleat. Then there was only the sound of sucking, and the small hard body pushing against her, anxious for contact, missing his mother.

Anna looked out of the window. The wind was bending the trees. There were overshadowing clouds, telling of rain soon. Time to put the dogs indoors. Time to make the feeds for all the animals. Time to take her mare inside. Time to shut the hens and ducks away. Time, soon, to shut the door and enclose herself in solitude, only Sam beside her while Mellie was engaged with pups, and the smoke grey cat on her knee, helping her endure the hours of darkness, her mind half on the television set, half on the future, not wanting to live in the present, or recall the past; when she had been secure, with Dan beside her, not imagining that half her life would be lived alone. Perhaps you grew used to that, in time.

18

She heard Susan remonstrating with the lamb. Susan lived in total darkness. Yet her voice was bright, her conversation was gay and there was never a trace of self-pity, even though her mother had enslaved her. Dora had always been possessive. Alec Randall had deserted her when he discovered his daughter was blind. He could not bear to look at the baby.

Susan brought the bottle indoors, and went to the sink to wash it through and leave it and the teat ready for Anna to sterilize.

'Dave wants me to live in at the Centre,' she said. 'But Mother won't hear of it. She couldn't manage on her own. She's not like you, Anna.'

I'm having to learn, Anna thought, but didn't say the words. She looked at the towering clouds, at the dogs outside, at the flowers just showing in the garden, things that Susan would never know or see, and rallied herself.

'Come back soon,' she said.

Zanta came for her harness, knowing Susan was leaving. She stood, patient, her eyes on Susan's face. No one else existed in Zanta's world.

'I'll be back,' Susan said, her cheek against Anna's face. Contact was important for her. Her hand took Anna's and she squeezed. 'Darling Anna. Don't be too sad.'

She was gone, and Anna wished she knew better how to hide her feelings. She could hide them from the rest of the world, but never from Sue. She sensed mood with the certainty of an animal, as Sam sensed it, spending the evenings bringing her presents. The gifts became absurd. A small mountain formed beside her chair, as he busied himself, bringing her his toys and his bones, her purse and her spectacle case, adding to the pile a small cushion, her hairbrush, an odd pair of tights, until at last she had to chuckle and, delighted that he had been noticed, he clowned in the middle of the room, chasing his tail like a puppy.

He came in now, head on one side, and barked.

Time for food.

He sat, expectant, ears pricked, eyes bright, as she mixed meat and meal and added broth to it. She still had the older pups, a litter of Alsatians almost ready for sale, to feed.

Her mare needed hay. She ought to sell Marble, but prices were low and she might go for dog meat and Anna couldn't bear that.

Worry returned as she mixed the dogs' meals. There seemed no way of adding to her income at all. There was the money from the investments Dan had made when they received the compensation for Compton Hall, but over fifteen years that had not accumulated; it had not even kept level with inflation, and seemed to buy less, every time her cheque came in. They had never carried a big insurance. Dan hadn't expected to die young.

There were the eggs to sell. And the chickens, but that was only pin money. One penny had to do the work of two, all the time. She sold dog food, and leads and combs and brushes; they didn't make a fortune, though it did ensure that people came to her door, and she wasn't entirely alone all day. Even a brief contact with a stranger helped.

The fence in the far field needed repairing. There were tiles off the roof, and the kitchen linoleum had a hole in it, near the door. It was dangerous; and Sue might trip. She could do without new clothes. Lisa was always tiring of hers and bringing them home for Jumble Sales; and she and Anna were the same size, though Anna could not bear the colours and styles her daughter chose; but dyed, or altered, they went with jeans or trews. She was becoming very clever at altering Lisa's castoffs.

The last visit of her day was to the whelping kennel with Mellie's food. She needed far more than the other bitches, with all those pups still to feed. They wouldn't be weaned for nearly another week. Mellie was suckling, her expression blissful. Anna counted heads. There should have been eight, but there were only seven. Gemma, the pride of her litter, was missing.

She set down the bowl.

Mellie stood up, shaking off puppies. Hunger made her impatient and she was ravenous. Anna looked down behind the box. There was the pup, stretched out in the corner, breathing unevenly, and coughing, her little mouth open as she tried to suck in air.

The pick of her litter. Why was it always the best? She

picked the pup up, cuddling her against her jersey to keep her warm, and raced indoors, to phone Scott and ask him to come quick, as she was sure the pup would die on her.

She had been counting apples again.

She would never learn.

She stood by the telephone, holding the small gasping body, remembering the words, Dan's voice ringing in her ears as clearly as if he were there.

Memory overwhelmed her.

Chapter 3

Scott Lewis had just begun his high tea when Anna phoned. 'Trouble,' he said, as he shrugged on his coat, and Roz, his wife, used to the procedure, took the plate, so that she could keep his food warm on the pan of hot water that stood always on the big Aga in her old-fashioned kitchen.

He couldn't keep Anna waiting. He knew that if she said urgent, she meant urgent. He and Dan had been friends, sometimes slipping out to the Saddler's Rest for an evening drink, and he missed Dan still. It seemed totally wrong to see the chair by the fire empty; not to have Dan coming to the gate to greet him, smiling, nor hear him turn his head and say to Anna, 'You're counting apples, again.' It had become a stock phrase in the village, over the years.

Now there was only Anna and since Dan had died, everything had seemed to go wrong.

Scott changed gear for the corner, and an old catch of Robert Burns came into his mind.

There's nae luck aboot the hoose,

There's nae luck at 'a,
There's nae luck aboot the hoose,
When the guid man's awa'.

This guid man was awa' for ever, Scott thought, as he
pulled up at the gate. He ran up the path. Anna had the door
open, the pup in her arms wrapped in a blanket.

Scott took the tiny animal. The soft fur was almost white,
the flap ears looked as if they would be Retriever-like, rather
than those of a Labrador. This pup, if she survived, would
favour Sam and not Mellie. The fur on the ears was golden
brown, a sign of her adult colouring. But it didn't look as if
she would survive to become adult.

The harsh breaths were quickening, as she struggled for
air.

Scott frowned down at the pup.

'I can't see a sign of anything wrong,' he said a moment
later. 'I thought it might be a twisted gut; but her tummy's
quite relaxed. Her throat . . . hang on, I'm a fool.'

He took the pup to the table, underneath the light, and
opened her mouth wide. He took a tiny pair of forceps from
his pocket. The pup was weakening; she did not struggle.
Her eyes stared up at Anna, agonized, and the shuddering
gasps racked her.

Scott put the forceps into the throat, and gently closed
them.

He brought them out.

'A piece of indiarubber. She must have found it on the
floor and chewed it, and it got stuck. She's better already.'

The gasping had stopped. The puppy flicked her ears.
Anna took her and put her on the hearthrug, beside the fire.
There was a whine at the back door, and a paw scraped the
paint.

'Mellie's missed her,' Anna said, letting the bitch into the
kitchen. Mellie grabbed the pup and nosed her and Gemma
began to feed.

'No trouble there,' Scott said.

'It was odd. Mellie hadn't missed her before. She was
outside the box, behind it, in the cold, and the bitch didn't
even care.'

'She may have thought she was dying and removed her from the litter,' Scott said.

'How did she know the pup was better?' Anna asked.

'They know. I've seen too much to wonder if I'm wrong,' Scott said. 'Their instincts are much sharper than ours. Like Sue. She lives her life far more intensely than we do. She notices things none of us see. She can tell you on a bright day whether she's facing north, south, east or west, if the sun is on her face, and she knows the time. Could you do that?'

'I expect Mellie could,' Anna said. 'People don't realize...'

She never needed to explain to Scott.

'She's right as rain now,' Scott said, looking down with satisfaction on the puppy.

'She's a corker,' Anna said. 'I couldn't bear to lose her. Tea, Scott?'

Scott was about to refuse. His evening meal was waiting for him, at home. Then he thought of the long evening ahead, and Anna alone. He nodded, and relaxed in Dan's chair, watching Mellie clean her baby, watching the pup nuzzle against her mother, small tail wagging. It was a beautiful puppy, well grown for its age, bonny with good bone, eyes bright, watching him, almost, he could have sworn, with amusement. She did have a solemn little wise face, far too old for her age. The wrinkles across her brow, parallel to her eyebrows, added to the impression.

Mellie had done her duty. She came to Scott and pawed at him, asking for affection. He stroked her head, praising her. She wagged her tail.

'Anna, I've a favour to ask,' Scott said, busy with his tea cup. He was anxious for Anna to say yes, knowing how slender was her income. He did not want her to guess that his motive was entirely altruistic. He did need help, but Roz could have done the job just as well as Anna.

'If I can,' Anna said. She lifted the pup and held her close. The small body, breathing and stretching, was reassurance, a beginning of hope. Life would be different in future; maybe after all there was a future and an end to grief. Perhaps she would be able to restore Dan's picture to the mantelpiece

24

and look at it without hurt. It was hidden in a cupboard now. It was too soon to bring it out.

'I've a client out at Walden who needs to go into hospital for a replacement hip. She's going to be out of action for weeks. She breeds racehorses. She's found homes for some, but the best mare of all is difficult; needs a lot of extra attention, which she won't get in a busy place. She's newly in foal; nearly eight months to go. Will you have her? The end stable's empty, and it would also make a foaling room when the time comes; it's a good big place.'

Dan's hunter had been sold to a farmer who wanted Jed for hunting. Anna had missed the horse. He was affectionate in his own way, more so than her mare, who was rather aloof.

'Suppose something goes wrong?' she asked, looking down at the pup. A few minutes longer and she would have been a casualty.

'If it's going to go wrong it will go wrong whether the mare is with you, or me, or a stranger,' Scott said. 'We can't foresee the future, Anna. We just have to do our best.'

Mellie growled softly as Sam came near her pup. She lifted the puppy gently and marched to the door.

'Time's up,' Anna grinned. 'Mellie's a nut.'

She took the bitch outside and closed the kennel on her, shooting the bolt. Mellie had ways of her own of getting free. She went back inside. Scott was standing by the door, ready to leave.

'I must go,' he said. 'Will you take the mare, Anna?'

'Yes,' Anna said. She enjoyed foals. It was a long time since they'd had one on the place. 'It's just that I don't trust Fate any more. First Dan; and then the fox got in and killed all my chickens; and that idiot shot the Muscovy duck thinking it was a wild duck. I feel jinxed.'

'We've beaten the jinx,' Scott said. 'We saved Gemma. That's the start of a new phase.' There was the sound of a car drawing up outside the gate. 'You've another visitor. I'll look in in the morning to make sure Gemma's none the worse. And I'll bring the mare over on Wednesday. I've promised to fetch her in my horsebox. Her owner doesn't want to trust her to a commercial driver, and an unknown groom. She's likely to be a handful. Roz is coming with me; she's used to awkward mares.'

'How's High Hopes?' Anna asked, suddenly remembering Scott's latest investment. He was always full of schemes for making a fortune before he retired.

Scott laughed.

'Just a hope,' he said. 'He's a daft little horse. I can't think why I was talked into buying him, except that Purdey trains him for free in return for free veterinary services. I've a feeling I'm a loser on that too; his horses produce the most complicated ailments.'

'Wasn't he running at Doncaster last week?' Anna asked.

'He came fifteenth out of twenty-one. An inglorious race. His jockey said he ran nice and steady and was a perfect little gentleman. Which won't win him races. I need a rip roarer for that. He's an easy ride though. He's running twice more and if he doesn't do any better he can come home, and you can keep him in the field for me to ride when I have time.'

Anna laughed. Scott's home was full of things he had bought to do when he had time. The golf clubs, only used once; the kiln for pottery; he had made her a jug so heavy that she needed two hands to pour milk from it; the rowing machine, now under the bed in the spare-room. Roz despaired.

'I must go,' Scott said, and grinned at the man who walked up the path. 'Hi, Dave. Come to look at the pups?'

'That; and to ask Anna a favour,' Dave said.

'Everyone's after me tonight,' Anna said, leading the way indoors. Dave Masterson, the Head Trainer at the Guide Dog Centre, was by now an old friend. He was as passionate as she about breeding good dogs.

'I've had an idea,' Dave said, when he was comfortably seated by the fire, with Mellie and the pups brought in for him to see. The pups were full fed and sleepy. They curled together in a mass of small bodies, heads against one another. Gemma's adventure had exhausted her. Mellie lay beside them, watchful. Sam leaned his head on Dave's knee.

Anna brought in a tray with coffee and cakes. Dave, though he watched his weight, being small and stockily built, with dark hair and a cherubic face that made him look ten

26

years younger than his forty-two years, adored home-made cake.

'You know we have been having to restrict the number of people we train to read Braille, and in getting around, because of the fire last year,' Dave said. Anna nodded, as she poured from the big earthenware coffee pot that was much too large for her now. The fire had destroyed the whole of one wing of the old building.

'Anna, would you take a blind lodger? We'd pay you what we'd need to spend on him or her if they stayed at the Centre. That way, an extra person can benefit. You won't be out of pocket. It would be far more than you could get with a sighted person, as there's much more to do; it will be someone newly blind; and both physically and emotionally there will be problems. It will be one hell of a challenge, and I know it's soon after Dan's death. But you'd be giving someone else a chance he might not get for months, and it would be well worth while. If it works out, we could fix you up with someone else when your first lodger goes. You're used to Susan; you know how to cope with blind people; it never seems to bother or embarrass you, as it does some people; and you don't indulge in constant sympathy which makes them thoroughly fed up. We thought of offering you a job at the Centre, but you'd hate to leave here; and also I need you for my pups. I've a new young bitch coming on, that should make as good a brood bitch as Mellie. You wouldn't like to change over and breed nothing but Guide Dogs? We never have enough. And of the next six, four are for people who are having new dogs, but the other two are replacements for retired animals.'

'I'm so used to Sue,' Anna said. 'Blindness doesn't seem to bother her. I suppose you don't miss sight so much if you never had it.'

'Sue's special,' Dave said, yearning in his voice. 'I wish she'd leave that ogress of a mother and branch out on her own.'

'She wouldn't be Sue if she did,' Anna said. 'Dave. I don't know if I could take someone on here. I'd have to think about it. For one thing, someone newly blind may keep falling over the animals.'

27

'Then he'll have to learn not to,' Dave said. 'Our aim is to return people to a normal life, not to shut them safely away with no risks at all. That's the way to a living death. Everyone today seems to think of safety all the time. You have to take risks; wrapping people up in cotton wool kills all adventure and initiative and fun. No racing driver would thank you for a nice safe old family saloon; no skin diver wants to be safely ashore; no mountaineer wants to be grounded. I don't want a five-day week and a fat pay packet and a pension to cushion my old age, while I sit in an armchair, doing nothing. I've a job I can do even when I am a bit decrepit.'

'I still need time to think,' Anna said.

'No hurry. The man I have in mind for you is nowhere near ready to come. He's weeks of healing of broken bones to do before we can help him. Also you have an added advantage, in that you live near Sue and when she's picked up in the morning, we can pick up your lodger too. I don't know what we'd do without Sue. I can help a lot, but I'm not blind. She is; and she can get around so easily she shames other people into trying to do as she does. Nothing like an example to fire enthusiasm.'

Anna listened as he drove away, hearing the engine sound die in the distance. Sue listened all the time, and constant contact with her had made Anna far more sensitive to noises.

She sat back in her chair, keeping Mellie and the pups with her. They helped to pass the time. Sam curled up beside her chair, staking his claim to the most important place in the room for a dog. If she took a lodger she would have company in the evenings. But what kind of company? Someone embittered, resenting the cards dealt out by Fate? Someone peevish and complaining, needing babying, flicking her own raw surfaces. She teased the thought in her mind as she took Mellie and the pups back to the whelping kennel, more than usually aware of the isolation of the place. She could scream, but only the cows next door would hear. She could lie ill, and unless someone came to call, she would lie alone. She thought of Dan, dying suddenly, between one heartbeat and the next, with no warning, and fear walked back along the path with her. Supposing she died like that too, with all the animals dependent on her and no one to alert help, to look after them?

The barn owl flew softly past her, hawking along the river bank. A night bird called, in the far distance. There were bright stars in the sky, and a promise of a growing moon.

The bobbity lamb bleated.

There was silence in kennel and stable; silence in the fields beyond her. A motorcycle revved its engine and roared through the night. There was a glow of light over the distant town, and at the end of the lane, the bright patchwork lights of Scott's home, half hidden by trees. In summer, with the leaves full grown, she might have been living in a forest.

Sam followed her into the house. Its emptiness hit her like a blow. She glanced automatically at Dan's chair. It faced her, an aching reminder. If only someone was sitting there. Anyone.

Anna cooked her evening meal. She ate, watching the television set that she and Dan had rarely had time to use. There had been so much to do; so many plans to make. So much to discuss.

Now there was nothing to discuss.

There was a schedule on the table for the next big Championship Show. She ought to enter Marcus, and try for the last certificate needed to make him a champion. There seemed little point. Who would share the excitement with her—Susan for one. And Dave for another. And if Marcus became a Champion she could double the stud fee, and more bitches would come to him. She could charge £25, and even once a fortnight, that would add to her income. She could sell the pups for an extra £10 or £15. And if she trained little Orry, and showed him, and won, she could get at least three hundred pounds for him if she could bring herself to part with him.

If only she had the energy to try.

If only she could afford some help. She could expand the kennels; could take in livery horses; could build the aviary she and Dan had always been going to start. She would like to breed birds. She had once thought of taking on pheasant rearing.

29

The programme ended. Anna hadn't heard a word. She switched off the set and unplugged it, always afraid of fire in the night and the animals at risk. Sam went upstairs, to his corner, where he could watch Anna and watch the door. His brown eyes were the last thing she saw before switching off the light.

She lay, listening to the ticking clock, the burr of the deep-freeze, the absence of sound outside. She was aware of Sam's fidgeting as he tried to settle. She would take on a lodger for Dave. Anything was better than this.

She fell asleep swiftly, not even realizing that she had turned a corner, had begun to make plans, and that she had begun to think of a future; not the future she and Dan had planned for, but something on her own; a new way of living.

She woke early, aware it was only five, unable as always to sleep on. She would have to change the furniture in the spare room; make sure there were no pitfalls for a man unable to see; she would have someone to cook for; no more picnic meals, barely considered, and eaten because she must. The deep-freeze was almost empty; she must start baking bread again; make cakes; the thoughts flickered through her mind.

She got up and played with Sam before starting on the day's routine, outside in the first light, and the fresh bite of frost in the air. Sam raced after his quoit and lumbered back to her. For the rest of that day he carried it hopefully. It was the first time Anna had played with him for months. He offered it to her at intervals throughout the day.

Anna worked more happily, aware that life would change. How it would change, not even she could guess.

Chapter 4

Steve was in a darkened world of blinding pain. He did not know that his father sat beside his bed for the greater part of two weeks. He did not know that a phone call to Mara was bringing her halfway across the world. In addition to his other injuries he had severe concussion.

He did not know that his mother, when told of his accident, had had a heart attack and was in the same hospital. Andrew spent his time between them. Nettie was recovering, but she would have to rest when she came home, and when Andrew had time to think, he was in despair. Without Nettie and without Steve, life would be impossible.

Steve did not know that he was a hero, his photograph, with Lig beside him, in every paper, telling the story of his failed brakes, and the way he had driven into a wall to avoid killing the children. The policeman who had been first on the scene of the accident confirmed that they would indeed have all been dead, if Steve had not turned the wheel. But

Steve was unlucky. The old car had no seat belts. He was thrown through the windscreen and hit the brick wall. He was lucky to be alive.

There were flowers beside his bed. Flowers from the children and their parents; flowers from people who had seen Steve working Lig in National and International Trials. He had won the Farmers' Trophy. He was well known. Flowers from the producer of 'One Man and His Dog', saddened to hear that Steve would not compete.

Steve drifted in and out of a frightening world, where noises drummed in his brain, where knives dug into his head, where pain was a constant companion, never leaving him. Pain in arms and ribs and legs; pain in his head; a deep-down driving pain that was only eased when he was sedated. He could not even remember who he was. He was aware of someone beside him, holding his hand, and then of time, drifting past, endlessly, on and on, in an abyss that had no bottom. He dreamed he was falling into space, and woke screaming.

He was aware of Andrew's voice, trying to soothe him but the voice had no reality. There was no reality. Mara came and sat beside him, but he did not know her, and Andrew would not let her come again. There was nothing anyone of them could do. And Mara was more efficient with the animals than he. Age and rheumatism had slowed him. He had never fully appreciated Steve's hard work, virtually running both farms.

Steve woke to reality on the third day of the third week in hospital. He could not move one leg. It was immobilized in plaster, held high in the air on a pulley. He could not move one arm. That too was in plaster. His ribs were bandaged. He put his left hand up to his face, to feel bandages round his head and over his eyes. He did not know if it were day or night.

His father, seeing the exploring hand, spoke gently.

'Steve?'

Reality surged back. Steve remembered the little car; remembered the brakes that failed, remembered seeing the wall loom towards him.

'The children. Are they all right?' It was desperately important to know; to be sure that he had not been injured for nothing. To be sure that no child lay dead because of him.

'They're fine,' said Andrew. 'They sent you flowers. Red roses.'

He put one of the flowers in Steve's hand. The stem was thorny. There was a faint scent from the soft petals. Steve held it against his lips.

'Is it day or night?' he asked.

'Day,' Andrew said. He waited with dread for the next question.

'When will they take the bandages off my eyes?'

'Soon,' a woman's brisk voice said close at hand. She straightened the sheet and shifted the pillow. 'That's enough talking for now. Here, this will ease the pain. Does your head hurt much?'

'Yes,' Steve said wearily. Pain seemed to have come to stay. The pain in his eyes was worst; a deep-down gritty feeling, with a shooting pain behind it. A vague fear began to form in his mind, but he dared not voice it.

There were firm hands on his shoulders. A feeding cup touched his lips. He swallowed, and lay back, exhausted by even that effort, wishing that the pain would ease, and even as he wished it, sleep reclaimed him.

'He's out of danger now,' the doctor said softly, a few minutes later. 'Go home, Mr Drake, and get some rest. Your wife is recovering too. You're all in.'

'When will you tell him?' Andrew asked. 'You will tell him?'

'I'll tell him, when the time's right,' the doctor said.

Andrew Drake looked at the bandaged figure in the bed. Nothing showed of Steve's face except his jaw. The windscreen had shattered, and he had needed surgery on both skin and eyes. One moment's hazard, one tiny link in an engine failing at a critical moment, and life was turned upside down. Steve, who had had everything only three weeks before, was now among the world's dispossessed. And Lig would never show the TV viewers what a champion

33

he was. Lig was almost a passion with Steve and he had set his heart on showing his dog's prowess to a larger audience than at the various trials.

There was a policeman standing in the car park, having come to take a statement from the victim of yet another crash.

'How is your son, Mr Drake?' he asked.

Andrew leaned wearily on the side of his car.

'He's recovering,' he said. 'But he's blind.'

He had not said the words aloud to anyone else till then. They fell, coldly, on the air.

'I'll drive you home, sir,' the man said. 'You're exhausted. They can send a car to your house for me. I'll phone when we get in.'

Andrew slept on the drive home. He was grateful to the man, who led him indoors, where Mara had food waiting.

'He'll be all right now. I'll look after him,' she said.

She watched Andrew eat his meal. He was almost sleepwalking.

'Does Steve know?' she asked, desolation in her voice.

'Not yet. I don't know how he'll take it. He isn't a patient man when it comes to physical disability. He's never had anything really wrong before. I don't even know how I'd take it . . .'

Andrew went upstairs to rest. Mara busied herself, cooking, cleaning, out for the evening milking, forcing her mind to concentrate on the job in hand and not to think about Steve, lying in hospital, never able to see again. Lig followed her, forlorn.

There was less pain when Steve woke again.

It was there, in the background, but it was bearable, so long as he did not try to move. He lay with his head against the pillows, aware of heat in his face and of sounds. The distant clang of the lift doors; a trolley wheeled along the corridor outside his room; an unidentifiable irritating buzzing, that was so persistent that he wondered if it were inside his own head. He was disorientated, unable to imagine his surroundings, unable to move or see, imprisoned inside his own body, trapped inside his own brain. He knew now that he was in hospital. He could smell disinfectant. He was aware of sound, more aware than he had ever been in all his life.

There was a blackbird singing outside the window. So it was day. The warmth on his cheek must be the sun shining on his face. Footsteps sounded, approaching his door, and then, disappointingly they passed, and faded into the distance. He began to listen for steps, and distinguish them; brisk light tapping steps; heavy ponderous masculine steps, and then an elephantine thump that stopped at his door, opened it, the click surprisingly distinct, and approached his bed.

A deep voice spoke.

'Awake?'

'Yes,' Steve said.

'Good. It's time you came back to us.' A firm hand clasped his wrist. He could hear the busy ticking of a watch. His pulse was being read. Daintier footsteps paced across the room. A thermometer touched his lips.

The darkness was infuriating.

'When can I have these bandages off?' Steve asked. 'It's horrible, not being able to see.'

There was a lengthening silence. Had it not been for the hand on his wrist and the quickened breathing of the nurse beside him, he would have thought they had gone away. He wanted to grab the hand and hold it, to be sure there was someone in the world besides himself. He was aware of the sheets, smooth against his chin; of the corner of a blanket, rough against his cheek; he needed a shave badly; there was a soft fuzz on his face. He detested beards. His eyes hurt, pricking grittily, as if they were full of sand. He wanted to rub them. He put a hand up to thrust impatiently at the bandages, but it was caught at once and held.

'No,' the voice said.

It was a patient resonant voice, belonging perhaps to an older man; Steve tried to picture him. Grey hair and a solid body. A kind voice and surely, brown eyes. It was a good voice.

'I'm sorry,' the voice said. 'You won't be able to see, not

even when the bandages come off. Your eyes were full of glass. We operated, but there's nothing more we can do. You will need treatment for some time; a year or two perhaps, to clear up the inflammation. Your father asked for one of the country's top eye specialists. He's done everything that's humanly possible.'

There was nothing to say. Ever.

Steve could not find words. He could not understand what he had been told. He would not understand. It was worse than a death sentence. Never to see the lambs again; or Lig, running on the hill, speeding swiftly over the heather, his eyes eager with excitement as he did the work he was bred for; never to compete again in the trials that he so enjoyed, with the best dog he had ever had. Not to marry Mara. He would never condemn her to life with a blind cripple.

The doctor stood, looking down, his face anxious. He was much younger than Steve imagined and already touched with the defeat that comes from the inability to make dying people well, or blind people see. He had not yet developed the shell that enabled him to blank out others' suffering. He would go away and sit in his small room, worrying desperately over Steve, identifying with him, knowing that he should learn to be indifferent, knowing that indifference would never be his.

This was something he had never done before. It had always been done by his superior, but John Morris had retired and he was superior now; he was in charge and he had to perform the unpleasant duties of telling those who were blind that they would never see; of telling the relatives of the dying that there was no more hope.

Had he done this wrong? Should he have waited? Had he misjudged this man's ability to withstand shock? He didn't know. Some could take it and some could not, but he did not want Steve to tear the bandages from his face and find the truth out that way.

There were so many things that were too difficult to know. Life seemed all trial and error; and Mark Lathom, not yet easy with his new position, felt that his lot was all error.

He tightened his grip, willing Steve to reply, willing him to overcome terror, to accept his new fate, willing the impossible to happen.

'Steve?' His voice held regret, held defeat. 'We're all sorry.'

Being sorry didn't help anyone. Steve did not move. He could not turn over, could not close his eyes against despair. He could not see. He would never see. He wanted to scream against the accident that had robbed him of everything worth living for; to rail against the man who had told him, but he swallowed his rage.

Mark knew it would be a long time before he absorbed the full meaning of the words, before he understood all that this meant. And there was nothing anyone could do to help him ride the shock. Later, they would put him into a ward, where other people would distract him from himself. They couldn't move him yet.

Steve wanted to sleep. Sleep banished thought.

'I'm tired,' he said.

Mark nodded to the nurse. The sudden prick of the needle made Steve jump. They should have warned him before injecting. But the prick brought temporary release, and eased the moment. The departing footsteps sounded like the knell of doom.

Steve slept.

He woke aware that someone was sitting beside his bed.

'Dad?'

'Your father's been and gone. So has your fiancée.'

'Mara's here?'

He didn't want her here; didn't want her close, feeling pity, pity banishing love. He knew she would marry him, stand by him, and he wasn't going to let her, but if she were beside him . . .

'She's not to come. Not to, do you hear?'

He tried to move, tried to turn, tried to make his words forceful.

'All right, love. I'll see she doesn't.'

Nurse Hancock had nursed for thirty years. She had seen it all; the suffering and the misery; had known it herself, and she guessed at Steve's reasons. He had to be kept quiet at all costs; had to be soothed; had to be babied; and she would have to tell the girl that her presence didn't help. Dear God, it's not fair, she said inside herself, but when she spoke her voice was cheerful.

'I'm Nurse Hancock. I'm sitting here knitting, mainly because it's my afternoon off and your armchair is more comfortable than the one in my room. I'm fed up, and need someone to talk to. So I thought I'd come and talk to you; as I'm sure you're fed up too. That makes two of us. Do you want a cup of tea?'

They'd offer tea on a death bed, Steve thought hysterically. He had an immense desire, all of a sudden, to laugh, to let the waves of mirth out and drown everything, and then came the desire to howl like a dog. He had better have a cup of tea. He was losing his grip. Drinking it would distract him and it was something to fill the endless hours.

'I'll bring it in a feeding cup; it's easier. Don't go away, there's a good boy.'

Irritation swept over him as she laughed and he heard her footsteps walk across the room and outside the door. The buzzing sound was interrupted by a few mysterious noises which suddenly clicked into place as the sound of tea being made in an automatic machine.

'Time to stop babying you,' Nurse Hancock said. 'Now, sit up and drink this.'

'I can't sit up,' Steve said peevishly.

'You can. Just wriggle yourself up the bed. You aren't paralysed.'

'I might as well be,' Steve said, suddenly furious with her and glad to vent his wrath on someone.

'Time to stop feeling sorry for yourself,' Nurse Hancock said, her voice crisp, reminding Steve of a teacher he had had at school. 'Of course you can do it if you try. I wouldn't have said you were the type of man that gave up. Life hasn't ended. It will take a new direction.'

'What life?' Steve asked.

'Drink your tea and count your blessings,' Nurse Hancock said sharply. Sympathy would only plunge Steve into an orgy of self-pity. 'It's in a feeding cup, but you can use your left hand. Here, take the handle. I'll guide it to your mouth; you'll have to learn to do it for yourself.'

Steve discovered he could move slightly in the bed; could ease himself on the pillows. He felt less helpless propped into a semi-sitting position. The tea was hot and sweet and welcome.

He did not want to talk. He was glad of company, of the busy clicking of the knitting needles that assured him she was still there; would answer if he spoke. There was time for thought and it was time to think.

He was a farmer; had always been a farmer. He knew life was unpredictable. Death came stealing in so many ways; taking ewe and lambs in the spring with twin lamb disease; coming to an old horse in the night, or a young horse, with sudden vicious colic; coming savagely by accident, when the bull had trampled his new pup, too bold by half, venturing into the stall under a gap Steve had thought too narrow to let the animal through. Coming when the fox savaged a goose.

He thought of birth. The new lambs in the field; the new pups in the kennel; the new kittens in the byre, so hard to bring, born in the early dawn.

'I'll never farm again,' Steve said.

'Five children alive and unhurt. Weigh that when you're on your own. Would you want your life and sight at that expense? The police say that you'd have killed them all. Your car was solid and big and heavy and they were in a little modern tin can. And you'd have hit them sideways; maybe you'd have died too, but it would have been seven lives gone; none were lost. You may think that a pity now, but time heals.'

'How the hell would you know?' Steve asked bitterly, and unfairly.

'I lost a husband in the war. He died in a Japanese prison camp. We'd only been married a few months. He never saw his son. Sounds corny, doesn't it? The sort of thing people read about in books and say is being laid on with a spade, but it happens. I wasn't the only one it happened to. I had my son for twenty-three years. He died when a bomb went off in a pub while he was on holiday. Stupid, wicked, senseless; all those. That was only last year. You can at least know that

39

you helped other women to keep their sons. That mother had picked up for five different families, if you include her own.'

There was nothing that Steve could say. Shame pricked, and then died. The click of the knitting needles continued.

It took Steve back to childhood illnesses, his mother sitting beside the bed, firmly capable, kissing him and making him feel better. Soothing him, and joking with him.

'Mother hasn't been to see me,' he said. He remembered Andrew's voice, in the days that had seemed like a nightmare, but never hers.

'She had a slight heart attack when she was told about your accident. She's in our coronary unit. She's much better now, but doctor doesn't think it wise to let her see you yet. She sent her love, and she bought the flowers that are beside your bed, from our ward trolley. Smell them.'

The scent of carnations. Bright colours and delicate petals. Steve touched them with his fingers, thinking of his mother, also in pain, because of him.

'She would have had an attack sooner or later anyway,' Nurse Hancock said. 'She's been overworking for years. Farmwork's far heavier than people realize.'

She had lugged the hay bales; helped with milking; painted the inside of the byres and the milking parlour, working alongside his father like a man, doing all the housework and cleaning and cooking; laundering for both of them.

He couldn't condemn Mara to that kind of life. If he married he would be a constant burden, needing far more help than most husbands, unable to take his share of responsibility. She was suddenly vivid in his mind, slender and tiny, with the lovely bones in her face, the big expressive eyes that laughed up at him. The sudden ache of misery was more than he could bear, but there was no respite from it. He could not read; he could only lie there, locked in with his own thoughts, and the despair that overtook him was like a black pit into which he was falling, unable to prevent himself from the fast downward slide.

He wanted Mara to cling to, for sanity. But that would be selfish. He couldn't ruin her life too.

40

He made a sound, and a hand took his and held it, pressing firmly, bringing human contact. Nurse Hancock was glad he could not see her face. Her expression would have belied the briskness in her voice. Her grip said 'I'm here; I'm doing all I can. I won't go away so long as you need me.'

Steve tightened his own grasp, holding on to her as if she alone could save him from total damnation and desolation.

He drifted into sleep, but in his dreams he was on the hills with Lig running free, and the little black and white lambs below him bleating for their mothers. There was something for him to do. Something for him and Lig. The outrun and the fetch; the lift and the drive; the shedding ring. It was all jumbled in his mind. The dog was working the sheep in the wrong order; they were making a mess of the competition, and the wind was blowing his words away. And then unbelievably Lig was running away from the sheep, running high on the hill, out of his reach, disobeying every command.

He penned the sheep alone, running round them like a dog, chivvying them with his crook, racing like a demented man, trying to put them safely in the pen.

There was the sound of thunder.

He woke, aware of footsteps approaching his bed, aware that the thunder was in his head, aware that he would never see Lig run free on the hills again.

'Steve?' It was his father's voice. The big hand gripped his tightly, and Steve gripped back, needing his father now more than he had ever needed him as a small boy, and aware that his father was old and needed him, and that he had failed him. They would have to sell The Nunneries, to cut back on Andrew's stock. He could never manage alone.

'Where's Lig?' he asked, his mind on the dog he would never work again.

'At our house. With Mara. She wants to come and see you.'

'No.' Steve's voice rose. 'I don't want to see her. You shouldn't have brought her home. She can't marry a blind man. It wouldn't be fair. My life is over—I won't wreck hers.'

'I should leave that to her, son,' Andrew said gently, knowing Mara better than Steve, it seemed.

41

'I'm not marrying. No way,' Steve said. He ached all over. He ached from the effort to see, even through the bandages. His eyes felt as if they ought to be able to see. His face was tight with stitches over the long gashes. She couldn't look at a sight like that every day. He would be scarred as well—a hideous mess—only fit to be hidden away. A ruin of a man.

'She's waiting to see you, Steve,' Andrew said patiently.

'I don't want to see her,' Steve said. Anger had come to stay, was boiling inside him; anger at the unpredictable fate that had snapped his brakes and rendered them useless; anger that might make him lash out at innocent people who had never harmed him; anger at the driver of the little car for being in the way; for not being hurt when he was hurt; anger because they could see and he could not. They could go places and he could not. And when his leg was free from plaster, what then? Was he doomed to creep around the world, crippled as well as blind? He dared not ask. He didn't even want to know the answer.

There was enough to bear without that knowledge.

Nurse Hancock glanced across at Andrew Drake, who sighed and sat heavily. He had aged ten years in the past three weeks and it was hard to pretend a confidence he did not feel. Steve had done so much for them; for him and for Mother, and only now did he realize he had been easing into retirement, letting Steve run both farms for him.

Mara had taken over, doing all she could, while her father had sent one of his men over to act as shepherd at The Nunneries.

'Is Lig all right?' Steve asked. He had also failed his dog.

'Lig's fine,' Andrew said. His thoughts went to the dog lying silent by the yard gate, turning his head eagerly when a car came along the lane, and the downcast body, every inch showing desolation, when Steve didn't come.

'When can I go home?' Steve asked.

'A long way to go,' Nurse Hancock said. 'You'll have to learn patience.'

Her knitting needles clicked again. It would be weeks before Steve was fit to leave hospital. She thought of the long weary hours in front of him, and caught his father's eye. The same thought was in both their minds.

Suddenly Andrew Drake was glad his son couldn't see his face. It would have betrayed him.

And somehow he had to go home and face Mara. He wished he could have been spared that task. She had taken over Nettie's work, without complaint, taking it for granted that even before marriage she was committed to them, to helping Steve. She went over to The Nunneries daily, to clean and air the house, and keep the heating going, to supervise old Hennessey, although he was a far better shepherd than she would ever be. To pick flowers for Andrew to take to Nettie. Someone had to stay on the farm, and watch over everything.

Steve couldn't talk. His thoughts raced through his head, and he felt that people must hear him screaming, but no sound came from his lips. The dark was pressing down on him, was palpable, was terrifying. Dark, and more dark, for ever and ever, world without end, amen. Dear God. It wasn't fair.

He began to laugh.

Nurse Hancock was ready. Drugs brought swift sleep, but he could not have them for ever. Andrew was left sitting by his son's bed, doing all the suffering for both of them. There was no relief for him.

Chapter 5

Most people underestimated Mara on first meeting her. She was small, with an appearance of extreme fragility that was totally deceptive. She looked impractical, but she could not only run both house and farm, she could handle most crises, from a terrified horse refusing to enter a horsebox, to a stampeding bull, fended off deftly with a pitchfork. She had once saved her father's life by her prompt action, enticing the bull into the field through a strategically opened gate and fetching the gun, using it swiftly and efficiently as he turned in fury to attack a second time.

'Told you you shouldn't have bought a Jersey bull,' she had commented, and been rewarded by her father's wry grin. Neither of them had told her mother exactly what had happened in the field that day. Least said was a maxim respected by both.

She listened to Andrew quietly. She had expected trouble with Steve. He was too fiercely independent to want to be dependent on anyone. Marriage this year was out of the question. He would still be in hospital when the date arrived.

'Mara?' Andrew looked at her anxiously.

'I'll try to persuade him, just once,' Mara said. She poured the tea, and passed over the cake she had made while she waited for Andrew to return. 'I won't push it. He needs time ... we all need time.'

'Why don't you go back to America?' Andrew asked. 'Finish the year ... Steve would prefer that. He wanted you to have the chance.'

'I've had seven months. I'm needed here. I'm going to rent The Nunneries from you; keep it going, till Steve's fit to return. And then we'll see about marriage. There's never been anyone else, and there won't be. I can wait.'

Andrew nodded.

He and Nettie had often laughed together over the little pigtailed girl who followed their son around. She had started chasing Steve when she was fourteen and he was sixteen. By the time Steve was twenty she hadn't needed to chase; they were there for one another and the future was assured, but both wanted a chance to achieve something first. When Mara wanted a partner, Steve was there; and when Steve wanted a companion for riding, Mara was always available. She had wanted to teach; had gone away to college, and then to several different schools, while Steve had built up the farm, ready for both of them. Neither were in a hurry. The future waited.

She had loved America; loved the frenetic bustle of New York, the constant happenings, the rush of a bigger city than any she had ever known. Had loved too the enormous spaces, beyond the city, the forests and the landscape that stretched for miles; the wild life, so much more varied and so much larger than anything at home; the children, alive, excited, provocative to teach, enjoying her English accent, wanting to hear more of England, of the legends and the stories of a country that was, for many, their father's or their grandfather's home. It was surprising to see how much emigration there had been. Her hosts were named Williams and came from Wales. Her headmaster's name was Ferguson, and his family still celebrated Burns's Night, and

45

his mother remembered Inverness, where she had been born and lived until she was nine years old.

Everyone had been kind when she received the news of Steve. Her luggage had been full of presents, hastily bought, but not hastily thought about. She packed them with an ache in her throat; the tiny phial of scent from Wistar; the teddy bear mascot from Al; the little black doll to remind her of Cara, who had been as dark as the doll herself, with a bright appealing face and an ability to do the most astonishing sums in her head.

Her colleagues had heard her admiring a new book of animal paintings. It was now on her bedside table, to look at at night; autographed by all of them. She thought of them now, part of her life only a few weeks before, when the future was all excitement.

She looked about the room. It was familiar to her as her own home, and she had no intention of giving it up.

'Steve has to go his own way,' she said. 'He always did, but I could push him in the end. I've always had to be cunning. It's a matter of time. He never would be told, would he?'

'Never,' Andrew said, remembering Steve, struggling to tie his own shoes, to dress himself at an age when most boys were content to be dressed; to feed himself long before he could properly hold the spoon, torn by terrifying rages because he wanted to do it himself, wanted, always, to outdo those around him, to be better than they were, and so often when he was little, frustrated by his own lack of strength as he struggled to help carry the little pigs out to the truck when it was time to market them, or to handle a horse too big for him, and he had worked the sheepdogs when he was only seven years old.

Lig was lying by the window. He never took his eyes off the gate. Steve would come, as he always did, down the lane in the car, and open the gate and take Lig home. The dog never gave up hope. He had not eaten for the first two weeks. Mara, as determined as Lig, had hand fed him with dainties, enticing him, trying to win his allegiance, but he had none for her. He accepted them all, but he needed his master. Whenever he heard an engine, he stood hopeful, his tail faintly wagging. A stranger appeared and Lig dropped down, defeated. Mara had brought the dog indoors, hoping that would break the gate-watching habit, but Lig merely took up a position on the window seat, something Steve would never have allowed, but that neither she nor Andrew had the heart to check.

Andrew had wondered, as he drove home, how Mara would react. He had forgotten her toughness and her determination. She had always been able to wait. No one could ever push Steve, though sometimes he could be guided and he did know when he had been pigheadedly wrong. Andrew suddenly remembered the wild argument they had had when Steve had mated one of his sows to the sow's father.

'You can't do it; there's bad blood in the strain,' Andrew had said, at the start of the experiment.

Steve, looking at fourteen dead piglets, all of them deformed, had apologized. It had meant a big loss on the litter. The next mating was much more carefully done.

'I'm running The Nunneries, whatever happens,' Mara said. 'Steve needn't even know. You can tell him it's rented, which will be true.'

'You're not paying rent, girl,' Andrew said. 'Merciful Heaven, I ought to be paying you.'

Mara put her arms round his neck and kissed him.

'You're going to be my father-in-law whatever Steve thinks,' she said. 'So I'm family already. I have been for long enough, haven't I? I made a dead set at Steve and I'm not giving up now.'

Her father had said as much on the phone one day, when Andrew had voiced his doubts to him. It was too much for Mara to take on. 'Rubbish,' said the robust voice at the other end, completely without illusions. 'She's tough as they come. Don't you be misled because she's tiny.'

'I'm going to see Steve this evening,' Mara said. 'He can tell me himself. I'll try and persuade him to change his mind. If we were married in the hospital, it might give him a future to look forward to. We could be, still.'

'I'll drive you,' Andrew said. 'We can do the milking before we go and lock the stock up for the night. Hennessey can stay on; he won't mind, will he?'

'He'll be glad to be used,' Mara said. 'He's been a pest since he retired, driving the men mad by coming back every day; he hated retiring. This has given him a new lease of life; he's whistling as if he's in love again. He probably is, at that. He adores sheep; "never 'ad no time for women, always 'ad me sheep,"' she mimicked the old man's voice, and laughed.

Later, in the milking shed, her thoughts were bleak. She knew Steve too well to imagine an easy victory. He would be quixotic and obstinate, and he would have nothing to do with her. And she'd have done the same, afraid of being married out of pity, she thought with agonizing clarity. All the same, she was going to try.

On the way out, she stopped to hug Lig. The dog barely acknowledged her, positive that one day that gate would open and Steve would come through and whistle to him and take him out on the hill. Steve had never been away before, not without Lig. Their only break from the farm was to travel to sheepdog trials, all over the country, staying with friends on their farms at night. The dog huddled back into the cushions, his nose on his paws. He was only half alive without Steve.

Mara did not speak on the way to the hospital. Andrew was going up to see Nettie. He was having it rough, too. Mara had been too occupied with her own miseries to have thought about Andrew till then. Nettie was going to be a semi-invalid for a long time, unable to help round the place, having to rest. She wasn't even to lift a full kettle at first when she came home, the doctor had said. Now she was recovering, they knew it had been quite a bad attack.

Parked in the visitors' car park, Mara stared at the hospital. It was a dauntingly ugly Victorian building, more like a prison. Steve would feel imprisoned. He was never a good patient. He hated inactivity. He rarely sat still, and even in the evenings worked about the place, repairing, painting, building, improving, with energy enough for two men. He was a restless companion at times.

Andrew left Mara at the end of the corridor and continued towards the cardiac wing. Mara looked about her. The ward numbers were marked on a board on the wall.

48

Steve was in room B4, still on his own. It was up the stairs, along a polished corridor and past the children's ward, where small bodies, all of them victims of road accidents, lay in beds, some with legs or arms plastered, all unnaturally silent. If it hadn't been for Steve there might be five more beds occupied. If they'd been lucky.

She thought of her class in her American school. She had nicknamed them the Riot Squad. They were full of mischief, but once they had learned that she would stand no nonsense, they had behaved for her. She had always been able to handle children, and dogs, and horses. The only person in the world she couldn't handle was Steve.

She had brought nothing with her. There were flowers on the table in the room, which was brightly painted, with gay curtains. Everything had been designed to appeal to the eye. Steve was lying quiet. All she could see of him was his mouth and nose. There was little damage there. A few scratches, now almost healed.

She fought back panic and managed to make her voice quiet.

'Hi, Steve.'

'I told you not to come,' he said tonelessly, after a silence that seemed to stretch for ever. His good hand clenched till the knuckles were white. 'Please, Mara. Go.'

'We could marry in hospital, Steve,' Mara said.

Steve heard the words, and thought of himself, useless, an object of pity and charity, unable to contribute anything at all to life. Farming was all he knew and how the hell could he do that any more? He would be tied to a desk job in some terrible office, have to learn Braille, sit around useless for the rest of his life. Mara needed to find a proper husband; a man who could see; who could give her a decent life. Could give her children. He would be dependent as any child, but a child developed and he would age and rot, becoming more of a liability with the years.

He was trying to make the biggest sacrifice of his life; to think of Mara, to let her go free, and she was resisting him. He had no energy to argue. He was driven by instinct, by the need he had once had to make a wonderful life for both of them, to offer her the moon and the stars on a golden plate;

dreaming of the future they would build together. He was sure she would understand. He was offering her a normal life.

His future was shattered beyond repair.

He had lost Mara and he had lost Lig. They would cling to him if he allowed it; he knew that. But Lig needed to run on the wide hills, to run free, to herd the sheep, needed to fulfil the deep driving urge inside him, stronger than in many sheepdogs.

He could not condemn Lig to a life by the fire; to a lapdog existence, dependent on the needs of a blind master. He could not condemn Mara to a lifetime of waiting on a man who could not see; who could offer nothing; who would demand more and more of her, needing her to be his eyes, his courage, his protection against a harsh reality that had condemned him to a lifetime of inactivity, to a world he could not endure.

'Steve. Nothing matters—only us. Can't you see?' It was the wrong word.

Steve could not speak. The words were caught in his throat. He wanted, passionately, to be alone with his pain and his misery, not to have to put on an act; not to pretend that he was a civilized man enduring stoically when he needed to rage against the ill luck that had brought him to this moment.

If only he had insisted that his brakes were thoroughly checked. If only they had been married in the spring—no need for decision then. He clenched his hands. Mara saw the movement and bent over him.

If only she could look into his eyes; could hold him, stroke his face; she leaned over him, her scent bringing back memory, and tried to take his hand. She dared not use words. Speech betrayed her. She couldn't even hold him tight; he was lost in a mass of plaster and pulleys and strings, looking like a grotesque puppet.

Steve had needed to scream for days. He had controlled himself, hiding terror. Trying to keep calm, trying not to show his feelings, but this was beyond bearing. Suddenly all the implications before him hit him with full force. He tried to push Mara away, tried to turn away from her, but the pulleys held him firm, the plaster was as rigid as a coffin, the bandages hid the light. There was no light. No relief from dark unending. The weeks of self restraint had frayed all patience.

'Get out,' he yelled, and pushed against the bed trolley with all his strength. It caught Mara off balance and she fell against the chair by his bed, gasping at the pain in her leg; the trolley travelled on and hit the wardrobe with a mighty crash, and everything on it fell to the floor, the soda siphon bursting.

Anger overcame everything else. The weeks of waiting, the pain in her ankle, the blind stupid unreason of Steve's rejection were more than she could bear.

'Stop thinking of yourself,' Mara shouted. 'Think of me; you know I want to marry you. I don't care if you are blind, deaf, and crippled...I don't care...I don't care.'

The awkward sobs were choking her. She never cried, and anger grew because of her tears.

Steve said nothing. He lay with clenched fists, enduring a hell beyond any imagining, willing Mara to go, before he cried out to her to stay, to bind her to him for ever, by bonds of pity. She could never love a half man, with no life of his own. And he would not condemn her to pity.

Nurse Hancock and the doctor both heard the noise, and were there, Nurse Hancock adjusting the pulleys and slings, Mark taking Mara by the arm, leading her firmly away from the room, down the corridor, into the lift, along another corridor to his own sitting-room, where he helped her into a chair and poured out a measure of whisky.

'I don't drink in the middle of the afternoon,' Mara said, trying to be flippant and not succeeding.

'Drink it up. It's medicine.' Mark sat down in his own armchair, and looked broodingly at her. It must make it worse for Steve, knowing what he was missing. Mara was very good to look at.

'Why won't he let me come?' Mara sipped at the whisky, not tasting it, not seeing it, her mind back in the room beneath them, seeing Steve, alien to her, wrapped in his bandages.

'He's a proud man; he doesn't want to be underdog in his

51

own home, and he would be, married, and dependent on a wife; especially a wife like you.'

'Like me?' Mara stared at him, astounded.

'From what Steve's father says, you're very efficient; quite able to run a farm singlehanded, and to make a man who has lost his sight feel inadequate; and Steve is sure that love will turn to pity and he couldn't bear that.' They had talked at night when the pain was bad.

'Also Steve is lucky to be alive; if he hadn't had a head as tough as a rhino's he'd be dead now. He went through that windscreen and hit the wall. He isn't totally rational and he won't be for a long time; he's a very sick man. People change when they're ill.'

Mara looked into the yellow liquid in her glass.

'When the devil is ill, the devil a saint would be; when the devil is well, the devil a saint is he.' She swirled the liquid in the glass. 'That's one of Hennessey's sayings. He's my father's ex-shepherd; he's old now, but a good man still. I think Hennessey brought me up. I was always tagging after him, wanting to help with the sheep.'

And life was good then, Mara thought drearily. There was a future. Now, the years stretch eternal, pointless, nothing. What goals do I aim for? What hope is left?

Mark guessed at her thoughts and had no comfort to offer. He could sedate Steve, but there would be no relief for Mara. Life was never fair. If there hadn't been Steve, he might have asked her out himself. There was no time for women in his life. And he was bone tired. He needed comfort. He pushed the thought away and took the empty glass.

'Steve's father is waiting by the car,' he said, looking down into the car park, where Andrew stood defeated, his shoulders drooping, unaware of watching eyes. Mara joined him and looked down.

'My life is there, whatever Steve thinks,' she said.

Mark nodded. 'Give him time.' It was all he had to offer.

Next day she took her horse out of the stable. Her father had sent him over for her to ride. She always found relaxation and relief from worry in the saddle. She rode out on the hills as soon as milking was over. There had been snow in the night, lying on the high peaks, smooth and untroubled, masking danger, like a blind man's face, hiding thought; she wished the words hadn't come into her mind. Spring was round the corner but it was winter here and the bare hills echoed her mood. They thrust into the clouds, or lay white and still, the crags and peaks hidden as the bandages hid Steve's eyes.

She came to a level patch of ground and gave the horse his head. The wind was in her face, and under her was the surge of power driving his legs, the thud of hooves on the turf, the need to control him taking all her strength, flying against the wind, until she was exhausted, and eased to a trot and then to a walk.

It was time to return.

Her father was waiting at the doorway. He looked at the tired horse, at the lather on his coat, the sweat dripping from him.

'Don't take it out on the animals,' he said, his eyes angry. Mara looked at him, recognizing the expression, remembering herself at twelve, having gone to bed and left her pony untended. Tom had made her get up and groom and feed the pony and get the straw for his bedding, scattering it across the stable floor, shivering in her nightdress.

'See how you like it,' he had said. 'Your pony needs comfort too.'

She felt equally guilty now, a small girl again. She removed the saddle and began to rub the horse down. Hard work was a relief from memory. Her father watched her, and then went into the house to make coffee and bring it out, offering her the only gesture he knew, of a small unusual service. He was as taciturn as Steve, unable to put feelings into words, only able to talk of farm matters, of sheep and cattle and dogs.

Andrew was out, working in the far field, where the bullocks he was rearing had pushed down a length of fence. The sound of his hammer was a backnote to the other sounds on the farm. Somewhere a lamb bleated for its mother; a deep baa answered; a hen cackled, an idiotic insistent noise.

'Maggie's laid an egg,' Mara said, watching the hen strut

importantly round the corner. She always announced the event loudly, as did Myfanwy, the big Rhode Island Red that ignored the other hens and slept in the greenhouse with Sooty the black kitten tucked under her wing like a chick. Myfanwy also had a habit of coming into the house and investigating each room, ending up amazed in front of the television set if it were on. It was hard to evict her as they were always helpless with laughter at her expression. Mara had never realized a hen could register astonishment.

'I can't think how people live without animals,' Mara said. 'There's always something to make you laugh, even when life's at its grimmest.'

There was no more time to think. The horse needed feeding; and there were the baby pigs to bottlefeed. Magnolia had no milk, although she had managed to eat about four times as much as any other in-farrow sow. Mara went to the sty, armed with the bottles, and watched the tiny animals rush to her, ignoring their mother, who had no function in their lives. Mara and Andrew were the only source of food as far as they were concerned. Magnolia grunted angrily, wanting her own supper, but she would have to wait.

Andrew returned, weary, putting the hammer away and joining her in the sty, taking over half the feeding. It was an irritating chore, and Magnolia was destined for other purposes as this was the second time she had proved to have no milk. Also she had a habit of throwing hermaphrodite piglets that were no use for breeding.

'Maybe she'd be better mated to another boar,' Mara said, following her own line of thought.

'Not worth trying,' Andrew said. 'We've too many sows anyway. It's all we can do to keep up with the extra work when something like this happens.'

They were both too tired to talk. The piglets squelched happily at the bottles, sucking them dry; both Mara and Andrew held a bottle in each hand, and presently Hennessey came in with his Collie bitch and took on two more bottles, while Sal, a benign expression on her face, held a third. There were fourteen piglets to rear. Sal was used to helping feed orphan lambs. Piglets or lambs, it made no difference to Sal. She was all maternal instinct, and she learned fast. Hennessey had taught her many things that were alien to most sheepdogs. He and Sal thought alike. Mara sometimes thought the old man closer to the dogs than to humans; or maybe to sheep. He caught her glance on him and grinned, a wide gap-toothed grin. Hennessey had no time for dentists or such new-fangled things as false teeth. Went against nature to put those things in your mouth.

At last they were done, the animals safe for the night, the ducks and geese and hens shut in against the raiding foxes, and it was time to eat. Mara had made a cold pasty, working at midnight the day before; there was salad and soup in a huge flask. She had learned to cut corners. Hennessey washed his hands and cut doorsteps of new-baked bread, and they ate on the kitchen table, not bothering about a cloth. The fresh butter and home-made cheese made a dessert fit for any king. The cats foraged under the table for the crumbs. Hennessey nodded goodnight and went.

'If I go on staying here the village will talk,' Mara said at breakfast two days later. 'I'm moving into The Nunneries tomorrow. Steve won't be coming there for at least a year; the doctor said he would go to a rehabilitation Centre for the Blind. Maybe by then he'll see sense.'

'And if he doesn't?' Andrew asked, wishing he could wave a wand and have the last weeks changed; wishing they were back when the children were small and life held nothing much worse than a cut knee.

'Then I'll be a maiden aunt,' Mara said. 'There's never been anyone but Steve and never will be. If he wants to waste two lives that's up to him. I'm here if he wants me. Dad says I can keep Hennessey; he'll be out of the men's hair and in fact he's by no means past working. He's as strong as an ox, though he does look a bit frail.'

'He's only six years older than me, girl,' Andrew said testily. 'I'll be glad to have you over there. The place will only get damp if it's left empty. But if you regret it, say so. I won't hold it against you, now or ever.'

Mara had gone to the window and was stroking the soft fur round the Collie's neck.

'I'll take Lig with me, and work him. I can do the shepherding on the farm with him, and maybe back where he belongs, he'll learn to be without Steve.'

The dog, hearing Steve's name, wagged his tail hopefully and looked up.

Oh hell, you and me both, Mara thought, but did not say. Andrew, looking at her, thought of the long courtship; fourteen years, ending like this.

There was the sound of a car in the lane.

Mara opened the back door and Lig flew outside, to race to the gate and stand with his paws on the second bar, looking through, his whole body expectant. Mara's father got out of the car, and watched the dog shrink into himself, and turn away, tail down, ears drooping, creeping back to the house as if he had just been whipped.

'He reminds us of Steve all the time,' Mara said, as she greeted Tom Hastings again. He came over frequently, wishing he could help, but there was nothing anyone could do. Like Mara, he had no illusions about Steve. Steve would think he was doing the right thing even when everyone else knew it was totally wrong. For all that, he would have liked Steve as a son-in-law, blind or not. He was right for Mara, and Mara would never change. She was just as pigheaded. Exasperation made him brusque.

'Letter for you from America,' he said.

Mara read it, standing against the gate.

The words danced in front of her eyes. It was from the headmaster of the school she had taught in. She had written to say she would not be coming back, and told him of Steve's blindness.

'The school are collecting for a Seeing Eye dog for your fiancé. They took to you in a big way and this is their way of saying thank you. I don't know how you work it in England, but the Guide Dog people tell me a dog costs £750. I've asked if we can donate that, and have a dog picked out specially for Steve. The kids have organized a concert for next week; they all have ideas for making money. We've nearly a hundred dollars already and some of the parents have chipped in. We're all so sorry. He sounds a great guy.'

She held it out to her father, unable to speak.

She thought of evenings spent with other teachers; of the homes she had visited. Everyone had been so kind and fascinated by her stories of The Nunneries, the little cottage in the hills on the site of an old convent; so small that many of her class, living in comfortable suburban homes, cushioned by wealth, could not believe it.

They had loved her stories of Steve and Lig and the lambs on the hills. They had been gunning for Steve, sure Lig would win the championship in the TV series. She had told them he was to compete.

Andrew had poured whisky for them. He read the letter too.

'They're great people,' he said sincerely.

Mara nodded.

She went upstairs, unable to face them, not wanting to talk to them, not wanting to admit defeat.

'You think that when they grow up, you lose them and their troubles,' Tom said heavily, over a second whisky. 'Somehow, it just gets worse; you're never free of them. Though it's as well it's happened to Mara and not to Lou. She couldn't have taken it and I always pray that she'll have life easy, as she's like Meg, who can't take things either. I don't know what she'd do if I die first.'

'Makes you broody,' Andrew said. 'I never realized Nettie was overworking, though I see it now. Depended on her too much.'

They had been friends for years. Neither needed words. Tom sat, smoking his pipe, thinking about his daughter. Nothing would ever break the bond between them. They had always been close. Lou, his other daughter, was closer to Meg. Whether she were with him or away from him, he would worry about Mara as if she were still a little girl, totally dependent on him.

But he would never interfere. Nor would she guess his fears for her.

He parked the car above the loch as he drove home, looking down at the water, watching the little waves break white under the moon. An owl flew by. Steve would never see either again, and Tom's senses were suddenly sharpened, so that long after he had put the car away, he stood by the farm gate, just looking, at the cattle, shadowy in the field; at the moonlight shining on the farmhouse, at the shape of a tree, stark against the sky, aware of nuances of colour and shade he had never noticed before, standing there so long that Meg called to him.

Far away at High Hollows, Mara lay with the light on. She was overwhelmed by the dark, dreaming of Steve and waking desolate, imagining endless night. She heard a scratch at her door. Lig had come for comfort. She opened it and let him in and he lay beside her bed. Looking at him, she wondered if the dog ever slept.

She drew back the curtains and looked outside at the moonlit yard. The moon banished darkness. She switched off the light, but sleep was only a memory and she did not know how to court it.

She only knew that tomorrow would be as lonely as today.

And that the future stretched before her, an endless road that led to nowhere.

Lig whimpered and she wished she could join in but she had never been the whimpering type. She thought of the whisky bottle, but that was no answer.

There was only one anodyne and that lay in work.

She had to plan.

She would buy a ram from her father; would upgrade the stock; would breed the best lambs in the country; would show them and win prizes, make a future for herself, show what she was made of, go out like Steve and win, though not on the hills but through the hills. She understood breeding; she understood showing; she had always shown her stock.

Mara Hastings would breed the best sheep in the country. Mara Drake might take over, one day, and on that faint hope of a future she turned over and slept.

Chapter 6

Steve's broken bones mended. The painful daily treatment of his eyes also ended, though he needed, probably for months, to endure a session of a few days, back in hospital. Daily, he hoped, as the bandages were unwrapped, that the doctors were wrong. Daily, he suffered bitter disappointment. The darkness around him seemed denser, instead of less.

Without even realizing it, he acquired new awareness of his surroundings. He identified noises, and equated them with the day's happenings. The early morning tea; the clang of washbowls and bedpans; the doctor's morning round; the wheeling past his door of the trolley burdened with books and with writing paper, with small extras to make life more comfortable for those who could see.

Daily Andrew visited with news of Steve's mother, now soon to go home; with news of the farm, and of the Nunneries. Steve listened, impassively and never commented. He never asked about Lig. He never asked about

Mara. He dared not. It hurt too much to think of either. Once he tried but the lump in his throat frustrated the words. He needed them both badly. He was lost in the dark, without contact anywhere; without interest in anything; without a future.

He was moved into a ward, where there was noise and bustle and the man beside talking to him. He made conversation remotely, with an effort, not wanting to be bothered, wanting to be left alone with his misery, aware that claustrophobia was becoming his constant nightmare; he had never been an indoor man. He was stifled by the heat in the ward, suffocated by the presence of so many people, and the yearning for the hills and for the sheep and for Lig mastered everything else.

Yet he couldn't bear Andrew to talk about the sheep. Couldn't bear to think of another man working The Nunneries, as he now knew it had been rented. Andrew did not mention Mara, or that the rent was non-existent; without Mara, he would be lost too, and he was afraid that if Steve did know she had moved in, as if she already belonged, and nothing had happened to change her life, except that Steve was temporarily missing, he would blow up. The doctor was afraid of that too.

Night without day made time endless. The meals punctuated the days. Food was tasteless, and he rarely ate a proper meal. Nurse Hancock, aware that the hospital diet, though adequate, was unimaginative, made savoury dishes and mouthwatering desserts and cakes for him in her room at night, having adopted him as the patient most in need of care. Blindness might be easier on a man who was used to an indoor life. She had been farm bred herself, and knew Steve would have never spent even a bad day indoors, unless confined to bed, fretting and impatient.

Steve was just beginning to get about, with help, on two sticks, when they moved another man into the bed beside him. Paul Duke was dying and knew it. He had a wry sense of humour, making jokes about life after death that shocked the man on the other side of him, unwilling to contemplate the ultimate fact of life, but that appealed to Steve. Death was part of living; he had been aware of its imminence from the time, as a small boy, that he saw the first pig killed in the farmyard.

'I've a seat booked Up There, in the stalls, so that I can listen to the Heavenly Choir,' old Paul said one day, after a concert to which both he and Steve had listened. 'I hope they play classical music. D'you think they've been converted to rock and jazz and the modern stuff?'

Steve laughed at the thought of an angel playing a frenetic roll on the drums.

He was aware that the old man was growing weaker, and often in pain. He listened, and began to try and talk, even when he didn't wish to. Talking seemed to help the old boy ride the days. Then one night he heard Paul moan. Steve rang his bell, but the night nurse was busy with a patient who was coming round from an anaesthetic after an emergency operation, and did not hear.

Steve climbed out of bed, found his dressing gown, and found his way to the chair by the old man's bed. He sat beside him, holding his hand. It was a long night, and the nurse, when she did come, brought drugs for Paul and helped Steve back to bed, but not to sleep. He lay, listening, and rang his bell when the heavy breathing beside him stopped.

'He was a great old boy,' Nurse Hancock said next day. 'He would have been a hundred next week. He was looking forward to just making it and getting his telegram from the Queen. We thought he might hang on till then. He always had a joke for us, no matter how he felt.' Steve had not realized Paul was so old.

Nurse Hancock was off duty in the evening, but came in when the supper was brought round, bringing with her a pasty she had made, and a glass of wine.

'Old Paul had wine with his meal every night,' she said. 'There was a little left. He would have liked you to have it.'

Steve drank the wine and thought of the old man; born one hundred years ago, before the days of cars and radio and TV; born in a world so different it was impossible to imagine. Somehow it reduced life to perspective; he was, for the first time, glad he hadn't died in the crash. If only he could walk on the mountains again and look up at the peaks and be healed.

That night he asked about The Nunneries; he asked about Lig. He did not mention Mara—the thought of her was too painful—and he did not intend to change his mind. She might resent him now. She would thank him later.

He lay awake a long time, with an ache in his throat. He would have to find a new way of living; a way of occupying his time; of earning money. He had visions of a lifetime of pity; of charity. The trolley ladies sickened him, not knowing how to talk to him, using the word 'see' and suddenly drying up. He didn't care if they did talk about seeing; he talked about seeing. When Andrew left each night, Steve said 'See you,' as he always had, and only afterwards did the irony strike him. Then he began to take the words for granted.

Nurse Hancock spent much of her off duty time beside his bed, with nothing of her own to go home to. She was full of common sense, used to helping the newly blind acquire new skills; suggesting ways of eating, of folding his clothes on a chair she brought to put beside his bed, so that they were close at hand, and in the right order. Daily now, he was getting dressed.

She taught him how to count the steps he took to the end of the ward; to memorize the way the doors opened, to go slowly, feeling with his stick to find out if they had been propped open. It was unnerving to feel for a door that had mysteriously vanished. Panic and a sense of disorientation set in at once.

He knew that he needed to take thirty steps down the ward; to turn left after he had passed through the doorway, and then fourteen more steps to the toilets. He managed to take a shower, and dress again, without help. He had not yet tackled stairs; he did not know if those at the end of the corridor went down or up; either way there were pitfalls, though falling up was probably less of a disaster than falling down.

There were often hazards.

Someone left a wheelchair outside the ward one morning and he crashed into it, sending it down the corridor and falling himself, so that the nurse came racing, terrified lest he had broken one of the newly-healed fractures.

He was bruised, but otherwise unharmed. Soon he could find his way along the corridor, and up a short flight of stairs to the physiotherapy room, where he exercised unused muscles, and was given massage. He did not know that there was always a male orderly behind him, ready to dash forward if needed. Arthur Coutts had learned to walk like a cat, keeping unobtrusive watch, so that no one suffered injury, yet those who were newly blind acquired a feeling of independence, unaware that there was a protector behind them.

Life could not be denied. Steve fought his way back to health, exercising, learning all the time, often without realizing it, developing new routines, and when he was able to shed his sticks, finding that touch would tell him a great deal that he needed to know.

He could make his way to the lift, where someone was sure to take him down to the ground floor, and outside into the sunshine, counting carefully till he reached the flight of steps down. Out of doors he was more his own man; there was the wind on his face and a freshness in the air that was lacking in the hothouse atmosphere inside.

One morning he ventured, using a stick to guide him, across the gravel drive and on to the grass, using the sun on his face as a guide, afraid of becoming disorientated and getting completely lost in what was probably only a small area.

He came to a fence and a gate.

Somewhere near his face was a friendly huff, and he huffed back and was rewarded by a horse's muzzle against his face; a very tame horse, used to being petted and fussed. He put out a hand to stroke its mane and encountered thorns. Gently he disentangled the stick from the long soft hair, and put it on his side of the gate so that it wouldn't get caught again. He stood for a long time, his hand against the warm hide, savouring the horse smell, longing to be back with animals.

And then he was released to go home, briefly, before going on to the Centre, where they would teach him new ways, and how to lead a new life. He did not want a new life, but life with animals would be impossible. He needed eyes to see.

'Is Lig here?' he asked, as Andrew guided him through the yard to the house. There was a strong wind blowing and he could hear the sheep. A dog sniffed at his legs, but when he put a hand down, he knew it wasn't Lig.

'He fretted terribly, son,' Andrew said. 'I didn't tell you. Wouldn't have helped. He didn't eat for nearly two weeks and he still goes to the gate when a car comes to see if it's you. He's settling now and Hennessey's working him; I can get him if you like, but you'll be away again in a week or so.'

'Leave him,' Steve said. It was bitter disappointment, but he couldn't bear to think of the dog hunting for him, desolate, day after day when he had gone away again. He would not condemn him to that. He had hoped the dog would not have fretted—then he could have his company. He knew too much about dogs to bring Lig back. That would be too cruel—the dog would never understand his second departure. It would be abandonment all over again. Nothing could be normal. Steve had to think of the dog and plan for Mara—and he did not realize that Mara did not understand.

Even home was difficult. He heard worry in his mother's voice; fell over things that people had moved and forgotten to put back against the wall; banged his head repeatedly on doors that he had once seen and ducked under, forgetting.

He could find his way to the milking parlour. He didn't need eyes to fix the cups; nor to hand-milk. Hand-milking was therapy, his head against any cow that had a touch of mastitis, keeping her milk separate from the rest because of the antibiotics in it. Leaning against the warm hide, shushing softly under his breath, listening to the rhythmic fall of the milk in the pail, able to dip a hand in to feel whether the bucket was full as this milk was only to be thrown out. Andrew wouldn't even use it on the pigs. Not with medicine in it. You never knew what came through.

He could groom the horses. It was like being born again in a different body, he thought, stumbling round the stable, trying to find the brush; swearing when a rake hit him on the shins or he tripped against a broom, refusing to be babied, shouting in fury at his father if he tried to help. Frustration made him angry, though he regretted his bad temper at once. He hated his clumsiness.

Andrew had a sudden memory of Steve at ten, grimly determined to work his own dog, competing in the local trials at the village fete and winning the junior handlers cup. He had worked daily on his Collie and it wasn't luck that had brought him to ownership of a dog that was a champion. Steve worked at everything, gave himself heart and soul to it, drove himself harder than he ever drove his animals, learning how to get the best out of a dog without being too hard on it, but teaching it to obey.

He had never chosen easy dogs or sensitive dogs. Just as he had always wanted a spirited horse, needing to prove himself master. Lig had been a devil of a pup; obstinate, self-willed, dominant; Steve had chosen him because of that, reckoning a soft dog no use at all; if you could get the better of a really difficult dog, he was yours for life and better than any other dog ever could be. Every good dog handler knew that. The easy dogs trained themselves—Steve liked a challenge. But his accident had changed him.

It had been a battle, those first two years with Lig.

Andrew thought of the battle now, wondering what was going on in Steve's mind. He had become morose, except when he was with the stock. He snapped at Andrew, and tried to keep his temper with his mother, but his mother rubbed him raw, cutting up his food, running to open a door though she was supposed to be resting, making extra treats for him at mealtimes as if he were ten again. He needed to be adult—to work things out for himself—to be independent.

Whenever he could, he got away from the farm, feeling his way with his stick across the yard, through the gate and out on to the bridle path that led down to the loch. It was easy going on soft turf, and out of doors, in the wind that often savaged the hills, he could visualize the day; imagine the marbling of cloud that masked the sun, so that warmth came and went on his face; knowing how behind him the tall peaks spired against the sky, their flanks covered in grey shaggy sheep that moved slowly across the green.

There was a rose bush by the cottage door; the scent

65

brought memory of the long red buds and the opening petals. His sister's husband was colour-blind. George saw flowers and leaves as if they were the same colour. Once he had pitied George; now he envied him. He could see the world, even if he never saw it as other men did.

There was too much time to think. Lying in bed at night, wondering if the moon was shining through the trees; listening to the calling owl; waiting for cockcrow when he could get up and be among people again, could reassure himself that there was a world beyond the darkness, where others still walked in sunlight and saw sights that would be memories only for the rest of his life.

He sat often by the loch, listening to the sound of the waves against the sand; listening to the sea birds crying; knowing that above him they were wheeling effortlessly, hearing them as they plunged after fish, his ears suddenly alert to sounds he had never noticed before. Once there was a slap on the water and he guessed that out there, not far from the shore, a seal was playing, somersaulting in the sunshine.

And everywhere there was the sound of birds.

He could distinguish them; blackbird and thrush and chittering starling; an angry robin, shouting a warning at something Steve could not see; perhaps one of the farm cats, for the fury was echoed all round him, an amazing din. He began to read the sounds, aware of small incidents that no one else noticed. Sitting on the grass, leaning against a tree, he tried to picture what was happening around him from wind noise and sea noise; days of high wind and the waves noisy on the beach; days of gentle breezes and a small murmur from the water; days when the wind roared and he stood in the doorway, his face turned towards the mountains, picturing the high hills and the excitement of those who walked on them, struggling against the unseen force that pushed them backwards and took the breath from their throats.

Andrew, watching, worried.

He could see no future for Steve. He couldn't farm, that was for sure; and what sort of outdoor job could a blind man do? Yet even on wet days, Steve wanted to be outside, feeling space about him. The house was a prison, compounding darkness, restricting movement, stifling him.

'You should have a Guide Dog,' one of his visitors said.

'What use is a dog I can't see?' Steve asked bitterly. 'Besides, I don't want to be dependent on a dog; I know too much about them. You need eyes to watch them all the time, or they get into mischief. A Guide Dog would be no different.'

It was useless arguing. He had always been as stubborn as the old horse that no one rode any more as Jumbo stopped dead at the gate and nothing would move him. Left alone, he lolloped back to the field and continued cropping the grass. It was too much effort to force him on. He was retired and left to his own devices, pigheaded to the last day of his life, when he had faced the gun, unaware that it was meant for him, still feeding. Andrew had hated shooting him, but he was almost blind and toothless and beginning to suffer pain from a growth on his hind leg.

Steve found he could do things indoors. He made tea for his mother, and took her cup to her, balanced carefully on a tray. Her gratitude was overdone and irritated him. She used the tone he used to a dog that had acquired a new skill.

She wanted him to marry Mara. Andrew had persuaded her not to raise the subject but she tried cunningly to introduce news of his nephew and niece, of Mara's sister's new baby, of the pleasure a baby brought to the house until Steve could have yelled at her. Such pleasures were not for him.

He spent more and more time beside the loch, away from the house, by himself. No one interrupted him there. No one knew where he was. Andrew worried but knew his son had to be left alone.

Cuckoo time was maddening. The bird never stopped. Its noise sounded over the hills, and echoed and re-echoed, drowning all other noise. Steve began to be irritated constantly by the smallest sounds; by the frantic rushing tick of his bedside clock. He buried it under his shirts in the drawer, unable to endure it a moment longer. The gasfire hissed. He had never noticed it before. Logs crackled and sputtered and spat.

His mother sometimes typed her letters. The clack of the keys annoyed him; so did the constant click of her knitting needles. He could hear the dogs breathing; hear the throbbing purr of the kittens in the basket by the window. He always jumped when one of them leaped to his knee or his shoulder, totally unprepared for a sudden assault.

They were still not ready for him at the Centre.

Impatience at his own shortcomings sharpened his tongue and his temper. He lashed against Andrew if he made the smallest suggestion to make life easier. Andrew suggested once that he put a thong on Steve's stick so that when he was out he could keep it on his wrist and not lay it down and have to hunt for it. Steve felt babied and resented it bitterly. He needed to get away.

Andrew took to driving himself across to The Nunneries, leaving the farm in the afternoons while Nettie rested, and Steve walked down to the lochside, swinging his stick angrily. Once the farm dog had gone with him, but Shell was sensitive, and she could not bear his moods, though he never harmed her. She could sense the anger in him and kept away.

Mara was thinner; she was tanned by the sun, was somehow older, more confident, but she seldom laughed. There was little to laugh about. She did not want to think about Steve and she knew from Andrew's comments that anything she did now would only worsen matters. He had to learn to accept; and until then no one could help him. And he'd always resented the smallest disability.

She drove herself and Hennessey. The farm had never been so trim, so well kept; the sheep so well tended. Not even Steve had been so fanatical. Mara was determined to make the place pay; to make a life for them both, when Steve saw sense. She refused to believe that he would never see sense.

Hennessey was giving her a crash course in sheep farming. She walked beside him, listening to the lore he spilled all the time, teaching without knowing he was teaching, keeping up a running commentary as they went.

Comments on the hay for the winter feed. Can't feed sheep on Timothy grass; that's best for the horses. We need hay from the mountain meadows; and we need to cut it at the right time, seeing these are hill sheep, not like your Dad's. He looked hard at the fields as he went, assessing each with an experienced eye.

Need good wether lambs. Need ewes with plenty of milk. That new young ram of your Dad's, he'd be good for this flock; they could do with making more milk than they do; market likes milky lambs. Only you can't deep-freeze them. Need to buy dips; there's ticks about, said Hennessey, parting the heavy fleeces. Need to book the contract shearers, never do it on our own, you and me. I could once, but...

Her one break each week was the long letter that came from America from the Riot Squad, telling her how they were faring with their money raising. She hoped that Steve would change his mind about a Guide Dog. If all that work were wasted, she wouldn't know how to tell the kids. Andrew, reading the letter with her, shared her hope.

'He's obstinate as that old ewe we had that always lost her lamb and never took another, not even when it was wearing her dead lamb's fleece,' Andrew said.

'Maybe he'll learn,' Mara said, but there was a note of despair in her voice, and Andrew went home angry, determined to talk to Steve. But Steve was in a blacker mood than usual, and glowered all through his tea, saying nothing; and Nettie was tearful.

'I tried to talk sense to him,' she said in bed that night. 'Told him it wasn't fair on Mara, and she wouldn't care if he were deaf, dumb and blind.'

'I told you to leave it alone,' Andrew said wearily. 'What did he say?'

'Nothing. Just went out of the house and slammed the front door. It needs a new pane of glass.' Nettie still felt very weak, and it was too difficult to cope with a blind son, recovering from an accident, hating the world he had been barred from, venting his wrath on everyone close to him.

Andrew went down next morning to find a letter for Steve in the mailbox.

'Read it,' Steve said, irritated. There would never be privacy again. He was not expecting any private mail, but the knowledge that others had to open his letters and tell him what they said had only just come to him, and it angered him.

'They want you at the Centre next Monday,' Andrew said, hoping his own relief didn't show in his voice. Nettie might improve more rapidly if Steve were away. 'There isn't a room for you there, as they had a fire last year and one wing was destroyed and is only just being rebuilt. You're staying with a Mrs. Anna Leigh at a place called Setter's Dene.'

Oh God, Steve thought. He could just picture it. A suburban villa and a too kind, over-cheerful hostess trying to jolly him up. And they'd teach him to make baskets and read Braille, and what other insane things would he learn?

He walked outside without his stick, and banged his head on the half-shut door. He had forgotten to put out his hand. Andrew had left a bucket on the cobbles, ready to feed the hens. Steve, knocking against it, kicked it savagely across the yard, spilling the corn. He walked to the low wall and stood beside it, driving his fist against it until the skin bled. Andrew, watching from the doorway, tightened his mouth.

There was nothing he could do.

He fetched broom and shovel and swept up the feed and took it to the hen house. The birds flocked, squawking, and Steve, hearing them, guessed what he had done.

As Andrew came back across the yard Steve touched him on the arm.

'Sorry,' he said harshly, and went indoors and up to his own room, where he sat by the window, his thoughts milling futilely.

Andrew wished he hadn't apologized. That only made it worse.

He locked the chickens in the shed and stood by the wall, looking down the hill and across the loch to the hills on the far side, blue in the distance. He wondered what he had done to deserve a sick wife and a blind son who wouldn't see sense.

Did a man only get what he deserved?

Andrew, bred from Puritan stock, with a sense of unease and guilt about his own actions, was far too hard on himself,

70

always, finding life too complex, too senseless, yet unwilling to believe it had neither form nor shape, but was made up of idiot happenings, like those that occurred in a house with a brain-damaged child.

Steve himself, sitting in his chair, knowing sleep would never come if he went to bed, was thinking along the same lines. Once he had a future, had been on the top of the world. He tried to recall the mood of that day, but it had vanished completely.

Life was a tale told by an idiot.

The words went round and round in his brain, until they stopped making any sense.

Darkness was pressing in on him; he hated the dark. Once it had been friendly, moonlit nights and brilliant stars. They were still outside, but he was barred from them. He was barred from all mankind, singled out to be different.

'Steve?' his mother's voice asked, as she came to his door. 'Are you all right?'

'Of course I'm all right,' Steve said, his voice savage, wanting to say how the hell can I be all right, trying to keep despair from his tone, but not succeeding.

His mother said nothing. Her footsteps died away and the house became a creaking place where everyone slept but he. Or had they all gone, and was he alone in a world with no one there? He opened the window and listened to the wind in the trees.

The door opened again.

'I've brought you a drink,' his father said. 'You didn't have any supper. There are sandwiches too.'

As if he wanted either. But he made an effort and said his thanks, wishing that the door would close again and Andrew go away. Andrew looked at his son, hesitated and then went out, shutting the door decisively behind him.

Steve sat down in the chair. He might as well drink and might as well eat. It would pass the time.

He was surprised to find a glass instead of a cup. Perhaps his father thought it easier to hold or perhaps he had brought up some of Nettie's homemade lemonade.

The whisky took his breath away.

He sipped, and savoured.

71

His father's special Glenfiddich, brought out only on state occasions. And the sandwiches were delicious.

Steve felt more miserable than he had ever felt before, hating himself for his impatience, but wanting to get away, to learn to be a man again, instead of a child to be humoured, and treated with such care.

Setter's Dene couldn't possibly be worse than this.

Chapter 7

Only the nip in the air told Steve it was autumn. Time had gone past and he was left behind. His mental clock had stopped with the lambing season. Now the lambs he had reared would mostly be sold; only the breeding ewes remained and it was past time for the rams to be with them.

His father bought him a little transistor radio to take to the Centre with him. Its triviality irritated him, so that often he switched off, wondering if the disc jockeys really were as maddeningly pat-on-the-head as they seemed. The country programmes he might have enjoyed were reduced to asininity by the most idiotic questions he had ever heard.

'Do you mean sheep think?' asked one bright spark, conducting a countryside programme, full of eager enquiry.

'What the hell does he think they do? Get wound up like toys?' Steve said to the empty air. He had thought his mother was in the room but she had gone to the yard to call Andrew for morning coffee. It was one of the stupider hazards of blindness. The radio had drowned the sound of her departure.

The phone-in programmes were even worse, with announcers who seemed to regard the general public more as if they were recalcitrant school children than grown people. He also began to hate television confrontations, hearing the acidity behind the interviewers' voices, more aware of bias with his eyes shut for ever than when he had been able to see. More aware too of the brainwashing that went on through the media, so that he felt that half the viewing and listening time was devoted to subliminal propaganda.

The farming programmes were the only ones that ever made sense and only those when they were factual and presented by working farmers. It took a professional to know a professional, he thought, listening to one interviewer who knew nothing of his subject being conned by a man who was almost as ignorant and whatever else he was, was not an expert on sheep.

Frustration was building all the time. He could not wait to get away, though he was sure that whatever life lay ahead would not be welcome. He could not see himself manning a switchboard, or working in a factory, and he did not want to be one of those the Government insisted must be employed, to ensure that the disabled had a chance of some kind of work. Whatever he did would be drudgery, away from the realities of life.

Mara had hoped to visit Steve before he left, but it was very plain that that would be unwise.

'Won't do any good, girl,' Andrew said wearily after a particularly dreadful day when all the men on the farm had conspired to leave objects lying around for Steve to stumble or fall over. 'He's like a tiger tied by the tail, and his tongue is getting more bitter every day. He's best left to work it out in his own way. We can't help, any of us. Maybe the folk at the Centre will; they'll have experience.'

The Riot Squad were writing more and more enthusiastic letters as they neared their target.

It was difficult to write back to them, to keep the tone cheerful, knowing that when Steve had been told he was eligible for a dog, he had rejected the idea with fury. He wouldn't be dependent on anyone, man or beast. And it was no life for a dog. A dog's place was out on the hills, among the sheep and Collies were no use as Guides; that would be cruelty. And he'd no time for any other breed. Now or ever.

'He's maddening,' Andrew said. 'The phone rang, and he went to answer it, instead of calling me, and left the bathroom tap running. We need a new ceiling as he didn't hear it; Nettie found it when she came in. She's beginning to get around a bit now. He will make his own tea, but he won't wait for people to find the crockery; and the kitchen floor's quarry tiles. Things don't bounce. And you know Nettie; everything must be put away. If she'd only leave the things handy, but she forgets.'

Andrew did not mention the fact that one of the farmhands had thoughtlessly moved Steve's milking stool that morning, and Steve had spent a black hour blundering round the milking parlour looking for it. It was in the barn, having been used instead of a ladder to stand on to repair a broken beam.

Steve had exploded with anger, yelling at the man who had taken the stool, who had promptly given his notice in, saying he wasn't employed to humour a lunatic and he'd go elsewhere.

Everybody had calmed down an hour later, but the incident had upset Andrew more than he realized. He was beginning to dread going back to High Hollows, where Steve would have upset his mother and Nettie would be sitting in the chair by the fire, silent, trying to restrain tears. She cried very easily these days, and Steve was making life hell for all of them. He knew it. He tried, but his nerves were rubbed raw.

Mara took her horse when Andrew had gone, and rode out on to the hills. There among the high peaks, looking down on the rich autumn trees that Steve had so loved and would never see again, she found herself more aware than ever of the gift of sight.

There was the blue loch, riffled with white; scattered farmhouses, roofs half hidden among the trees; the fox-colour of the turning bracken; the grey roving sheep; the eagle soaring above her, idle, sliding down the air streams, playing with the sky. He showed little of the power and thrust and surge of his flight, until something far away caught his eye and he beat strongly, his shadow fleeing over the hill, so that her horse shied, and she rallied herself, knowing that she had been inattentive and that if she were thrown and injured too, life would be impossible for all of them.

It was impossible to imagine Steve's world. Impossible to break into his desolation. Perhaps it would be easier for him once he was away, in unfamiliar surroundings that did not constantly remind him of all he now missed.

Hennessey was waiting for her, eyeing her with concern, having known her all his life, since she was a little lass, black determined to do her own thing, always laughing. She never laughed now.

She drove herself harder than ever, up on the hills at all hours, watching over the sheep. She brought in a ewe that was sickening. Hennessey thought it had yellowses, a form of poisoning due to eating weeds, causing a form of jaundice; they isolated it, but the vet reassured her. Not very much wrong; it proved to be a minute abscess under a tooth. Once lanced and drained, the ewe recovered and went back to her place, beside three rocks and a broom bush, regarding that as home. Hennessey had imagined the yellowing eyeballs. He was a born pessimist.

Mara soon recognized the haunts of each particular beast and if one were missing sent Lig to seek and find. He was an adept at finding them; she sometimes wondered how he knew which were theirs, as he never brought one with a wrong mark on its back.

Steve had determined to travel alone by train. He did not want Andrew fussing round him. He could manage. Besides, it wasn't a good time to leave the farm. Nettie shouldn't be alone and it would mean an overnight stay for his father.

The night before Steve travelled was the longest he had ever spent.

Sleep was impossible. He tossed and turned and thumped his pillow and listened to the clock outside his door tick on and on and on.

Somewhere in the house something hummed with a maddening persistent sound that he began to think was inside his head. The bed was hard and the sheets rumpled and the eiderdown fell off and he couldn't find it again. It had slipped between the bed and the wall. He gave up and began to count the ticks. He thought suddenly of Lig and the thought was an aching torment, longing for the dog, longing to walk on the hills with the wind on his face, to see his dog speeding upwards, a black and white streak, dropping when commanded, stalking when told, creeping gently, easily, never panicking the sheep. Lig had a mind of his own and could use it, often to good advantage.

That was in the past.

And in the future was isolation. The people talking to him did not always seem real; sometimes when the darkness pressed even more heavily than usual he wondered if he were inventing the world about him; or living through a long nightmare. There was nothing to reassure him, except touch.

He fingered the beard he had grown. He had it shaped and his hair cut by Bob, the barber in the village who had known him all his life, but who had found blind Steve a daunting person, and had made uneasy conversation, sometimes babbling too fast and nervously, and then drying up, afraid somehow he had said the wrong thing. Unaware that everything was wrong in Steve's present mood. Steve went home with every nerve pricking.

He would never be able to accept other people's reactions to him.

He was suddenly a freak in a world made for people who could see. In the country of the blind the one-eyed man is king. Who said that? And Milton; long ago he had learned the sonnet on his blindness, never guessing that one day it would apply to him.

And that one talent, that is death to hide...

Lig, he thought desolately, Lig. Lig on the hills, and the sheep.

Lodged with me, useless.

He couldn't lie there. He got up, blundering across the room, forgetting the chair and knocking it over so that Andrew woke and lay, in his turn, listening.

There was a sharp night frost; and Steve had gone to bed,

77

leaving his window wide, knowing that the night air would relieve the feeling he had of being penned in for ever. The loss of his bedding had made him cold. He would go down, make a hot drink, sit for a bit by the gasfire, feeling warmth on him. He was glad of the automatic ignition switch.

He sat, huddled into himself, and the cat came to curl against him, glad of company.

It was three in the morning.

He did not move. He sat on, aware of warmth, lost in an abyss of despair.

Andrew, creeping downstairs, worried by the silence, opened the door, letting the light from the hall flood into the room. He took one look at his son's face and retreated, going back to bed to watch clouds sail over the moon, his own body aching with misery.

He slept briefly and woke again.

No sound from downstairs. He lay rigid, wondering if he should go down, not knowing what to do. Words etched on his mind, come from nowhere, a tag from his schooldays when Shakespeare had been compulsory learning for all of them.

'Put out the light and then put out the light.'

He remembered the war years and the doom voice of the announcer on the eve of battle.

The lights are going out all over Europe.

Downstairs Steve sat on enduring a darkness so tangible that it hurt his head, knowing that the lights would never shine for him again.

Andrew lay, listening. There was no sound. And then, with a sudden lurch of his heart, he thought he smelled gas. Had the fire gone out? North Sea gas wasn't poisonous, but there was a risk of explosion. He ran downstairs. He switched on the light. Steve was still sitting silent, looking into himself and into a future that held no savour whatever. The gaslight glowed.

'I forgot to set my alarm,' Andrew said. 'Thought I'd over-slept and it was past time for milking.'

'What time is it?' Not that it mattered any more. Daylight, sunlight, moonlight, starlight, firelight, gaslight, man lived for light. And light had gone.

'A quarter past four. I'd have to be up in half an hour anyway. Like a coffee?'

'I'll get it,' Steve said. He could blank out thought by concentrating on action. Ten steps to the kitchen, feel for the door; open, so where was the lintel? A hand told him. Three steps to the left and the kettle on the tabletop beside the cooker. He blundered against the cooker painfully, having taken a smaller step than usual. Turn from the table to the sink, just behind it, and feel for the tap, waiting, till the kettle felt heavy enough and then plug in. Find two cups and two saucers; spoons and the sugar tin for his father, feeling along the top, praying he wouldn't send anything flying to the floor. He had learned to be cautious. The refrigerator, to the right and five paces on. The milk bottle, lodged in the door, and feel to see if the top had been removed. That was one of the more defeating chores; he always smothered himself in milk. Not that the cat or the dog minded.

He could hear the kettle boiling; Andrew had bought a steam whistle to help. Mind the steam. He felt carefully for the handle, poured the water on to the coffee, using sound to help him, stopping too soon. Andrew topped the cups quietly, careful to make no tell-tale sound, and added the milk.

'Mother's getting better,' Steve said, unable to think of a single thing to say.

'They said it would be slow. She's always done too much.' Andrew thought of the past; Nettie had been beautiful, a slim girl with a mass of dark reddish brown hair caught in a pony tail down her back. She ran everywhere, always had. Somewhere life had caught up with them, buried hopes and dreams alike. He had thought one day he would have a big farm; breed wonderful pedigree stock, but instead it took all the money he earned to keep up with the yearly increase in prices. Now the world had gone mad and was whirling away to disaster and nobody saw that they needed the men on the land; that when all the factories had ground to a halt; when all the jobs were lost and there was no money to buy anything but sheer necessities, everyone would have to go back to producing food in order to live.

Sometimes, watching the news at night, Andrew had a

feeling that everything was grinding to a halt, that the world they knew was disappearing and that the Dark Ages would soon return when it was every man for himself, and a fight to survive, instead of being cocooned like a baby from the cradle to the grave in the insanity of the Welfare State that made it as profitable for a man to be idle as to work. He had one man, a good man, Harry; Harry's brother-in-law was out of work, and Harry himself earned £3 a week more than the State gave to Joe. Mad, Andrew thought, preferring his thoughts to thinking about Steve.

He had never had enough.

He had done it all for Steve, wanting to hand over a good farm and good land to his son; to his son's son; and to those who came after. A family home, to carry the past into the future; that was what life was about. Providing for generations yet to come, husbanding the soil and keeping it in good heart; building for posterity.

His coffee tasted sour in his throat.

'Time to start milking,' Andrew said and went to dress. When he came down Steve had dragged the churns in, and sent the dog to fetch the cattle. They came from the byres, udders swinging. He swabbed them down and Steve fixed the cups, swearing as a tail flicked across his face. Soon the place was alive with cattle, with the milky smell of clean cows; with the noise as they munched placidly while they were milked.

Steve sat down beside old Follie, who had had a sore teat, and couldn't yet bear the cups on her. He felt the udder warm and full against his hands and then he didn't need sight, for the familiar skill was there and he squeezed rhythmically, thinking how much man missed by using machines. His head pressed against old Follie's warm and rumbling side; she shoved against him and stood on his foot. He shoved back and she dipped her head to feed again. She didn't know he couldn't see. She wouldn't care if she did know. Her life was simple and basic; the fields and the grass; the byre on cold nights and the calf that she bore every year. If only man could live as simply as the animals instead of having a computer mind filled with hopes and fears and wild imaginings.

80

He would only do this when he visited home briefly in future.

And then it was breakfast time and the taxi was at the door. And Steve was inside it, sitting back, tense, all the way to the station. Jock, the driver, talked of last week's football results and the horse that must have run backwards and then made Steve laugh by describing how he had entered his prize-winning bitch in a little local exemption dog show.

'Only two dogs of her breed in it and the other went for the judge,' he said, negotiating a huge roundabout, making Steve wonder if they were ever going to go straight again. He sighed with relief as the car took the last exit. 'Guess which won.'

'Yours?' Steve asked.

'The other. Temperament like a mad fox and it beat mine and mine gets prizes at much bigger shows. I only entered for a laugh.'

'You got your laugh,' Steve said, and the man chuckled.

'Oh, aye, ye can say that again. Want a lift to the platform, Mr. Drake?'

Jock had an easy knack of saying the right thing, offering simply without embarrassment. OK the man couldn't see and so what? No pity anywhere. Just one of those things. The matter-of-fact acceptance made it easy for Steve to take help; to take Jock's arm, and hand over his case.

'You keep behind me. There's steps down, remember and it's no so easy.'

Down the steps and through the tunnel. Voices and footsteps echoed and distance was difficult to judge. It was noisy, more noisy than Steve remembered. The unintelligible gabble of the tannoy shouting the arrivals and departures and destinations; the rattle of trolleys; the whine of an electric truck, navigating the crowds.

People were all about him. They bumped into him, or he into them. He wasn't sure which. Some apologized and some didn't. No one was aware he couldn't see. He was almost glad to be treated so roughly. It meant that his inability didn't show to a casual eye.

'Mr Drake?' British Rail knew he was travelling. There was a porter to meet him. The man took the case, and Jock was away, before Steve had time to thank him. He was led to a seat at the far end of the platform.

'It's no so busy here, and it's out of the rain. It's just beginning and by the look of the sky we're in for a drenching.'

The man had a Glasgow accent, and a cheerful voice.

'I'll be back just before the train comes,' the voice said. 'Ye'll hear it announced.'

Steve sat, unaware of the curious glances of two girls standing near him. Both were extremely pretty and were not used to men who ignored them. Steve, with his dark beard, which hid the scars from his accident, was a remarkably handsome man.

A woman sitting at the other end of his bench wondered why he stared with such fixity at an extremely ugly poster, advertising a building society, as if he were trying to memorize every word. She concluded he was a misogynist, hating women and trying to pretend neither she nor the girls existed. She was startled when the porter came back and had to touch Steve before he was aware of his presence.

'Train's just due, sir,' he said. 'Mind how you get in. The step's very high and you'll no find it easy.'

She hadn't realized he was blind.

Steve hadn't considered that the journey would be tedious. There was no way whatever of passing the time, other than sitting and listening to the wheels race on, to feel the swaying, unable to balance himself properly, thrown off balance at every jolt, unable to anticipate even the train drawing into a platform.

Another train passing in the opposite direction produced a noise so terrifying that he thought they were about to crash, until he remembered the sound, and identified it, and relaxed again. Someone coughed. He didn't know if he were in a corridor compartment or not and hoped suddenly and fiercely that he would not need the lavatory as he would never find the way and he would never ever ask.

At the next station a man got in beside him.

He was conscious of a strong smell of tobacco and a stronger smell of sweat. The man hit him with his elbow as he sat down.

'Sorry, I'm blind as a bat. Never see a thing unless it's in front of my nose,' a rough cheerful masculine voice said. 'No offence, I hope.'

'No,' Steve said stiffly. He was blinder than a bat.

'Paper?'

'Thanks, no.'

He listened to the rustle of the paper; to heavy masculine breathing, trying to picture the man, whether young or old. There was a woman talking in the far corner. Her cooing voice went on and on, reminding Steve of the pigeons in the tree outside his bedroom window. They never stopped either. Boo-to-you-too. Over and over.

Somewhere down the train a young baby was crying.

The only sense of journeying came when the train jolted or stopped.

The guard came along.

'Would you like a meal, Mr Drake?'

The other passengers looked on in astonishment, wondering why Steve should be singled out for special treatment.

Steve was hungry and it would pass the time. He tried to stand, but almost overbalanced.

'Steady does it, mate,' the man beside him said cheerfully. 'Taken a load aboard, haven't you?'

'The gentleman's blind,' the guard said, anxious to stop any more comments that might hurt. 'Mind your feet, folk.'

Steve stumbled over legs that seemed unable to get out of his way, horribly and ridiculously aware that even if he were being led to an open door and thrown out on the track there was nothing he could do about it. The rocking of the train made movement difficult.

It was a relief to sit down at a table, and also to know he was travelling forwards. Going backwards made him feel slightly sick.

'I think sandwiches would be easiest for you, sir,' the guard said. 'It can't be easy to eat a meal you can't see on a moving train.'

His matter of factness did not hurt.

'Sandwiches would be much easier,' Steve said gratefully.

'How on earth do you manage?' a feminine voice asked.

Another voice without pity; just interest in the tone. An older woman he thought, perhaps his mother's age.

'I'm only just learning,' Steve said.

'An accident?'

'A car accident. About six months ago, I think. I've lost track. It's the first time they've let me out,' he said and he grinned, wondering why it was so easy to talk to a total stranger. 'Is this a table for two?'

'Yes. We're very tête a tête. I don't think there are any hazards for you with sandwiches. I'll see they don't fill your cup too full. A lap full of coffee can be nasty.'

Steve laughed.

'Thanks,' he said. 'Where are we?'

'Just approaching the Lake District. The autumn trees are lovely. Great masses of red-gold and yellow leaves everywhere. It's a sunny day; blue sky and small clouds and sunshine on the water. I'm not sure which lake it is.'

"It's hard to realize it's already autumn,' Steve said. The spring had never happened.

'I know your voice; and your face is familiar. Why?'

It hurt to remember, but Steve had to reply. 'We compete in a lot of trials. You probably saw me in one of those. Do you go to them?'

'Of course. You're Steve Drake. The beard makes you look different. And Lig. I remember now. It was beastly luck. Your brakes failed on a hill, didn't they? It was in all the papers. Those children did you proud when they were interviewed.'

Steve had never considered that kind of publicity. He had not realized his accident had hit the headlines and for some days he had been a hero, everyone caught up by his act, everyone sad because he would never be able to prove his dog's ability.

'What's happened to Lig?'

'He's back on my farm,' Steve said. 'There's a tenant running it for me; and he's got Lig'

It was a bitter fact to digest. Lig working with someone else. He knew Hennessey though and knew the old man would be kind. But who was living at The Nunneries? Somehow Andrew had always evaded the question. Steve hadn't considered the matter before.

'Pride comes before a fall, I suppose,' Steve said. 'I was sure I would win the TV Trophy. I was so pleased when they asked us to compete.'

'No one deserves that kind of fall,' the woman said sharply. 'Lig's exceptional. I breed working sheepdogs. I bred one of your rivals. That dog has everything. I bred little Ellie.'

Steve remembered her; an ugly little black prick-eared dog, with tremendous potential. She had every chance of outdoing Lig in a year or two.

'I remember her,' he said.

'I saw you work Lig two years ago at Coniston. Do you remember? You won there too.'

As if he could forget. It had been a hard day with a high wind blowing from the dog to the sheep; and as tricky a bunch of sheep as he had ever had. They might have been bred for a rodeo. He had earned that win by sheer determination, using his brains. Lig had had to use his too, or with one false move the sheep would have stampeded, running every which way. As it was he had prayed and held his breath and the dog had worked like a dream. No luck that day. He had needed all his skill.

'Are you giving Lig a chance to go on working?' The voice was matter-of-fact.

'Yes,' Steve said. 'I haven't seen him—' He broke off. 'It's tough—but it's the only way—it's cruel to half own a dog that was once all yours.'

It helped to know he was right and it didn't help at all. He wanted Lig. And the sheep. And the hills. And his sight.

The ham sandwiches were excellent and the waiter brought biscuits, cheese and celery. His companion had ordered a full meal and was eating fish, which he could smell. She also ordered a half bottle of wine and surprised him by inviting him to share it.

'I never thought I'd meet Lig's owner,' she said. 'It's something to celebrate. Please don't go back to your compartment unless you prefer it. I'd love to go on talking. I don't often have the chance to talk to a dyed-in-the-wool Collie man.'

The rest of the journey passed swiftly. His table companion knew all the great dogs and their breeding; she had made a hobby of the study, and then started out on her own when her husband died. She bred with care and her dogs were in high demand. He recognized her name and her kennel prefix when she told him. If he'd ever needed a successor for Lig ... realization returned and she guessed by his expression that she had touched an exposed nerve.

'I've a litter at home now,' she said. 'Three dogs and a little bitch. I had a major problem as the mother had eclampsia and though she had calcium injections which saved her life, she's no milk. I've been hand rearing.'

'Did she mother them?' Steve asked. That made all the difference.

'Luckily, yes. They're weaned now; soon be ready to go to new homes, though I'll keep the bitch. She looks as if she'd be a good mother too. I get off soon. Good luck.'

'Thanks,' Steve said. I'll need it, he thought, after she had gone, when he was left to his own thoughts and the rattle of the wheels. Darkness had returned with her going. She had broken his isolation; had sparked his interest; had made him laugh, and though she had only been a disembodied voice across the table, and he had no idea how she looked or whether she were old or young, he missed her.

'We've arrived,' the guard said, touching his elbow. He had already collected Steve's case from the compartment. Steve stood, easing himself out with difficulty. They were in Manchester, at the terminus, and the guard had waited until the train had emptied.

Steve wondered what lay ahead.

Surprisingly, he felt sun on his face.

'I thought it always rained in Manchester,' he said.

The guard laughed.

'Not always,' he said, and handed him over to a porter, who led him along the platform and down some steps, and out into the sunshine again.

'Mr Drake?' a voice asked, close by.

'Yes,' Steve said.

It was a good voice, with warmth in it. Steve had begun to study voices; they gave a good deal away. He could detect mood, and sharpness; and read behind the voice, knowing if his hearer were not listening.

'I'm Anna Leigh. And this is Susan. She works at the Centre. They gave her the day off to meet you. She'll help you to the car. It's just a little way along here.'

'Anna has your cases. Take my arm,' said a voice. This voice was young, with overtones of laughter. A carefree voice. Steve felt sudden bitter envy as he took the girl's arm and she stepped out confidently.

'Hold on,' she said. 'Zanta's telling us to wait.'

'Zanta?' Steve was bewildered. He hadn't realized anyone else was there.

'My Guide Dog. I'm blind too.'

Steve stood beside her, too startled to speak.

'OK. Road's clear. Did you hear that car go by? You'll have to learn to use your ears all over again. I've had lots of practice as I've never known what it's like to see. I've known only darkness. It must be awful to have the light taken away when you've lived in it for years.'

Steve could not answer. He ducked as Susan indicated the car, and climbed in. Anna and Susan were in front. Zanta came with him and leaned against his knee. He put his hands over her head. He could feel an animal without embarrassment but he could not feel a human face; he would never be able to do that. He had lived without touching people for too long.

Soft fur and flop ears. Smooth coat and smooth tail. An eager tongue licking his hand. Labrador. He thought of Susan and her quick compassion, pitying him when she had nothing to remember, and he had had thirty years of a bright world.

He felt bitterly ashamed.

Chapter 8

Anna, concentrating on her driving, was vaguely aware of Susan trying to make conversation with Steve; finally she gave up and lapsed into silence, aware that travelling alone had exhausted him and that his taciturnity was due to tiredness, and not to rudeness.

Steve, sitting back, with the dog's cold nose thrust against his hand, was fighting against an overwhelming desire for sleep. He began to wonder about Setter's Dene. He had never lived in a town and was not at all sure he would care for the place.

It was difficult to judge his surroundings when at last they drew up in the yard. He used his ears, expecting to hear traffic. Instead he heard the bleat of a kid; a frenzied barking; the baaing of an impatient lamb; and beyond it was the coo of doves and the mew of a cat.

The lamb bleated again, a bleat that was neither juvenile nor adult, but somewhere between the two.

'That's my idiot ram lamb,' Anna said, laughing, as she

opened the door for Steve. 'He's far too old for a bottle but I can't break him of the habit. It's almost feeding time now.'

'Is this a farm?' Steve asked, puzzled. It was the last kind of place he had expected.

'A smallholding,' Anna said. 'Odd animals; and I mean odd. My mare likes ice-cream and dolly mixtures; the lamb ought to be weaned and isn't, and my stud dog mothers the kittens. They all creep into his pen to lie against him while their mother rushes round dementedly outside, mewing for me to come and rescue them. That's what's happening now. Marcus has four tabby kits with him and their mother is waiting for me to do something about it!'

'This way,' Sue laid a light hand on Steve's arm, as he stood beside the car, wondering which way to turn. 'There's a path, and then four steps up; duck your head as you go under the lintel; most men have to, and I expect you're tall too.'

'Six foot,' Steve said.

He stood, sniffing country air. There was a smell that could only be cows. 'Are there cattle?'

'Over the hedge,' Sue said. 'They don't belong to Anna. There's quite a big farm next door.'

Anna came in and made tea. She had baked scones; and a sponge cake, which she had filled with cream and jam. Steve's chair was comfortable, the cushion behind him soft, and when he had finished his tea, sleep claimed him. Sue went home, and Anna busied herself quietly about the room, aware that her guest must have endured great strain, travelling alone for the first time, and that to be alone and unable to see, among strangers, must also be daunting.

She finished her chores, and sat by the fire, lifting a box from the hearth. Inside were four blind Siamese kittens, only three days old. Scott had operated on the mother, but she had died during birth. Her owner was too elderly to bring up the litter, so Anna had been pressed into service.

Sam watched the kitten-feeding operations with great interest. He had barked at Steve and then accepted him when it was obvious that the man had come to stay. Sam knew about cases full of clothes, brought by visitors. He also knew when Steve woke. The dog stretched, and went to find a present. There was nothing lying around but the hearth brush which he dumped with great determination on Steve's knees.

'What on earth?' Steve began to wonder if he were in a home for the insane and some fellow lunatic had thrust the brush at him.

'I'm sorry,' Anna said. 'Sam's a Retriever and come hell or high water he retrieves; never mind what. You're lucky; it might have been wet or even mucky; he's a fiend.'

Steve, relieved to find he was the victim only of a dog's practical joke, relaxed, and felt for the soft ears. Instantly Sam's paw came up into his palm and the dog leaned against him.

There was a faint soft mew from the kitten Anna was feeding. It had lost the teat of the doll's bottle she was using, and protested with all its small voice.

'Whatever is that?' Steve asked.

'A three-day-old Siamese kitten. The mother died, and I'm hand rearing them. I'm already beginning to wish I hadn't taken it on. Feeding every two hours is no joke, especially when it's day and night.'

'I could probably manage the night feeds, and sleep by day,' Steve said. 'I gather they don't intend me to start at the Centre for a week or so, to give me a chance to settle in here.'

'I'd be more than grateful,' Anna said. 'There's a lot to do here. I've four brood bitches and one stud dog; several pups I'm running on. There's Ninny and her kid, and my mare; and a bitch with pups, as well as an in-foal mare I'm looking after while the owner is in hospital for a long stay, having a new hip joint.'

'Have you two bottles?' Steve asked.

'I prepare four and keep three warm,' Anna said. She picked up the second kitten, and put it into Steve's hand. He had never handled so tiny an animal before, and for a moment was afraid he might squeeze it and kill it. The farm cats always kittened in the barn, and brought in walking babies, well grown. It moved against his palm, and he traced the shape of the body with one finger, feeling the delicate ears and claws; the fragile paws and head, the surprisingly vital movements. Anna gave him the bottle, and at once the small mouth closed on it and the tiny animal began to suck.

'The worst part's getting them clean after feeding,' Anna said. 'I massage them with cotton wool dipped in olive oil, but it's already making them mucky.'

'Why not try one of the bitches?' Steve asked. 'They're used to the process. Cats might be dangerous, and try to kill strange kittens, but I think a very maternal bitch might well be your answer.'

'Tonka kills other cats' kittens. But Mellie is very maternal. Can't think why I didn't see the obvious,' Anna said. 'Mellie would save me a lot of work. She mothers everything; and nursed two orphaned kits two years ago. The bitch that has just whelped wouldn't take kittens either.'

Steve concentrated on the kitten he was feeding. It was far from easy to be sure he was holding it at the right angle. He heard the telltale suck of air from the emptying bottle, and then Anna removed the little animal from his hand and gave him the last kitten and bottle. Sam leaned his head on Steve's knee, always fascinated by this more peculiar than usual human activity. He was used to bitches feeding their young; he hadn't realized before that the human could take over.

'Sam can't make people out,' Anna observed, and laughed.

The door opened. Steve was aware of the quick patter of paws, of solid bodies pushing against him, sniffing him with interest, taking news from him of his own home and his father's dogs; and probably of the cows he had milked the day before. Animal scent clung no matter how hard you tried to eliminate it. You couldn't fool a dog's nose.

He had a sudden vision of Lig, coming to scent him, to try and find out where he had been; what dogs he had touched; what food he had eaten.

Lig.

He had pushed the thought of the dog out of his head, trying to forget the sheep and the windy hills; trying to forget the racing Collie speeding on his work, slipping upwards to bring the sheep down to his master, obeying every command without hesitation.

91

Now came total realization.

Lig was lost to him for ever.

He would never see the dog again; would never work him again. Memory overwhelmed him. He cradled the kitten in his hand, aware it was still, and sated with food, its small body breathing rhythmically.

He sat, looking inward, seeing the hills sweep up to the sky and the dog running, a flash of movement against the grass, dropping at once to a signal, creeping on, the sheep steady in front of him. His last Championship Trial was suddenly vivid in his memory. It had been a splendid day, with a fresh breeze and the sun bright on the hills, the wind ruffling the water to whiteness.

Memory was a traitor.

He thought he had conquered bitterness but bitterness returned, and the dogs at his knee were a tormenting reminder of all he had lost.

He sat steeped in misery and Mellie, always sensitive to mood, puzzled by this man who did not look at her but who stared at the wall beyond her, put both paws on Steve's knees and tried to look into his eyes. He did not know and did not move his head. She butted him with her nose, and leaned against him, licking his hand, offering all the sympathy she had, trying to comfort him, only too aware he was sad.

Sam, also anxious, pawed at his knee.

'I'll move the dogs if they bother you,' Anna said, coming in to the room to see the tableau and take in its significance. Steve had not heard her leave to fetch the two bitches. They always came in for the evening as company. She could not change the habit now. They wouldn't understand and would consider exclusion punishment for some inexplicable misdemeanour.

Anna took the kitten and put it on the hearthrug on a blanket, the other three beside it, and whistled to Mellie. Mellie came over, and bent her head to smell. She sniffed again, aware of babies; of extreme youth, of the milk round their mouths, which she carefully cleaned.

Then memory was triggered and she cuddled down beside them, and carefully licked each one clean. The kittens, up to then motherless, at once moved in to nuzzle at the dog's fur, and Mellie lay watching them, her eyes bright.

'Mellie's taken to them,' Anna said. 'I've had them in a box with an old teddy bear as mother figure; and a hot water bottle. Now they can have a living mother figure instead. Thank goodness you thought of it.'

Steve had been listening to the crackle of the fire without identifying the noise, his mind on the past, the future unknowable. Feeling the heat on his face, he said: 'There's a fire.'

'It's well guarded,' Anna said. 'I've been keeping the heat up for this litter. Their mother and father were both champions; the kits are worth a lot of money, so it's up to me to see they don't die on me. Their owner is old, and needs the money. She's very upset at losing her cat. I think she plans to keep one of these little ones; there are two females.'

There was a noisy bleat from outside and the sound of kicking hooves.

'That's Racket,' Anna said. 'I'll have to send him away; he's impossible. It's a good job we've no close neighbours. He wants his bottle.'

'I can do that,' Steve said. It was good to find things he could manage; he was tired of being superfluous while everyone else had a job to do. 'How old is he? Is he horned?'

'No,' Anna said. 'He's a North Country Cheviot. About six months old. The farmer next door was born in Scotland and he despises the sheep down here, so he bought lambs from the flock he left behind him. He was dispossessed by a road-widening scheme, like us. We had a lovely old farm, but had to sell everything and come and settle here. It was in the middle of the Herefordshire country, but they built the South Wales motorway link; and that was it. We were right in its path. I hated it here at first; hated the flat Cheshire plains and missed my hills.'

'We live in the mountains,' Steve said. 'I love them, sharp against the sky; changing shape all the time under the clouds. I gave my mother a picture for her birthday last year, of mountains and the sea, all blue and green and white, the hills hidden in mist. The artist captured the feeling perfectly, but people who have never seen the hills on that kind of day can't understand the painting at all.'

He had forgotten all about that picture. It hung over the sitting-room mantelpiece in his old home. Had he ever looked at it and taken it in, when he could see? He thought of his father, coping with both farms, having to supervise a tenant; having most of the work in the house to do as well as on the farm, with his mother out of action. And how long would that be?

He was glad when Anna took his arm to lead him outside to the shed where Racket was now thundering small hard hooves against the wood. His angry, hungry bleats sounded above everything. Steve walked carefully, afraid of falling. The yard was cobbled and uneven. He had lost all sense of direction. Anna had led him in zigzags, trying to avoid the worst hazards. The yard ought to be properly paved, but she hadn't the money.

'Here,' Anna said. 'Duck your head, right down. It's a very low shed.'

Steve stooped. A small hard fleecy body butted at his legs and he almost went backwards. He knelt, holding the ram tightly, and held out his hand for the bottle. The hungry mouth grabbed the teat and almost snatched the bottle out of his hand.

Then as he began to suck, the beast relaxed.

Steve listened to the sucking. He put out a hand to the sturdy well-covered body; felt the shape of the head, the forward pointing ears, knowing every bone by heart. It was a well-made animal. He suddenly wondered if it would be possible to judge cattle and sheep without being able to see them. But he wouldn't see colour imperfections; or see if the beast were bright-eyed and alert, or moved uneasily owing to bad conformation or to incipient illness.

He sighed.

He knelt by the lamb, savouring the sheep smell, the farm smell, and then as the animal relaxed, satisfied now he had had his own way, Anna pushed the ram back into the pen and bolted the door, led Steve outside, and closed the shed door and bolted that.

Steve, waiting for her in the garden, knew it was night, by the feel of the air and the muted sounds. Cattle were breathing in unison in the next field, a sibilant sound like an old man snoring. He heard the rustle of leaves as the cows moved against the hedge; a deep sigh as one shifted her position.

A nose pushed against his leg.

Steve put a hand down and felt Sam beside him. Anna was out of hearing, having gone to fetch the two mares and put them in the stable and forgotten to warn Steve that she would be some time. He was tired and wanted to sit down. He was aware of aching bones. He still limped slightly on one leg. Acting on impulse he put a hand into Sam's collar, and waited. The dog, used to leading Susan, led Steve inside. Sam often led Susan when Zanta played. She and Anna had been curious to see how much they could teach the big dog. Put on his lead, he led Susan round house and garden. They had never risked the lane. Sam hadn't been trained to guide. He entered the doorway, and Steve forgot to duck, hit his head, and swore.

'Never mind,' Anna said, from behind him. 'Dan could see, but he was always doing that. He never did remember not to barge straight through. You'll have to tie a knot in your handkerchief.'

'When did your husband die?' Steve asked.

'Almost a year ago. Very suddenly. It was a dreadful shock. But all changes are sudden in the end, aren't they? You wait nine months for a baby, knowing it will be born, but never guessing how the first one will change your life so completely. You're never prepared for the reality. They grow up and each time there's something new, different, unconsidered. They leave home and though you know they will, that's sudden too; one moment they're there and then the door closes and they're gone. You spend your life adjusting and you can get used to anything. I never thought I'd build a new life without Dan. But I have; I find I can cope. When I feel down I think of Susan who's one of the happiest people I know.'

'Perhaps you don't miss what you never had,' Steve said.

'I don't know. Can you imagine sight if it was never there? I often wonder what Susan makes of her world; she must know less than the dogs in some ways. She can feel the shape of the smaller things, but she can't know colour; can't see the life in the eyes of a dog or a bird or a human, can't see what makes Sam different from Marcus in appearance, though she can feel and tell Retriever from Alsatian. What about things like trees? She can feel a model, but the real thing, towering high above her, the shape of the branches, the fabric of the leaves? It must be unimaginable.'

'A different world,' Steve said. It hurt to think of it, but the pain meant that he was returning to life; he had been numb with grief for himself till old Paul died that night in hospital. Now he was able to think of others. He had never considered the plight of those blind from birth.

It was time to feed the kittens again. It was a small beginning; very small, but even here, from the beginning of his stay, he could ease a little of Anna's load. He was in surroundings that were in many ways familiar, among animals again, and there was more he could do than he had realized. He could feed the ram, could groom the mares, not needing eyes for that. But it wasn't a man's life. A man's life was in the fields with his dog at his heels and the sheep bleating and the lambs being born.

His hands smelled of Racket. The smell triggered memory so that all the time he sat, listening to the contented sucking of the kittens from their bottles, he was out on the high hills in imagination, watching Lig, with a pain in his chest and an ache in his throat and a feeling of total futility.

Chapter 9

Neither Anna nor Steve was ever aware that they were both part of a carefully worked-out experiment. Sue often talked of Anna; of the dogs and the goats and the smallholding; and it was through Sue that Dave had realized that Anna was the perfect person to breed litters for him. He hadn't the time or the staff for puppies. If he could find her a good brood bitch and help her with its mating so that they bred carefully, choosing dogs with all the qualities they needed, they might have a higher record of useful pups. There were always some that had to be sold as pets, in every litter, without the ability to make Guide Dogs.

Dave was as constant a visitor as Sue. He was dedicated to his work, thinking daily of ways to make the dogs steadier, more reliable, to learn quickly; to help the girls who helped with the training; to provide easier ways of teaching new owners, especially those who had never owned a dog in their lives. Few people realized there was far more to a dog than four legs, a mouth to eat with and a wagging tail.

It was also necessary to work out a diet for each so that they wouldn't be overfed. A Guide Dog was too expensive an investment to risk and some dogs, like some people, needed very little food, or they grew fat; others stayed lean and needed quantities. It was also necessary to make sure those that were cheapest to feed went to those with the smallest incomes.

The letter about Steve had arrived one morning on Dave's desk. It would be a long time before Steve was ready for a dog; he had to learn a whole new way of living first. But the doctor's report showed that he also needed to have his confidence restored and to be shown that life in his old surroundings was possible; and that many blind men married very happily and successfully. Steve had to be remade.

He needed to be put among animals; and Anna was the perfect person for him. The lodging scheme was born in a moment, at the next committee meeting. Dave went to see Scott, who promised to make sure Anna was genuinely overloaded and had to have help. If Steve and she couldn't cope alone, he could easily salvage the situation. He and Dave between them schemed and planned, and before long, half the village was involved. The Siamese kittens were a find; and with luck, there would be more animals in need of care, and Anna could never resist an appeal to her heart. Nor could she resist an animal. Scott, visiting two days later, found Anna on one side of the kitchen table, with a kitten on her knee, while Steve was mothering his, Mellie having cleaned it for him. Gemma, bright-eyed, was watching intently, intrigued by the yowls of the tiny animal.

Steve already knew Scott's footsteps.

'Never thought I'd be mother to a kitten,' he said, with a grin. 'I like this fellow. He gets so hungry he sucks on my fingers while he's waiting, and nibbles at my ear when he's on my shoulder. He swarms up as soon as he's fed, going high. What colour is he?'

'All white still. He's pure bred Siamese. His father's a champion and so is his mother. That litter is worth one hundred and fifty pounds apiece and their breeder needs the money, so don't you let me down. We can't afford to lose any of them.'

'It's hard to think of cats as worth so much,' Steve said. 'I suppose they hope for show animals from all four?'

'Greedyguts looks as if he will be a champion; he's gorgeous,' Anna said. 'The little one ought to be a good mother, but I'm not so sure about her shape. Though it's not easy to tell when they're so tiny. They don't really look like cats yet.'

'Thought I'd choked one this morning,' Steve said. 'It sounded like a rusty saw, and then I realized it was purring. Or trying to. It suddenly got the hang of it. It's an astounding noise for anything so small.'

'Sue loves feeding them, too,' Anna said. 'She'll be here later. I think you're due for a lesson in Braille. I have to go out. Would you like to come? Or to stay here and cope? I'll put the phone on the table. I'm expecting a bitch to come to Marcus tomorrow, and they're ringing to confirm.'

'I'll stay,' Steve said. Scott had gone away, the tyres of his car screeching as he turned on the gravel of the lane. The dogs had stopped barking. Their noise was a constant background of sound, and Steve began to suspect that Racket thought he was a dog too, as whenever the dogs barked, he added his bleats, and if they were in the compound and ran to the wire, he charged behind them, trying to keep up.

Anna had described the scene to Steve the first time it happened, and now he could picture it for himself; the four Alsatians, and Mellie and Gemma, and the ram. Sam stayed with Anna.

That had unexpected hazards too, as Sam had been bred to retrieve, and lacking pheasants, he spent his time carrying objects round the house. Anna was used to having to hunt for her purse or her spectacles, if she had not remembered to put them high, out of Sam's reach. He could open drawers, and he did, pulling on the handle to find out what was inside.

Steve's first annoying encounter with Sam's retrieving instinct happened when he wanted his shoes one morning.

Sam had slipped into the room and carried both downstairs. Steve, having learned always to undress by the bedroom chair and put each article down carefully, was certain the shoes were under the chair. He felt.

Nothing.

He must have put them somewhere else, but he had been so sure. Frowning, he sat on the chair and explored the floor.

Nothing.

Irritation was building, and he began to crawl round the floor, finding nothing whatever. He wondered if he were moving in circles. He stood up, nearer to the bed than he had realized and banged his head.

He swore.

'Something wrong?' Anna asked, from the doorway.

'I can't find my shoes,' Steve said, swallowing rage. 'I was sure I put them under the chair.'

'Was your door open last night?'

'Yes. I was too hot and couldn't breathe,' Steve said. It was one of his constant hazards; he was beginning to feel penned, needing the wide outdoor spaces to which he was used, small rooms caging him as surely as any zoo animal was caged. He couldn't bear the door shut.

'Sam's been in, I bet you. I'll look downstairs.'

Anna found one shoe in the kitchen and the other in the yard. Sam, scolded, was unrepentant and proudly carried one of the shoes upstairs, dumping it in Steve's lap. It was impossible not to laugh at the dog.

'He's so proud of himself,' Anna said. 'I'm sorry, Steve. It's one of the penalties of living with a Retriever. He carries the newspaper and the post, and if he won't come and I call him to take in my glove or my purse, he comes immediately, delighted to be useful. It's a major need, to carry.'

Like Lig's need, right from a tiny pup, to herd.

Anna went out, and Steve sat by the window, feeling the sun on his face. He remembered Lig at ten weeks old, herding the farmyard ducks and chicks; and Lig, learning, among the sheep, quick to know what he had to do, and when he was grown, using his brains, to bark at Steve if a lamb were in trouble or a sheep caught in wire or bramble or overturned, rolled on to her back, unable to get up.

'Anyone there?' Sue called.

Steve answered her, listening to her heel taps, and to Zanta's panting.

'First lesson today,' Sue said. 'Is Anna out?'

'She's gone shopping,' Steve said.

'Then we'll get to work. You'll need to learn the alphabet, and once you can read, you'll find you can have a sort of notebook and make notes and read them back to yourself. And you can touch-type and write your letters that way. Would you like me to read to you for a bit before we begin?'

It would pass the time. Time stretched endless, between meals, and food was becoming too important; there was so little to look forward to, and Anna was regaining lost skills and trying hard to make Steve recover an almost forgotten appetite for food. She was beginning to succeed. He had a sudden memory of being a boy at school, of the endlessness of Friday afternoon and the knowledge that this night of the week there was always a special meal, as everyone was tired and his mother knew that good food would overcome the frictions and irritations that sprang up so easily at the end of the day.

'Please read,' Steve said, and sat listening to the soft voice, as Sue read from a book about the country; the story of a sheep farmer and a dog; and he wondered if she had meant to be kind, or to trigger pain, for pain came, and he ceased to listen and saw only Lig running on the hill again, and himself striding carelessly over the rocks, unaware that life was superb at that moment and that it would never be the same again.

'You're not listening,' Susan said, knowing he had left her in thought, sensitive as always to mood, feeling the change in the air.

'I'm sorry,' Steve said. 'Sue, how do you bear it? I was remembering a piece of verse from schooldays; my memory's doing funny things. I suppose it's due to having so much time to think for the first time in my life. I never had time before. Now it's all time.'

101

'What is the verse?' Sue asked.
'Thomas Moore wrote it, I think.

I feel like one who treads alone
Some banquet hall deserted
Whose lights are fled, whose garlands dead,
And all but he departed.'

'That's only one aspect,' Susan said. 'You don't need to
feel like that. There's a whole world waiting. You have to
reach out to it. I remember Thomas Moore too.

"Come, come," said Tom's father, "at your time of life,
There's no excuse for thus playing the rake
It is time you should think, boy, of taking a wife."
"Why so it is, father. Whose wife shall I take?"'

'Did he write that?' Steve asked. 'I never knew.' He
laughed.
'I like nonsense verse best,' Susan said. 'I can never
remember whether it was Browning or Wordsworth who
wrote

Joy and Temperance and Repose
Slam the door on the doctor's nose.'

'I know a better one than that if you're verse swapping,'
Anna's voice said from the doorway.

'Her lips are redder than coral
That under the ocean grows
She is sweet, she is fair, she is moral,
My beautiful Georgian rose.'

Steve joined in the laughter.
'I haven't taught him a thing,' Susan said. 'I'll make coffee.
Come on, Zan. Kitchen.'
Steve heard her footsteps tap away and the scratch of the
dog's claws on the linoleum.

'I picked some roses for Sue's mother,' Anna said. 'Don't they smell lovely?'

The roses were Alec's Red. He had planted them all round the door for Mara, and the scent brought desolation worse than anything he had ever known. He could see the bushes clearly, well-grown, bright with flowers, and the scent brought back The Nunneries and everything he had lost. And Mara's face.

He went outside, to stand in the yard, and then walk carefully towards the field gate, where he knew the mare would come to him and put her head against him. She was a gentle creature and loved handling.

'I did the wrong thing,' Anna said forlornly. 'I thought he'd like to smell the roses.'

'Scent brings memory,' Susan said. 'It will take a very long time, Anna. There will be traps for all of us. Not even Steve will know the traps. We're bound to make mistakes. Words, places, smells, even the dogs...I read the wrong book today. I thought it might help. It didn't.'

Anna stood at the window looking out at the dark beaded man stroking the mare. Behind them the trees were burnished by the sun, and the mare's coat shone copper. The robin on the bush by the gate had a breast that was fiercely, fierily red. Colour flamed at her, almost overwhelming her, as she stood there, aware that only she could see, and that the world to Susan, and to Steve, had no shape at all and maybe little sense at times.

Susan gripped her hand.

'I'll save the lesson for another day,' she said. 'Give him time, Anna.'

She went out of the gate, her dog leading her. Anna watched them walk briskly down the lane, only the white harness betraying Susan's own disability. Time. For Steve it must be endless. She would have to fill it for him, find him more to do, take care with every word she spoke and every action.

Susan had forgotten the roses.

Anna took them to the end of the field and dropped them in the ditch, where they lay like broken promises, spilling red

103

petals dark as blood.

Steve came in later, to feed the kittens. He knew the way round the room now, and could find the box without difficulty. The kittens knew him. He only had to put down a hand and they swarmed up him, needle claws gripping. He sat, feeling the sun on his face, as they cuddled against him, squealing for the food that would soon be ready for him to give.

They were stronger now, sucking hard at the teat, digging against his hands, full of life, and full of the need to survive. Scott was pleased with their progress and they seemed to grow daily. Steve could feel the changes in them; the hardening of their claws, the stiffening of minute whiskers, the soft silky fur that grew more densely, the needle teeth that came through, occasionally burying themselves in his hand when he was too slow with the teat. They chewed the teats. Their ears were growing, and twitched away from him when he touched them; he could feel the shape of them; could feel the soft pads on the paws; he grew to know them better than he had ever known any animal, although he couldn't see them. He was familiar with every whisker. Those were now growing too.

He knew which was which; Greedyguts moving lightning fast, along his arm, towards his shoulder after feeding, and after Mellie had cleaned him; the little female snuggling against his hand, purring, the second little Tom, slow and ponderous, heavier, moving solidly against him; and the last female, reluctant to be put down, needing much more nursing, far more affectionate than any of them, so that she was first to reach him and always clung to him, not wanting to go back in her box.

'We'll have to keep that one for you,' Anna said. 'She's adopted you completely. You can take her home when you go. I was promised one as a thank you.'

That was in the distant future. There were letters from home; Andrew telling of the daily happenings; and how his mother was getting stronger and able to go out in the car, and visit friends again; how The Nunneries flock was increasing and the new tenant had bought in from another flock, and had bought a good young ram.

Steve had been feeding Racket the night before. The ram was a good one and would match his own herd. Perhaps he could take Racket back with him; their flock would benefit from new blood. Racket had a beautifully shaped head; an excellent fleece; and a good body. He was all a sheep should be, and he was in riproaring health, full of his own strength and becoming a major nuisance, butting the dogs, quite unafraid of them. Mellie hated him and ran when she saw him. Gemma played with him but the games were getting rough.

Anna went off daily with Gemma and was often away for three or four hours. Steve was too occupied with his own miseries to wonder where she had gone. It wasn't till Sue commented that Anna was out training the bitch that he did ask.

'Training her for what?'

'She's going to be a Guide Dog. Anna's breeding Guide Dogs for the Centre now. The rest of that litter is being puppy walked with other people. Some in towns, some by the seaside; the puppy walkers have to teach the dogs a little work; to sit, to go down, to stay, and to walk without being too boisterous. They have to walk a little ahead all the time, not at heel, so you let them pull a bit. And they get taken into shops, through busy streets, out among the stock; getting used to everything under the sun. You can't have a dog that suddenly decides to rush after sheep, and drags you after it. And they have to be taught so that they know how to use their brains as you depend on the dog.'

'I can't imagine that,' Steve said. 'My dogs have always been dependent on me; I'm boss.'

'I'm Zanta's boss too,' Sue said. 'All the same, I trust her to know when cars are coming, or if there's an obstacle in my way. I don't let her play me up. She can. She hated buses at one time; no idea why, but we went by bus twice a day for nearly six months to get over it; I got fed up with buses, but now she doesn't worry whether it's train, bus or car. She loves trains. Cars are OK, but trains are a big occasion for her.'

'Is each dog trained to a different environment?' Steve asked.

'They have to be. Some will be country dogs and have to cope with lanes without pavements; others will be in the middle of towns and in and out of crowded places all the time; how would Lig react if you took him to London?'

'He'd probably go crazy with the noise,' Steve said. 'He never did like busy towns. I rarely needed to go there with him. That seems a world away,' he added. 'I suppose Gemma's destined for a country home?'

'Yes,' Sue said. 'She's been hand-picked. She's one of the brightest little bitches Dave's ever seen and he's dying to get her to train. She's due to go in a week or two. Anna will miss her. And then, within four months or so, she'll be ready for her new owner, and the owner will have to be trained with her. It's a slow job.'

Everything was slow. Steve hated his Braille lessons. His fingers were insensitive and he confused the dots, or couldn't feel them properly. It was a new way to think; a difficult way to think. Sue, who had read Braille for years and never known any other way of reading, had no problems; her fingers flashed over the words, reading at almost a normal pace.

But he did make progress.

By the time he had been with Anna for five months, he was beginning to be able to read again. It took time to construe the words, but it was an occupation. The radio still infuriated him and he more often than not turned it off, wondering if everyone felt that they were being treated like morons, condescended to by superior beings who felt the world was composed of school children, needing to be chattered to and entertained. He wondered women could bear their programmes, especially when prepared by men.

'Steve,' Sue said when the day's lesson was completed. 'It's Anna's birthday tomorrow. When Dan was alive we all went down to the Traveller's Rest for a meal and then stayed in the bar afterwards. She won't come by herself; would you partner her?'

Steve hadn't yet mixed with a large group of people. He could now talk more readily to those who came to visit Anna, many of them not realizing that he was unable to see. He could walk easily about the place, handle the dogs, hold a bitch if she played up, when brought to Marcus, and fetch the big stud dog from his kennel. Marcus recognized authority, and never played Steve up, though sometimes he teased Anna and refused to come when she called. It only needed Steve to shout his name and he came at once.

It was easy to talk to Scott and his wife; to visit their home, and spend the time discussing animals. Easy to talk to Dave who lived among blind people, and who somehow always stimulated him to make yet more effort, to tackle something else for himself, to work about the place, carrying hay for Anna, lugging the big bales, lifting the sacks of dog feed, not needing eyes to find his way around to barns and storehouses, to kennels and dog runs. He could let the dogs out of the kennels in the morning, into the runs, always bolting the run door before he undid the kennel door. The dogs came to greet him, bounding into freedom, jumping up at him excitedly, delighted to be free.

The new pups came to know him, and when pups came into the house, he helped Susan play with them, stroke them, fuss them, accustoming them to human hands. He helped Anna make noises about the puppy kennels; carrying in an alarm clock every time they went to feed, sometimes setting it off, first far from the kennels then closer, dropping bin lids and dog pans, so that pups taken from her home into a home where no one ever considered silence, would not have too traumatic a change. The transistor radios were often put on loud and left outside the runs; Anna reversed her car beside the run; ran the engine, or sounded the horn; Steve stood by the run clapping his hands one morning, feeling absurd, but realizing that Anna was wise. These would be no cherished pups going from a gentle placid home to the hurly burly of life; they were being prepared deliberately for thoughtless noisy families, to whom the dog was an adjunct, loved, but ignored, and hopefully, not neglected.

They were never handled with undue gentleness, lest when a child came to pat and stroke with heavy uncontrolled hands, they turned and snapped. It was necessary, all the time, to remember they were destined to live in the house, subjected to the stresses of modern life.

They were played with in front of the television set; Steve nursed them while Anna used the vacuum cleaner, or the food mixer, or beat eggs noisily, clattering in the kitchen, banging plates against one another. Scott always slammed his car door outside the puppy run.

The pups came to see what was causing the noise, jumping up to lick at hands through the wire, leaning companionably against legs indoors, trying to gnaw at shoelaces or trousers, or at Steve's fingers. Each pup was different. He began to try and work out how, without being able to see. There were differences in shape and in ear set; there were differences in movement, and he could feel how one was light on its paws and danced to him and another came ponderously. The pups ended up with absurd petnames that Sue devised; Plod and Quicksilver; Flopears and Prickears; Squealer and Fluffface. One of the pups born in Steve's first few weeks with Anna was sold without the owner's knowing he had been nicknamed Awful, as he had more ways of getting into mischief than any pup either Anna or Steve had ever met.

He tore up a cushion so that there were feathers all over the room; he ate half a tea towel and had to be dosed with liquid paraffin; he overturned the kitchen bin, and dragged the contents all over the newly-washed floor; he uprooted newly-planted wallflowers; he tried to chew Scott's tyre; he tore Anna's scarf, having taken it outside to play tug of war with his sister.

'I can only hope they don't sue me or want me to take him back,' Anna said when the car drove off, but Awful, renamed Rascal, was replacing an old dog that had died, and could do no wrong. He was a triumphant success, helping to soothe memory. They had had the old dog for fifteen years and he had been a major part of their life. Anna liked replacing animals; the new pups benefited by their owner's experience and settling in was always much easier than in a home that had a dog for the first time.

By the time Anna's birthday came round there had been three new litters, the last only a few days old. The kittens were all sold, except for little Sukie, who was now Steve's own pet, sleeping on his bed, coming to him first thing in the morning to wake him by patting his cheek, snuggling down at night, sure she was the most necessary thing in all the world to him.

She was a comfort when the nights were long and sleep would not come and there was only memory. He had never had much time for cats before; had not realized how much character they had and certainly Sukie had more than her share. She was demanding all the time, needing attention, yelling for food, yelling if she were shut in a room away from Steve; and she followed him outside like a shadow.

'She's always there, just behind you,' Anna said. 'Don't ever turn suddenly or you'll step on her.'

Steve took to calling her before he turned and was always rewarded by her flying leap onto his shoulder. She leaned against his face, purring loudly, looking down scornfully at the dogs from her vantage point. Both Mellie and Sam had learned to keep out of Steve's way, having been trodden on before he remembered their habit of always lying in the gangway and never tucked in a corner of a room like Lig.

On the night of Anna's birthday he put on an unfamiliar suit, noting with dismay that it was tight across the shoulders and the trousers were distinctly uncomfortable. He was sitting around too much, and gaining weight. He needed to walk but there was no one he could ask to take him around. Susan was at work, and Scott and Anna were busy. But he couldn't manage long walks alone.

He was dreading the evening.

'It's only just down the road,' Anna said, taking his arm. 'I've locked up the kennel dogs and Mellie and Sam guard the house. The lane's a bit uneven. You had better take my arm.' Dave had collected Gemma the day before.

He hated being led, but said nothing. He had asked Scott to buy flowers for Anna from him; Scott had chosen carnations; he could smell them when he came into the room. Anna was delighted with them and with the thought that had prompted buying them. It was her first birthday without Dan.

The Traveller's Rest was old; low black beams, and black settles. Steve had to duck his head. He was aware of pipe smoke, and the smell of beer almost caught him off guard; he hadn't been in a pub for so long. It was overwhelming and he longed to fight his way out of the room again into the fresh clean air; he wanted to run back to Setter's Dene, and stand in the quiet yard, beside the dog runs, listening to the night. The noise was an assault on his ears, and panic set in when someone put a coin in the juke box and the sounding beat of the modern music drowned all conversation.

He wondered that he had ever taken pleasure in such a place. He sat, silent, unable to speak, while Scott and Roz Lewis and Sue and Dave and Anna chattered, and presently Mike Redwood, Marcus's show handler, came to join them, and the corner was brisk with conversation.

Steve sat sipping a pint of bitter, a being apart in an alien world, unable to visualize his surroundings. Anna had forgotten to describe them, and Sue was caught up in an argument with Dave about some improvement she thought necessary at work. Mike and Anna were animated, discussing Marcus's chances at the coming championship show. Scott was exhausted, having been up half the night with a calving cow, and Roz was listening to Sue.

Steve was in a vacuum without shape, packed with people. A man jostled his shoulder; someone spilled a few drops of beer onto his coat sleeve; a woman passed, drenched in scent. Someone sat on the arm of his chair, back to him, talking, and he felt as if he were invisible, suddenly vanished, a ghost to be ignored. The words 'a spectre at the feast' came into his head and the beer tasted sour in his throat. He couldn't swallow.

He sat, the darkness more tangible than he had ever known it, the noise of the place a terror that couldn't be borne, the beat-beat of the music a pounding in his head. His hands clenched on his knees, and Dave, turning his head, saw the white knuckles and cursed himself for stupidity.

'God, it's hot in here,' he said. 'I need a breath of air before we eat. Coming outside, Steve?'

Outside was an escape. It was peace, and Dave walked Steve down the shadowy garden, to sit by a bench against the wall and listen to the soft splash of a little river, grumbling softly to itself as it sped over stones. The air was fresh and clear, the sky bright with stars, and the half moon low over the trees.

The music from the inn was muted and somewhere an owl called. There was a scent of flowers, and of newcut grass. Slowly, the panic died. Dave sat quiet, looking at the night, knowing Steve's need.

'Time to eat,' he said after a few minutes. 'The dining-room's at the other end of the building, away from all the noise. It's a nice room; red velvet curtains and old-fashioned cloths with bobble fringes; red plush chairs; and there are two pictures. "Love locked out" and "When did you last see your father?"'

Steve laughed.

He knew both well; the girl leaning against the door in her long dress, and the boy facing the Roundheads; the Victorians had loved them and his grandmother had both in her house, one at the top of the stairs, the other over the big heavy old-fashioned carved sideboard. He had forgotten all about them.

They went in through french windows. Everyone else was already seated, and Steve took his place beside a radiator, feeling it warm against his arm.

'There's pâté,' Anna said. 'It's good here. Would you like it, Steve?'

Steve thought of battling with toast and an invisible paste.

'I'm having it,' Sue said. 'The waiters know about us, Steve, and it will be all ready to eat. They're sweet here. I love coming. Mind your legs. Zanta's under the table.'

Steve had known that. He had been greeted by a cold nose dipped into his hand, and felt the harness, as he stroked her, lying across her back. She would stay there quiet until she was needed. If he had a dog maybe he could go for the long walks he craved, up over the hills. But a gundog was no use; he needed a Collie and wished that the memory of Lig would cease haunting him, triggered over and over by Anna's dogs and by Zanta.

He couldn't help comparing.

The meal was made easy for him. The pâté was spread on the toast; he ordered roast pheasant with game potatoes and broccoli; everything on his plate was cut into manageable sizes; no need to struggle. Even the broccoli stalks had been cut. He chose cheese and biscuits for dessert; he was always afraid a mushy sweet would drop off

111

his spoon, messing his clothes. It was still not easy to eat without seeing either plate or knife and fork and spoon.

Dave had spoken to the landlord. When the meal was finished they retired, not to the big bar, but to a smaller private room, where two farmers, both friends of the landlord, were sitting drinking whisky, after a good day at the Beast Sales.

They looked up as Anna's party came in.

Dave put Steve on the settle beside the two men, and drew up a second table.

The men looked curiously at Steve.

'This is Steve Drake, Mr Long,' Anna said. 'Steve, Mr Long owns Racket. He breeds the North Cheviot sheep.'

'And I watched you work Lig,' the man said. 'Pity you can't go on working him, but that's life. Always something; some good and some bad. And sometimes good comes out of bad, though you'd never think it.'

Steve half grinned, wondering what good could ever come out of being blinded; but at least they were matter-of-fact and not full of false sympathy. Their comments were easier to bear than those of people who either gushed or were embarrassed.

'I like Racket,' Steve said. 'If I were going back I'd ask if I could buy him; he'd do my flock good. Anna says your ewes are good ones; full of milk and breed twin lambs.'

'You can have him for a song,' the farmer said. 'Mrs Leigh's the one who's reared him; I'd have lost him as there wasn't time to bottle feed. We're pushed to the limit all the time. We're dipping next week. Could do with an extra pair of hands. Would you like to help? Don't need eyes if we feed the sheep to you to push in.'

It hadn't occurred to Steve that he could be of use. But so long as he had hold of the sheep and knew where the trough was he could feed the sheep in; someone else would be needed anyway to lug them out again. He could provide hands, and a sudden yearning for a familiar job came to him. It was all very well helping with kittens and puppies, and they'd done a good job on the litter of Siamese; the breeder had netted four hundred pounds from the sale and gladly donated Sukie by way of thanks, but reality was among the sheep and cattle, earning a living in the only way he knew.

112

Reality was The Nunneries, cuddling under the Scottish mountains, and the sun setting behind it on an autumn day and the trees massed with colour. Reality was Lig, racing down the hillside, keeping a lamb back from the cliff edge, or barking to him because a ewe had tried to climb the drystone wall and trapped a leg. Reality was a couple of hundred miles from here, among his own people and he was a stranger in a strange place, and the dreadful awareness of being different, an outsider, an object of pity, swept over him.

He barely spoke after that, and longed for the evening to end, though he made an effort whenever Anna asked him a question or Scott offered him another drink.

He drank more than he wanted or needed and the drink only served to add to his misery. There was no lift to gaiety, as with the others. Only a yawning abyss of nightmare into which he was falling, so that he was thankful when Scott said it was time to call it a day and Mike Redwood took his arm and led him back to the house, where Mellie and Sam went mad, groaning with delight at seeing them again and Sam covered the floor with his offerings, which included Steve's wallet that he had left on his bedside table.

Sukie waited while he washed; rubbed against him as he struggled with his clothes, feeling partly fuddled. Anna was busy with the late-night chores; checking locks and bolts, making sure no one had intruded while she was away, locking up the house.

Steve heard her door shut at last and then there was silence. Sam and Mellie were on the landing. Sukie was curled against him, tucked beside his shoulder, her warmth more comfort than he had imagined possible. He had not had enough beer to make him drunk; he had had enough to open up yawning terrors that he had not yet imagined, so that he dozed and dreamed he was in the dark, fighting to find a light and then woke to reality, lying with the moon across his face, knowing it was there, feeling the walls of his room shut in on him like a prison, knowing that the proud future he had once dreamed of was no longer there, had been torn from him by one fateful mishap. His father had written to say he would receive heavy compensation but what compensation was possible for the loss of light?

Chapter 10

Mara was busier than she had ever been in her life. The demands of the farm were constant, and she was glad of them. The days passed; the day came on which she should have been married, and she stood at the window, looking out on the hill, a lump in her throat. The unused wedding dress hung in her wardrobe, protected by a polythene bag. She took it out, and looked at it, at the delicate stitchery, at the fragile embroidery. Nettie had loved making it, and put all her heart into every stitch.

Downstairs, Lig was waiting. Steve had never kept the dog in the house, but Mara needed him. He was company and protection, guarding her against importunate travelling salesmen who tried to trick her into buying products she did not require. One flick of the finger behind her and Lig was beside her, his teeth showing. He was capable of the swift Collie nip, a dash in, a bite, and out again, if she needed it, but only then. She wondered miserably what Steve would make of Lig's training now.

Hennessey took him on the hills, leaving his own dog behind him. Craig was growing old but he'd been a wonderful dog in his time and many of his pups were working in farms around the area. He was a more solid dog than Lig, heavy-bodied, with an honest working face and flop ears that made him look unlike a Collie. His muzzle was grey and the fur on his shoulders was also tinged with grey. He had a lame foreleg and walked stiffly. He had adopted Mara with enthusiasm, as most dogs adopted her, and did not begrudge Lig his work with Hennessey. Craig was a better guard dog than Lig; his angry growl prevented many a man from pushing his luck too far. Mara had to husband her money. She was intent on managing the farm, on paying her own way, on making a future for Steve.

If he ever changed his mind.

She pushed the thought away and hung the dress back in the wardrobe. Everything was there; the white shoes, the long slip, the blue handkerchief that her mother had lent her. Something old, something new, something borrowed, something blue.

She went downstairs with another thought echoing in her head. The cherry stone counting. This year, next year, some time, never.

Never. Never. Never.

The word echoed in her mind. She would be an old maid, left here on her own for ever, in a place justly called The Nunneries; living the life of a nun, without a man or a child to give her pleasure.

She went to the basket where her new hobby lay; Xoxes was a Cameo cat, a beautiful rich creamy long-furred animal with translucent eyes. Her mate Xerxes lived outside in a roomy cage and run. He was far too male to live in the house and both cats had won prizes. She had bought them from their breeder, who had to move home, and was unable to keep them for at least another year. She had promised her a couple of kittens from the litter.

There were four kittens. Xoxes growled at Lig, who kept well out of the way. Mara sighed. If Steve ever came home, there would be problems as his cats were farm cats, and never house kept. They only came in when there were signs

115

of mice. He would banish these to the barn. He would never tolerate a cat indoors. She was not even sure he liked cats. She loved them and had always bred her own litters of Burmese at home, showing them from the age of ten on, when her parents went to the big agricultural shows and took their stock. She had shown her rams as well. One of them was out in the field now, butting thoughtfully at the gatepost, as if his life depended on it.

The mountains rose stark and straight and splendid, devoid of mist. The autumn bracken was fox-coloured. There was a fringe of snow on the highest peak that was seldom without its white cap. The sun never shone on that side of the hill.

She took her jacket and whistled to Lig. She couldn't even face a slice of toast, not today when the village bells should have been pealing, and she should have been dressing in her bright attic room at home, her mother fussing, her sister with her, her little niece dressed in the blue dress Nettie had loved so much; knowing that by eleven o'clock Steve would be at the church, waiting for her.

She ran outside and up the hill, leaving memory behind, stopping to tease a thorny twig out of a lamb's woolly oily-smelling fleece; stopping to look down at The Nunneries, hiding its grey roof under the trees; walking up to the second field to look at the sheep and check them, one by one, knowing that this was now her life, world without end, amen and if Steve never came back to her, and never came back to farming, she would save until she could buy the place and live with her memories and build a new life among the sheep.

She needed to phone the contract shearers. She couldn't shear her own.

She needed more food for the hens.

She needed to feed them and to feed the two pigs in the new sty that her father had built for her; and she needed to go over to High Hollows where Nettie still had to build up her strength, and needed too comfort on this day she had hoped for so much. Mara had been in and out of the house all her life, and now she was their adopted daughter, calling in daily, doing all the jobs that Nettie couldn't manage, trying to cheer Andrew up, looking around to see where he was findings things difficult, helping as Steve would have helped.

Except that she wasn't strong enough to lug great bales and enormous sacks of feed; and neither was Andrew and nor was Hennessey, but she only had to give the word and one of the men from her father's farm would come over. Paddy or Big John who prided himself on his strength, and could lift a young bullock at the country fair for the sake of the silver tossed in his cap. Only she hated asking for help.

She wanted to manage on her own.

When she returned to the house there was a letter from America, this time from Jimmy Williams, the youngest member of the Riot Squad.

We've gotten all the money needed for a Seeing Eye dog for Steve. Wistar wrote to the Centre and they sent us a picture; she's lovely, a lady dog, called Gemma; a cross bred, half Labrador Retriever, half Golden Retriever. They say she's been picked out for him only he doesn't know it yet. Maybe sometime we could visit with you and see her; and see The Nunneries. It sounds a great place. We miss you; if you would like to visit with us again we would all be proud to have you come. And Steve too.

She had a sudden vision of the classroom and the eager faces; of Jimmie, with his carroty hair always on end and his snub nose and his pockets full of animals. She never knew what he would bring next. Gerbils, hamsters, white mice and one day a white rat that slid in and out of his sleeve. She hated rats.

There was a hoot at the door.

Her parents were there, dressed to go out.

'In and change. I've brought Big John and Paddy over to help here. You can bring Lig, but that's all. We're having a day playing hookey. Time you had a break. Lou's gone in to help Andrew and Nettie. Hurry up.' Her father was out of the car, her mother was hurrying her in, choosing a dress for her, taking out a coat, and chivvying her back as if she were ten years old instead of a grown woman who should have been married that day.

And then they were speeding down the road, with the loch beside them and the eagle soaring and The Nunneries

117

only a memory in the distance, on to the main road, and through to Perth to eat at the Royal George, and then back along the road, to stop at a sheep market and argue endlessly with her father over the merits of two separate rams, one of which he thought she should buy and the other she wanted.

'You haven't got an eye for a ram yet,' her father said irritably. 'Don't try and run before you can walk,' and then looked at her as she started to laugh. A moment later he realized why, as they walked round the pen and saw the red SOLD notices on both rams, not visible from where Tom had been standing.

'That settles that,' Mara said.

'You're coming home to supper and staying the night with us,' her mother said. 'You've been on your own long enough. I've made your bed up, so no arguing.'

It was good to sit back and be looked after; to be spoiled; to eat the meal her mother had provided, and to relax by the wood fire with Lig at her feet; to look round the familiar shabby room; the big chintzy armchairs; the Stubbs picture, of horses by a tree, hanging over the sideboard, the pattern of the rug she had hooked for her mother's birthday the year she was sixteen. Sixteen and the world in front of her and life composed, even then, of dates with Steve; to play tennis or row, or walk on the hills; sure that the only future for her was with Steve; learning about sheep so that she could talk to him.

She sat, listening to her parents arguing over who should do the dishes; and then discussed the sheep with her father; the possible price of sheared wool; the future of the market, and went to bed to lie awake and watch the moon finger the trees, see the flickering of light on the wall where the leaves moved in the wind, and to know that Steve would never see such a thing again and that she was lucky, luckier than she had ever realized.

And to know that she would gladly give her eyes if only he could see again, and come home and marry her, and set up as they had always meant to set up, at The Nunneries, where the roses he had planted for her were blooming freely and the garden was a recurrent miracle, changing each day, laid out with so much care, and as yet only half finished and she had no idea how to finish it.

It would remain a memorial to him.

As if he were dead.

As he was now, to her, just as Lig was to him.

She stood by the window and looked out over the hills.

Dear God in heaven, why is life so cruel?

No one could answer her.

Shivering, she crept back to bed, and made no protest whatever when Lig crept from his corner of the room and eased himself gently on to the covers beside her feet.

She half smiled in the darkness. If Steve could see his dog now.

And then she whistled and the dog came to her and she held on to him as if he alone could save her from the desolation that swept over her, shaking her from head to foot, so that she lay in bed shivering, her teeth chattering, as the moon slipped out of the sky and the room became black and she knew what Steve saw, all the time.

The dreadful nothingness.

There was a switch beside her hands, but it was hours before she reached to flood the room with light and watch Lig sit up and shake his head, and stretch and then lie close again, against her, as she watched the clock tick through the endless minutes until daybreak came and she could dress and join her father in the milking parlour.

He looked at her face and wondered if their plan had been such a good idea after all. His voice was carefully neutral when he spoke.

They watched her drive away in a borrowed car. They would visit at the weekend and her mother would drive it home. They moved away from the window, not looking at one another, not wanting to give voice to the fears they had for Mara.

She reached home, parked the car and changed her clothes, and then took her horse and whistled to Lig and left the men working and climbed to the high hills, up among the clouds, where the rain on her cheeks mingled saltily, and Lig loped tirelessly behind her, never letting her out of his sight.

She sat, looking down.

The Nunneries was a doll's house, and the cars on the roads were midget cars and the people walking were puppets. Tiny creatures, who were here for a brief moment and then gone, their agonies forgotten. The hills would be here when she was nothing but words on a grey stone in the churchyard.

One future had vanished.

The wedding day that might have been was best forgotten.

She went down the hill again and fed and groomed her horse, and then took the wedding dress from the wardrobe and folded it gently, in stacks of tissue and put it in a case, which she pushed to the back of the store-room.

She had to start again.

She went to the phone to ring the contract shearers, to order the animal feed, to ask her father to look out for a new ram for her and then went to talk to Hennessey about the things that were important; the dipping and the inoculations; the time to put the rams in; and the perennial problem of stray dogs, worrying the sheep.

She rang Andrew. Nettie was busy, and all was well.

She worked until midnight and then went to bed and slept dreamlessly, having set the pattern of her new life.

Nightly she watched the sun die over the hills, in flaming colour, or in black clouds edged in gold; and slowly, she and Lig were a new team, working together in a different way, the dog having at last given her all the allegiance he once owed to Steve. She wondered if he remembered Steve, and then knew he did when the dog found one of Steve's old gloves in the closet, and sat over it, and howled.

She wished she could join in.

Chapter 11

Steve had never imagined life could hold so many hazards. He had only once tried to walk alone in the lane, on a bright sunny morning, after a night of heavy rain. Tree branches caught his hair and water poured down his neck. The lane, he discovered, was unmade, a mass of heavy ruts and potholes, into which he plunged his feet, ankle deep, in thick muddy ice-cold water.

Also the unevenness was impossible to cope with without eyes. He blundered from one side of the road to the other, and then caught his sleeve in a thick thorny stem that lacerated his hands as he tried to remove it. It clung like a burr and as soon as he had freed it from one part of his arm it fastened, leechlike, to another, until he felt like one of the Ancients wrestling in the dark with unseen terrors and could have howled in desperation.

Scott, driving along the lane, saw Steve struggling and came to his rescue.

'You've tangled with Mrs Halliwell's prize Giant Blackberry,' he said. 'It's a devil of a thing. I curse it every time I walk down here in the dark.'

'I'm soaked to the ankles, in a foul temper, sore and frustrated,' Steve said.

'I was coming to find you. Let's go back to Setter's Dene and make coffee, and you can change out of those wet shoes and socks and into some dry trousers. I'll put something on those scratches. You have pasted yourself. Jump in.'

Scott's car smelled of dog. A cold nose butted Steve in the neck as the newest recruit to the household, a black flat-coated Retriever pup, made delighted overtures to this newcomer, who also smelled of dogs.

'I have plans to take him to Field Trials,' Scott said. 'I doubt if they'll come off.' Even Steve was now aware of Scott's never-realized ambitions. He laughed.

Steve was so familiar with the lane that he knew when they turned into the yard. Barking dogs confirmed it. Marcus's deep bay was unmistakable.

Anna was busy in the kennels and came out to greet them.

'I didn't want to discourage you,' she said, taking in Steve's wet feet and bleeding hands. 'But it's a terrible place, our lane, even for those who can see.'

'I don't think I'll try alone again,' Steve said. 'I don't know how Sue manages.'

'Zanta's clever,' Scott said. 'You should see her eyeing the ground, then looking up at the trees and the bushes, and taking avoiding action. A dog would give you a lot of freedom, Steve.'

Steve refused to discuss the matter. He only wanted his Collie; and his sight, and his walks on the hills. Bitterness overwhelmed him, and he sat for a long time in his chair in his room, reluctant to make any move at all, not wanting to go back downstairs, overcome by defeat. He had hoped to be able to walk down the lane and find the newspaper shop, and bring Anna's paper back for her. It was only a small chore, but it took her time each day. The newspapers were not delivered in the lane. The newsagent wanted an added charge, for the inconvenience, as it was right out of the way, and Anna refused to pay the extra amount. It was simpler to walk up and get it. Sometimes she forgot.

She was now in the habit of reading parts of the news to Steve over the breakfast table. They discussed the world beyond their gates; the politics and the tragedies; the fears that beset everyone; the rising prices and the falling pound. Both of them saw an old age spent in poverty, without the money to pay for their needs. Both were doomed to live mainly on invested money, Anna on Dan's savings for her, and Steve on his compensation. He could never make The Nunneries pay now.

He roused himself when Scott called to say that coffee was made, but his thoughts were dark and he forgot to concentrate on the stairs. There were ten steps, and so long as he counted all was well. This time, he was far away, back on the hills, with the air fresh and clean and the smell of the seaweed on the wind, far from Cheshire and its stuffiness, its dead air that rarely seemed to have any lift or life in it.

He thought he was at the bottom of the stairs when he was not and tried to walk on the level, falling down the last two steps with a tremendous crash that brought Scott and Anna running, while Mellie, disturbed by his position on the floor, rushed round him, barking.

He had wrenched his ankle, and pulled the muscles of the leg that had been broken in the accident. He felt sick, but above all he was furious with himself. He let Scott help him to the chair by the radio that was now his accepted place in the room. Anna took great care to see that it was always in the same position and that the path to it was free from obstacles, though she could never guarantee freedom from cats or dogs. Sukie was waiting, and at once came to nuzzle against Steve's chin and purr noisily. She was so much part of his present life that it was hard to remember he had once had little time for cats; so long as they stayed outside and caught rats he tolerated them, but no cat ever came indoors at The Nunneries except to mouse.

He wanted a home of his own. He sat, drinking coffee, deep in his own thoughts, scarcely aware of Scott and Anna who were discussing the date of Trina's litter. It was a first litter. Trina was one of Marcus's daughters, and had been mated to a dog in the next county, a well-thought-of dog, with a future ahead of him, but both dog and bitch were relatively untried. Anna, always looking for a perfect pup, daydreamed, while Scott tried to bring her back to earth again.

'Remember Dan always said never count apples,' he warned.

Anna sighed.

'I never learn. But Scott, there's no future for any of us without hope.'

The words drummed into Steve's brain. He sat there, with the echo beating.

Without hope. Without hope. Without hope.

The darkness was darker, was absolute and he was sinking into a void, into a deep pit, and there was no one to pull him out again; no one to shout to; no one to hold on to. He gripped Sukie, and she wailed and sprang off his lap, to go to Anna for comfort.

'I must learn not to grab her so hard,' Steve said, trying to make his voice light, but Scott caught the echo of despair.

'Steve, I came because I'm going to need you in a day or two. I can't think of anyone else who'd be any good. I've a patient; a young and skittish little mare, that was bought by one of the businessmen in the village for his daughter to ride. They didn't know a thing about horses; got her at an auction, and she was already six weeks in foal. The foal's due any day. The father's no use with animals; he can't bear blood. The child's only ten. The mother's useless too, she cries all over me if her dog needs an injection and is sure that if I squeeze his anal glands he'll probably die next week. I spend my life praying that nothing serious will go wrong with the dog, though the day will come when it has to go; and goodness knows how we'll cope then. Would you mind if I collect you, and take you to hold her for me? It's not going to be an easy birth as I suspect the foal's the wrong way round. I may have to turn it. And she'll play up, as no one's known how to handle her or even school her. She's half wild.'

'It sounds dangerous,' Anna said.

'I don't think so. Steve's so used to animals he'll know what to do. I'm going over to look at the mare now. Come and get to know her.'

Anything was better than sitting there, waiting for Sue to come; waiting for the next meal; waiting for a decent programme on the radio; waiting for Anna to finish her work and come in and talk to him. Waiting for the days to pass in unbroken endless sequence, day after day the same, without the ability to climb the high hills and look down on the world and know that man was insignificant. He was locked inside himself and no one had the key to release him.

Scott guessed something of the turmoil in Steve's mind. He began to make controversial statements about the breeding of sheep, knowing Steve would rise to the bait, and thankful to hear an alert note return to his voice, to show that his old interests were alive, ready to take over when Steve gave them a chance and recognized that life hadn't ended.

It would take time.

The mare was dainty, too lightly made, and heaven knew what stallion had mated her. No one seemed to know or care about her previous history. She had been bred on a Devon farm, but the farmer sold her at a year old to a family who kept several horses. They had to cut down on expenses and sold the mare again. She had been handed from person to person every few months and she trusted nobody.

Scott was spending more time than he had free in an effort to gentle her.

'She's enormous,' he said unhappily. 'I reckon she was got at by a cart horse; God knows what sort of time she'll have bringing that foal out into the world.'

She had come to the gate, and Steve took the carrot Scott pushed into his hand and held it out. Soft lips nuzzled against his fingers. He breathed softly into her nostrils, and she turned her head and breathed back, sensing that here was a man she could trust. His hand on her neck was very gentle, and he spoke softly, soothingly, as he had talked in the past to a calving cow or his own foaling mares.

The voice at his shoulder made him jump.

'Mr Lewis, are you sure that foal will be all right? Suppose poor Ginny dies? What on earth will I tell Sara?'

'You'll have to tell her the truth,' Scott said, and Steve was aware of the impatience behind his voice. The woman's

125

voice was high-pitched, an irritating buzz saw of a voice. Voices were important now; the only clue to character. Anna was soft-voiced, gentle; Sue was serene, a lilt of laughter often present; this woman was a shrew of a woman, petulant and foolish, and he disliked her without even seeing her.

'You could get out of my way,' she said, and he guessed she was talking to him.

'I'm sorry,' he said, but he moved the wrong way, not realizing how close she was behind him. His shoe knocked against something, a stone or a tree root.

'You trod on my foot. Are you blind or something?'

The words were a sudden shock, a realization, a slap in the face.

'Yes,' Steve said, and Scott heard the rawness in his tone. 'I am blind. I didn't know you were so close.'

'You poor man. Mr Lewis, why ever didn't you tell me?'

'There's not usually any need,' Steve said. 'Most people are considerate.'

There was a silence.

'Will the mare be all right?' she asked again.

'I'll do all I can and I can't do any more,' Scott said. 'The foal is going to be enormous for her; you've no idea what stallion mated her; not even the date so we're going on guesswork. I'll look in daily and Mr Drake will help me.'

'Help you?'

'I can hold her head and soothe her,' Steve said. 'I'm used to horses. And this one's going to need someone with some sense about her.'

He was shaking with anger, longing to hurt this fool of a woman who didn't know a thing about the animal she had bought for her daughter the way most people bought a teddy bear or a book without investigation; without knowing how to feed or look after her. He put down a hand to the hoof nearest the gate.

'Her hooves need paring. And she shouldn't have her shoes on now.'

'I did mention it,' Scott said.

Steve bit back his words. This was Scott's client, and he

couldn't be as rude as he wished. He stroked the mare again and turned to walk back to the car, hating the woman and all she typified. He could imagine her home; fake everything; and the way she lived, flitting from one interest to another, settling to none, the bright and brittle conversation at coffee mornings, the useless daily round of insignificant routines; the child brought up in unnatural surroundings, except for the mare, which she had probably wanted and had bought for her as a status symbol, because other girls had a pony too and a pony showed the family had arrived.

Arrived where? Steve wondered and was caught up in a deep longing for Mara who had often helped when a birth was tricky and whose plain down-to-earth practical commensense would, one day, be like Anna's. Anna lacked Mara's quick temper—but perhaps she had had that too, when she was young. Life had rounded her corners. One day, in about twenty-five years' time, he thought Mara would be exactly like Anna. They were two of a kind. Country women with knowledge of animals, farmers' wives . . . only Mara would be married to someone else. She still wrote, but her letters were non-committal; having to be read to him, she dared never say what she felt, and the need to pretend she was not at The Nunneries also hampered her. She longed to be able to write and tell him his favourite ewe had twins again and that there were more live lambs on the farm this year and Hennessey had caught a marauding dog, and she was learning to work Lig. Instead she wrote about the weather and her parents' home as if she were there now her year in America was over.

It was a relief to write to the Riot Squad who had adopted Steve completely. They had raised the money for a Guide Dog; and the Centre had 'given' them Anna's Gemma. Photographs of Gemma were sent across the sea, to be pinned on the classroom notice board and then on the school board; the children, seeing 'their' dog, were fired with fresh enthusiasm, and when Steve's birthday came round he found himself the possessor of an extremely expensive and beautiful cassette recorder and a library of tapes; tapes of music; tapes of books. Mara had written to the Riot Squad and told them of his favourites; and of the sort of library he liked, and they were all there. The soft lilting tunes of the Isles.

Anna put on the cassette.

If you're thinking in your inner heart the braggart's in my step,
You've never smelt the tangle of the Isles.

It had brought it all back to him; the soar of the hills, the sweep of the sky, the blue loch beneath him, the orange weed around the shore, the tangle of the Isles.

Sitting in Scott's car, on their way back to Setter's Dene, he thought of Mara, and of the time she must have spent remembering all he had loved so well. He never dared to write. She wrote as if nothing had changed; the little gossipy notes about her parents' farm were a contact from the past.

But the barrier between them was there. He wouldn't live dependent on her. He hated accepting help, even from Scott or Anna. He knew it was necessary as it had been that morning, when he ended up in such a stupid predicament in the lane; and when he had relaxed his care and fallen on the stairs. His ankle was still painful.

Are you blind or something?

The words mocked him. The woman hadn't known when she said them that they were true, but even so . . .

Anna was out and Scott had calls to make. Steve poured himself coffee from the flask left on the draining board and found the sandwiches Anna had made for him. She was spending the day in town, shopping, buying a new trouser suit, having her hair done, lunching with an old friend.

He reached for the cassette player.

'Speed, bonny boat, like a bird on the wing . . .'

Prince Charles, exiled from all he loved. Steve had a sudden memory of his grandmother singing the song as she worked and then telling him the story of the Prince who had fled across the sea; not the sad and squalid story unearthed by historians, but the old legend that had put fire into many a Highlander and brought him with the pipes proudly sounding, and kilts swirling to rally to the flag of the man who

128

was born to be King, and who was outcast from his own land.

Sukie was back on his lap, purring. He stroked her gently, apologizing for having grabbed her too hard and she rubbed against his chin and sat, staring at him so that he sensed the stare and wished he could see the cat and her wise blue eyes, see the delicate shading of the fur, and see Mellie who had come to lie at his feet, her nose on his shoe, waiting for Anna.

Far away, he had a dog. A black and white dog that roamed the hills, and sought the sheep and barked to warn him of the hovering eagle, and its speeding shadow. A rough dog—a tough dog, fighting off the foxes that threatened the sheep, fighting stray dogs that worried the sheep.

Sue came only three times a week. He missed her. She made him laugh and she could say things to him that Anna dared not, because Sue too was blind and knew the darkness in which he lived.

He switched off the recorder. A car sped into the lane and into the yard. Scott's car, by the sound of it, and then there were quick footsteps on the drive and Scott's voice calling.

'Steve, the mare's in trouble. The foal's half born and the owner's going spare. Are you ready?'

He was always ready. He grabbed at the chair on which his anorak lay, and found the edge of it, dragging it on. Scott was in the room, doing up the zip, taking Steve unceremoniously by the arm, hurrying him into the car. They were off, down the lane, into the main road, and then into back streets, going far too fast, to turn into the road where the mare was giving birth, her only attendant a terrified woman who could not get near her, because of the flailing hooves.

Scott sent the owner home. Steve took the mare's halter, and began to talk to her, soothing her, humming to her, softly passing his hands over her neck while Scott tried to get near her to examine her.

'Need help?' a voice asked. An old man's voice, Steve guessed.

'Gunter. The Lord be praised. Yes,' Scott said. 'The grapevine works fast, doesn't it?'

'That it don't. I been watching the mare. It's dull for a man to live with his daughter when he's been his own master, and had the horses I've had. I know she's in bad hands; stupid hands, not unkind, though they've no sense and they won't listen. Hey my pretty, giddap there and give over. We're here to help you. You hang on hard, Mr Drake and keep that end occupied. I reckon the foal's a dog sitter, Scott.'

'I thought maybe a breach.'

'No. You feel while she's still. I'll bet you a pound I'm right.'

'You're right,' Scott said a few minutes later. 'If we get the cords on the front legs and I can get those hind legs back . . .'

The mare was panting and straining against Scott's hands.

Steve was aware they were in some kind of shelter, but it was a mortally draughty place; no place for a mare and young foal with frosty nights due; the straw underfoot was sodden and dirty. What on earth were they doing with a horse, Steve wondered.

His hands on her neck comforted her. The birth process was so familiar he had no need to ask what was happening; Scott grunted as the hind legs fell into place and then he and Gunter held a one-sided conversation, mostly Gunter's voice, as they fixed the ropes.

And then it was necessary to pull, going with the mare, helping the foal out, and then there was a release of tension as the small creature came free.

'My God, what did she mate with, the Great Horse of Wicken?' Gunter said. 'Damned foal's nearly as big as she is.'

'Pigsty, not a stable,' he added a moment later. 'I'll put clean straw in the corner for her and get her over there. Mr Drake can hold the foal to her and get its first milk. You get on. People like this didn't ought to be allowed to 'ave 'orses. Poor brute.'

'Couldn't we bring her back to Anna?' Steve asked, as he pushed the small head against the udder. The mare's head was close to him, smelling the foal, licking the foal, already forgetting the birth ordeal.

'I'm going to try,' Scott said. 'I'll invent a few complications. They can pay Anna full livery though. They can afford it. And I'm inclined to charge double. It's lucky I had you and Gunter to help, or we'd have been in dead trouble.'

'You can call on me any time,' Steve said. 'I'd like to get her home and get her hooves pared. And those shoes off her. They're only held by a few nails. Her feet are in a mess as well.' His hands had been busy.

'If you could see her you'd know everything's in a mess,' Scott said wearily. 'She's not been fed for foaling; I doubt if they've given her extra hay and this stuff... smell it.'

Steve took the haynet and sniffed.

'They expect her to feed on that?' He was suddenly and fiercely angry. 'They ought to be prosecuted for neglect.'

The voice at the door was unexpectedly meek.

'Is the mare all right?'

'No,' Scott said. 'She needs a lot of nursing and attention. I'll give you a full breakdown of what's necessary. You'll need to spend the night with her.'

'Here? I couldn't do that... I don't have time...'

'I could ask Mrs Leigh to take her,' Scott said, reluctance in his voice. 'She's extremely busy and nursing the mare and foal will add to her load. She will have to be properly paid; this is a lot more than just livery, you know.'

'I'd be glad if she would,' the woman said. She had heard Steve's angry words, sounding loud and clear as she came up the field and she was frightened that he might report her. The mare wasn't well looked after, she knew that, but there was so much to do, all the time, and her husband had wanted it for the child. Sara rarely even came to see it and hadn't been able to ride it at all with the foal coming. It had been just like Martin, the woman thought, irritation at her husband flooding over her.

'I'll pay anything Mrs Leigh asks; I couldn't possibly look after her.'

The signs of the birth had made her feel sick. The foal was not yet clean, a messy looking little rumpled object, trying to stand on legs that wouldn't take his weight. They would sell the mare and buy Sara a gelded Shetland pony; there couldn't be any problems with that.

'I'll come over with my horsebox later,' Scott said.

'I'll stay with her for now,' Steve said. 'I haven't anything else to do.' He laughed suddenly, without amusement. He never had anything much to do.

'I'll stay too,' Gunter said. 'Be out of Mary's way. She's for ever turning me out of me chair to hoover, or dust, or shake the rugs, or take off the tablecloth. Proper fidget she is. I'll clean this place up; been getting on my wick for months.'

He vanished and returned again, to put an orange box against Steve's leg. 'Sit on that, and keep her happy. I don't suppose you've a pound or two to spare? I'll go down to the farm and get some clean hay for her; and a bran mash. This woman's never heard of a bran mash.'

Gunter talked as he worked, glad to have an audience. No one ever listened to him now at home. His grandsons were impatient with him and Mary was always busy about the place, short-tempered with him there all the time, and Joe when he came home picked up the paper and buried himself in that and then slept in front of the telly all evening, till bedtime. Old Gunter sometimes wondered if he had a voice left.

'Young Sue's the only one as ever listens,' he said, when he had been down to the farm for the mash, and the hay. Steve held the pail for the mare. She was ravenous. 'More of a gruel than I used to give,' Gunter said.

He was busy forking out great lumps of soiled straw.

'I'm seventy-seven, and still can handle a pitchfork with the best. Don't do to give up. That way you go soft and die early, like my brother Mick. Mick retired at sixty from a desk job and sat around the house reading, or went down to the betting shop. Never lived out his full span. He died at eighty and would have gone on for another twenty years if he'd taken exercise.'

'What did he die of?' Steve asked, restraining an impulse to yell with laughter when Gunter said, 'Fell under a bus.' It sounded more as if Mick had been cut short than died of inactivity, but Gunter was quite unaware of disparity in his words and the facts.

'My Dad had eight sons,' he said. 'Used to poach a bit, did Dad. Kept us well fed, and he bred the best pigs I ever seen. Loved his pigs, Dad did and spent all evening leaning on the sty wall, scratching 'em and smelling 'em. Smelled of porridge.'

'Oatmeal before killing,' Steve said.

'Forgot you were a farmer. Sheep, isn't it? I seen you work that dog. He's a cracker.'

'I'd give anything to work him again,' Steve said, voicing thoughts he had not shown to anyone before. Gunter was easy to talk to.

'Why not? Don't need eyes. He can bring the sheep to you. You done a good job then and you could have done as good alone on the foal. Many's the time I've calved a cow on a night dark as the pit, with a failing lamp and no eyes to help me. You don't need eyes to farm well.'

'I'd be useless,' Steve said.

'You think about it. Helping dip sheep tomorrow, aren't you? Takes time to learn to get around, but it happens all the time; there's plenty of folk as blind as you doing good jobs all over; and getting around. Get yourself a Guide Dog; and she can lead you on your hills. Give you freedom, like young Sue. Gave her a new lease of life, that dog did. She's only had a Guide Dog for five years. Think on, young man. And don't give up. You got a nose and ears and legs and arms; you can walk and talk and you can 'ear. You got all that knowledge, years of it, learned the 'ard way. Don't think I don't know. 'Ere, what's this then?'

Steve was aware of a forkful of muck shoved towards his face.

'Faugh,' he said. 'Don't they ever clean this place out?'

'I told yer. Don't need eyes, do yer? Yer know more than that fancy lady without even seeing. Don't take me wrong,' he added. 'I don't mean no 'arm.'

'I know that,' Steve said. Gunter accepted him as he was; no pity, no sympathy, just a message there. Get on with it, lad, and don't moan about your lot.

'I suppose I got to go back to that daughter of mine tonight,' Gunter said.

'Come and talk to me when you've time,' Steve said. 'It's good to talk farm talk and Anna's busy.'

'Time? I got as much time as you have,' the old man said.

Steve tried to imagine him, small, old and shabby with teeth that didn't fit. He could hear them click. Smelling fusty, rank tobacco on his clothes.

'I'll bore the pants off you, as my grandson says I do him,' Gunter said. He was suddenly anxious. 'You do mean it?'

'Mean it? You'll be doing me a favour. For God's sake, come,' Steve said.

'Me grin'll split me face if I don't take it off,' Gunter said. 'Mare's a chestnut, did Mr Lewis tell you? Got a white blaze on her nose and nice kind eyes, but she's been treated bad.'

'She's gentle and she's scared,' Steve said.

He went outside and felt the sun warm on his face. He had a quick feeling of brightness, of flowers about him, their scent heavy on the air, and for the first time since his accident, he felt the quiet air relax him, and had a vision of willow trees, and a lake with duck swimming, while behind him the birds sang and he thought of that morning's post which had brought him yet another gift from the Riot Squad, of all Ludwig Koch's bird records, taped ready for his cassette, so that he could identify the birds by their song.

'You want to get a wife,' Gunter said at his elbow. 'That's one thing you don't need eyes for. Make up for a lot.'

'Here's Mr Lewis and the horsebox. Work to do.' Steve had heard the engine.

Steve listened to the mare dancing on the ramp. He turned to find the foal and led him into the box. He felt the mare treading hastily behind him, anxious not to lose her newborn baby.

'Steve, you mutt,' Scott said. 'You had me scared. She might have trampled you.'

'Done it too often. She only had a mind for her son,' Steve said, and felt a glow of accomplishment that lasted through the day and took up the evening, when Gunter shyly knocked on the door, and came in to talk.

Steve, sitting over the coffee Anna had left for them, while she went down the road to see Susan's mother, who was ill in bed with bronchitis, was caught up in a world that had become remote, talking of lambing and the price of wool, finding himself totally out of touch.

That night, he slept soundly, and woke, looking forward

to Gunter's coming. The old man had promised to come over each day. Together they could explore the real world that Steve had left on the hills.

That morning he held Sukie close, purring against him, and wondered if perhaps there was a chance to remake his life.

Chapter 12

Mara had no choice but to live in the present. Memory was a trap that led to despair. The future was unknowable. Steve did not write, and she did not know it was because he dared not write. He wanted to write to her to come to him; to spend her life with him; he couldn't do without her, but he thought she was learning to break from him, that she would find another man, a whole man, a sighted man, who could give her the things he had once dreamed of giving her. The knowledge that he was offering her a better future helped him endure the loneliness, and the longing, which came at night, when the walls hemmed him in and the stifling darkness turned him in on himself. By day there were other people and a need to learn to adapt.

At night there was only the black pit of desolation and the memories that mocked him, of striding on the hill. He longed for Mara and he longed for Lig. He sent small messages, sure Mara only wrote to cheer him up, and not because she chose to spend her life with a blind and useless man. Anna wrote for him. He did not trust himself to write; he dictated words devoid of emotion, words offering no hope, words indicating what he could not say. I give you up for ever, for your own future; not mine. Memory was too bitter. Mara was merging with Anna; he had almost forgotten her ways, though never her looks, nor the days spent together.

If only he could spend the night talking; or listening to the radio, but he had nothing but the black company of his own thoughts. He sent brief notes only. Enjoy yourself. Have a good time. Words that hit Mara each time she read them, as major insults; words that hurt, because they seemed to her to show that he was not changing, that he did not need her, that he had flung her out of his life as if she had meant nothing. Time was endless; time and aloneness; no one to share the days.

She went over to Andrew and Nettie. She went home. She talked to Hennessey. Nothing seemed important any more. She no longer punished her horse. Instead she took Lig and climbed the steeps, looking over the sheep and lambs, working as hard as Hennessey, growing thin and tanned, and emptier day by day.

Anna wrote saying Steve was learning Braille; was helping round the house. Mara was jealous of Anna; jealous of Sue. They were close to him, sharing his life; and she was marooned in the hills, listening to the sheep and the soft unnerving sorrowing of the curlews, echoing her mood.

She was exhausted by anger; raging futilely against Fate, that had dealt her as hard a blow as Steve, depriving her of all hope. She wanted to take her father's car and drive down the motorways, drive to Cheshire and shout at Steve to remember her, that there was no life for her without him, to shake sense into him. He seemed to have become a different person, remote, uncaring, and she resented every letter that Anna sent, turning Anna in her own mind into a young and pretty rival, seeing sinister implications in Steve's references to Sue who was teaching him Braille.

Anna wrote regularly to Andrew Drake, but she hid some of the truth from him. The black moods that lasted for days, that neither Scott nor she could charm away. Nor could Sue who was unaware she was adding to Steve's problems because her voice reminded him of Mara's, and she had been given a gift of the perfume that Mara had loved and that he always gave her on her birthday. With Sue came memory so that he saw Mara's face and the background of the past unrolled itself tormentingly over and over in his mind. He could not break away from memory.

One morning Sue, coming over to read to him, chose 'La Belle Dame sans Merci'. It was difficult to find books in Braille that were suitable for Steve. The choice was limited, and so Sue tended to choose her own favourite reading; it helped fill the time, whatever the words.

Steve only half listened, until the third verse caught his attention.

I met a lady in the meads,
Full beautiful—a faery's child,
Her hair was long, her foot was light,
And her eyes were wild.

Memory was unrolling events in front of him, a relentless camera in the mind. The words drifted over him until his attention was caught again.

And there she lulled me asleep,
And there I dreamed...ah, woe betide!
The latest dream I ever dreamed,
On the cold hill's side.

The words were bitter; the voice was Mara's. Sue had no reality for him. The perfume lingering on the air was Mara's too and she was there, reading to him; and she was not there, not anywhere; she was out of reach and unobtainable. He was alone for ever, locked up in darkness, imprisoned by futility, aching for the past, longing for the wide hills and the scent of sea wrack and the surge of the waves on the shore; for the beat of a horse's hooves on the ground and Mara at his side, looking up at him, laughing up at him. There had been so much to laugh at.

Now there was nothing.

He was once more conscious of the words of the poem,

and of Sue, knowing he had been daydreaming, knowing he was in a distant place, far from home, with a girl who had been blind from birth and had known none of the pleasures he had always taken for granted. Until now.

His dog's brown eyes, looking into his.

The blue-green moving waves, flurrying white against the rocky shore.

The white wings of seagulls, soaring against a blue sky.

The eagle soaring above the lambs, and the white fleeces against green grass and grey rocks.

The words of the poem meant more than they had ever done before. He had read it, in school, and forgotten it, had never recognized the bleakness contained in the lines. He wanted to cry out to Sue to stop reading, to let him suffer alone, not to put his suffering into words, but her voice went on, unaware of the misery she was causing.

And this is why I sojourn here,
Alone and palely loitering,
Though the sedge is withered from the lake,
And no birds sing.

Mockingly outside, a blackbird heralded the sun; the sun he would never see again. He was lost, as lost as the knight caught by the faery lady; but Mara had pity; and he had thrust her from his life; had thrust himself into the cold world. Had become his own enemy.

His resolution was faltering.

The telephone in the hall would link him to her in a moment; he could call to her and say, come, come and rescue me, come and help me.

But he had vowed that his disability would be his own responsibility; he would not burden her; he had to face life on his own. The thoughts seethed inside his head, and Sue, aware of the changed atmosphere, sat silent, knowing she had roused feelings she did not understand, and too wise to talk.

The moments lengthened into minutes.

'What shall I read now?' Sue asked.

He only half heard the words. He was back in time, on his

horse, with Mara beside him, her long dark hair a silken mesh about her face, as they galloped beside the loch. There was wind in the air, and the scent of the sea, and the sound of surge against the sand; and Mara's scent close to him as they stood, locked in time, their horses cropping the grass.

Sue, aware of the overwhelming misery that seized him, did not know what to do or say, and could not guess the reason. He couldn't ask her to wear a different brand of perfume; and he couldn't ask Anna to buy one for her, without the gesture being misinterpreted.

'There's a right miserable way to cheer a man up,' Gunter's voice said from the doorway. 'Eh, lass, I'd a thought you'd more sense. He needs rousing chorus not a miserable mardy old rhyme like that. It's a bright day and a wind blowing and a time for a man to be stirring himself, not sitting indoors like a maid, dreaming of poetry, begging your pardon, Sue. I know you means well.'

'All right, Gunter, you cheer us up,' Sue said. 'This book's full of poems like that and I only wanted to read to Steve, and then pass it over to him for his lesson.'

'All dots and dashes, and hooks like Morse gone mad,' Gunter said, inspecting it.

'It's all dots,' Sue said.

'Sooner you get a dog to guide you and get back to them sheep of yours the better,' Gunter said.

'Who says I'm having a dog or going back?' Steve asked, jerked abruptly out of apathy.

'I says. What the 'ell's the use of wasting all your knowledge? You can teach a shepherd, teach a dozen shepherds for that matter; get the lads as is going to be vets up on the farm and get them to 'elp you; and teach them while you're doing it. What's more, you'll 'ave more time than most. I never did have time for a man that sat feeling sorry for 'isself and that's what you're doing here. Get on and marry that lass you've left up there; it's only yer eyes that 'ave gone. And now I'll recite yer something. I came over special to cheer you up and I'll do it or burst.'

'It's easy to talk,' Steve said bitterly, not meaning to challenge Gunter, but suddenly and swiftly angry because other people seemed to be planning his future all the time.

'Easy to talk, yes,' Gunter said. 'And easy to sit and think on yer bad luck. Look, matey, I'll tell yer something I never told anyone else. Sue here's close as the grave; never talks about no one. So I trusts her and I trusts you. Me dad, he were a wrong un. Drunk nine nights out of ten and mean vicious when he were sober. We all liked 'im better drunk. As long as he couldn't stand up and thrash us. He kicked us when he were sober; and 'e wore 'obnail boots. He went to jail for murder when I were nine years old. They made a song about it at school, and me uncle took us away, up to live with 'im, on the Yorkshire 'ills. He changed our name too. 'Is wife were me dad's sister, so names were different.'

Sue was quietly busy, making coffee for the three of them. Gunter watched her deft movements appreciatively. Never dream she couldn't see.

'Me uncle apprenticed me, if yer can call it that, to a shepherd in next farm. Old Joe taught me all I know, and he were a man in a million. I dreamed sheep and I thought sheep and I trained me dog. I married and I were shepherd on a big farm. They were good days. We 'ad two kids. And then a third, and she were born wi'out any sense to her. Lived seventeen years, like a baby, never grew up, did Stella. She were prettiest girl I ever saw, but she never walked, nor talked, nor even sat up. And when she died, all the life went out of my wife, and she took flu and it turned to pneumonia and that were it. And then came the war, and our Jack went to fight, and never came back.'

He drank his coffee, remembering. Steve, listening, began to feel his own troubles were minor.

'Farm went broke and got sold up, and I travelled from farm to farm, getting work while I could while uncle took the little girl and brought her up too. She's a great lass, is my girl, but we're on top of one another. I saved up for me own farm all those years, and then was able to rent one. Me and me own sheep. I bred good uns; won prizes at the shows; thought of wedding again, but some'ow I got along all right and couldn't face a woman underfoot. And then they put an order on the farm; compulsory purchase and bought it up for a council estate. That place never got built though they threw me out. I pass the farm every day; the 'ouse just falling

141

into ruin. There's land there still for sheep, but it's all nettles and docks; nothing on it. And where I grew me tatties, there's just weeds. It's crazy, and it's a crazy world. No sense to it and you make the best yer can and fight all the way; 'it back, whether it's the sky that fell on you or the council that busted you. I writes letters to 'em. Don't get no replies mind; I'm just an old fool and too old to farm now any road. But I gives them as good as I gets. What yer wants is a wife, and a Guide Dog like Sue's; and go back and farm. It's what yer were born for, matey. For God's sake don't give it all up. Yer own farm; just imagine what I'd give for me own land again; even if I did rent it. But I can't do it, so what the 'ell. I can walk out and look at sheep. I can enjoy me pint at night; I can still sing a bit; and still play darts and still enjoy a pretty leg. Just for looking, mind.'

'You were going to tell us a cheerful poem,' Sue said. She was close enough to Steve for her scent to drift across his nose, bringing Mara to mind again unbidden, however hard he tried to forget.

'I don't rise to much,' Gunter said. 'Rhymes for Mary's bairns. Little lass's favourite is about a schoolmaster.

Mr Rhind is very kind
He goes to Church on Sunday
To pray to God to gi' 'im strength
To skelp the bairns on Monday.'

Steve and Sue both laughed and suddenly Steve's mood lightened. Life was a bad joke, so long as you remembered to laugh at it. Gunter, highly delighted with the effect he had created, and with having an audience, racked his brains for something equally successful and Anna came in to hear him declaiming gustily, in almost a chant:

'Here's to the maiden of bashful fifteen!
Here's to the widow of fifty!
Here's to the flaunting extravagant quean;
And here's to the housewife that's thrifty.
Let the toast pass,
Drink to the lass,

I'll warrant she'll prove an excuse for the glass!

Anna laughed at him.

'There's educated you are. That's the song you sang at the village concert, isn't it?'

'I always did like it,' Gunter said.

'Here's to the charmer whose dimples we prize
Now to the maid 'oo 'as none, sir.
And 'ere's to the girl with a pair of blue eyes;
And 'ere's to the nymph wi' but one, sir.'

Anna and Sue joined in the chorus. Steve listening to them fooling, relaxed completely, smiling to himself. Sukie, resting against his neck, on his shoulder, kneaded his jacket blissfully with her paws, loving music.

'Here's to the maid with a bosom of snow.
Now to her that's as brown as a berry.
Here's to the wife with a face full of woe,
And now to the girl that is merry.'

This time Steve joined in the chorus, letting his voice rip. He had a good powerful voice, and the others had never heard him sing before.

Gunter led the last verse.

'For let them be clumsy, or let them be slim
Young or ancient, I care not a feather.
So fill a pint bumper quite up to the brim,
And let us een toast them together.'

Dave coming up the drive heard them singing, and came and listened to the final chorus.

'Let the toast pass.
Drink to the lass
I'll warrant she'll prove an excuse for a glass!'

'That's quite a voice on you,' he said to Steve. 'We can

use you; there's a concert coming soon and you'll bring the house down. I'll fetch you for the rehearsals. Have you ever belonged to an operatic society?'

'Never had time,' Steve said. 'I sang in the school choir, and after that only in my bath or sometimes out on the hills. Lig used to listen for the echo and bark at it.'

It was the first time he had remembered Lig without an ache.

That night he asked Anna to write and ask Mara to go over to The Nunneries and see if the new tenant was treating it well, and he wrote to his father to ask for details of the tenancy, in case he wanted to come back. Anna, writing the words at his dictation, felt an elation, and hoped that some of the change in him came from her, as well as from Gunter, who was worth his weight in hay.

'Can you help me unload the bales from the estate car?' Anna asked. 'They only need to go into the corner of the end barn. We're running out of hay. And the price goes up all the time. I wanted to take a crop off the big field, but without Dan it's been impossible.'

Steve that evening found himself giving time to Anna's problems. He had been so engrossed in his own he had not even thought about her.

'I'll miss you when you go,' she said, as if reading his thoughts. 'It's good to have company. Before you came I shut the door after the dogs were put to bed for the night, and sometimes never spoke to another soul till late the next day. I don't know what I'd do without the radio and TV.'

Steve thought of the evenings alone; the days and the endless nights alone; the rest of Anna's life stretching in front of her, needing to be filled; needing to be lived; and her invariable cheerfulness when she spoke to him.

'What sort of evening is it?' he asked.

'Dark clouds, almost black, edged with gold,' Anna said. 'A deep red sun; and a streak of light in the west. And the rest of the sky is soft eggshell-green. A little wind moving the trees. And the birds flying home.'

The wind on the hill, and the darkness coming, and below him the sound of sheep. Did he need eyes for that? A dog at his heels. Not a Collie dog, but a dog like Mellie, who was sitting at his side, her head on his knee. She enjoyed being stroked for hours on end and Steve had time for her. Anna was always busy.

And then Steve thought of Mara. She wrote, daily; wrote of the Riot Squad, but never of her own doings. She was home with her parents; leading what kind of life? Busy rushing about, or waiting for him to change his mind? Only now, rousing himself, feeling as if he had been very ill for a very long time, and was just beginning to convalesce, did he realize how brutal he had been. He had thought only of himself; not of her. Gunter's words had been to the point, and he wondered if perhaps she were waiting for him to change his mind, to return to as normal a life as possible. He now knew that Sue practically ran her own home, as her mother had retreated to a fantasy world, sitting most of the day dreaming of the past, of what might have been if her husband hadn't left her to deal with a blind baby; 'We would have been rich, Sue. I wouldn't have had to work so hard.'

Sue remembered the long years and the devoted care she had had, and babied her mother, making her little treats, bringing her home bunches of flowers, which Sue had to arrange as her mother left them to wither.

The world of 'if only' was a hard world to inhabit when the curtains were drawn, and the dark came to stay, but Sue coped with it cheerfully as she coped with those that came to the Centre, soothing their fears, teaching them all she knew about living with a disability that many people found too daunting to contemplate.

No one except Dave ever guessed how lonely her life was once she left for home or how difficult Dora had become. He had called one evening, and discovered for himself.

'Why don't you come and live at the Centre?' he asked Sue. 'It's time your mother learned how to live on her own.'

'She won't learn,' Sue said. 'She gave up a lot for me; now it's my turn. I don't mind. I won't ever marry. You know the kind of blindness I have is inherited. My father's grandmother had it, and he knew it could affect his children. I think that's why he ran away from us. He couldn't face the knowledge that it was in his family.'

Dave couldn't make her change her mind.

145

Sometimes he wished he were not so involved with his job. He was watching now over Gemma whose training was progressing well. She was just the dog for Steve. Right height, and would be easy for him to handle. She was a very sensitive little bitch. You could never raise your voice to her if she did wrong. It worried her far too much and she went to pieces. So long as she was handled firmly and kindly she did excellently. There would be no problem with Steve. He was used to dogs. On that score at least Dave had an easy mind. If they got Steve to agree to having a dog, there would be no more hurdles for him to jump. Unlike those who had never owned dogs in their lives before and were a little afraid of them.

Anna finished the night's work and lit the log fire. She sat down, picking up her sewing. She was making a shawl for her new grandchild. All was finished except for stitching a wide band round the work to make a patterned border.

Steve put on one of the cassettes in the record player that the Riot Squad had bought for him. He could not yet read the Braille legends, and had to take pot luck. It was more interesting that way. He never knew what was coming next.

He had picked out the 'Songs of the Hebrides' again.

This time, he joined in the singing, his voice soft and deep and true.

If ye're thinking in your inner heart the braggart's
*   in my step,*
Then you've never smelled the tangle of the Isles.

And he was back in time again, with Mara beside him, looking down on the orange sea wrack and the loch edged with foam. And he realized that he could still walk on the hills, perhaps with Mara beside him, and smell the salt on the wind and hear the waves and the curlews crying; and the sound of the wheeling gulls; and life would hold some flavour. He had condemned himself to a living death, not seeing any future, but a future was there, if he reached out to it and grasped it.

'I'll have that dog. Do you think they'll have one for me soon?' he asked.

Anna looked at him, and her voice was gay as she answered.

'Oh, Steve. I'm so glad. We were only waiting. Gemma was picked out for you long ago, as soon as the Centre heard about you and knew you were a farmer. She'll be ready in about five weeks' time.'

He could use the waiting time to make plans for the future and to find out about The Nunneries, and to hope for news from Mara.

'The Riot Squad collected the money for your dog,' Anna said. 'Mara's been waiting to write and tell them that you were going to have Gemma. They've adopted her; and you.'

It was a sudden warm feeling; those kids out in the States, giving up their time for him; collecting money to help him; sending money for the cassette player and more money came through Mara all the time for more cassettes.

'I must write to them,' Steve said. 'We'll do it tomorrow.'

He was beginning to plan again. Only a small plan, but before he had been content to wait, to take no initiative, though he willingly did all she asked. It was the beginning of a breakthrough.

After Steve had gone to bed Anna wrote to Andrew Drake.

'Steve has agreed to have a dog. There's one being trained for him now. It will make all the difference.'

She added a little about his health, which was now very good, and also asked Andrew to tell Mara how much he appreciated the cassette player. She sealed the envelope and wrote the address, and stamped it, putting it on the windowsill beside her car keys, to remember to post in the morning.

Sukie had been waiting for food. She fed the little cat and watched her go upstairs and call through the door to Steve. Steve opened it and the remarkably heavy paws pattered across the floor.

Sam and Mellie were waiting too, for their last night run, their last night biscuits and their titbit of hard cheese. And then it was time to switch off the lights, and go upstairs, the dogs behind her, to lie one each side of her bed. Sam came for his last fussing, his brown eyes soft and sorrowful, as he

147

revelled in the touch of her hands.

She switched off the light, and lay with her own memories, wishing the clock back and Dan beside her.

Steve had a future.

She had none.

Night, releasing him, took her in thrall, so that she could not sleep, but listened to the night owl and the creaking of her little electric clock and the dogs' soft breathing and wished for cockcrow, to get up and be so busy there was no time to think.

Her own favourite poem came into her mind, and she wished she had not remembered.

The night has a thousand eyes;
And the day but one,
Yet the light of the bright world dies,
With the dying sun.

The mind has a thousand eyes,
And the heart but one;
Yet the light of a whole life dies,
When love is done.

The moon was full. An owl cast a shadow and hooted, long and shrill, and Mellie roused her head and barked softly.

Anna quieted her, and deliberately turned her mind to the new litter that was due in a couple of weeks' time; to the next show for Marcus; to the urgent need of finding more money to pay for the horses' hay.

At last she fell asleep.

Chapter 13

It was a year since Steve had crashed. Mara was thinner than she had ever been, tanned by her work outside, firmly living in the present, ignoring the future and the past. She watched Hennessey walk across the farmyard towards her, one fine spring morning, wearing his working suit, sacking tied firmly round his waist, a lamb under one arm, his crook in his left hand. His blue eyes were fierce, peering out from under shaggy grey brows that just showed beneath the battered trilby he always wore, summer or winter, indoors or out. It was so much a part of him that she wondered if she would recognize him without it.

'Trouble?' she asked, knowing the expression well.

'More bloody dogs. Killed the ewe this time. If I'd had a gun...'

'Did you see them clearly?' Mara asked. Wandering dogs were a constant hazard. Half the village seemed to let theirs out to roam wherever they chose.

'A half-bred Collie cross; and a Spaniel pup, well-bred,

and someone's a fool to let it wander. No collars. They're both at the police station. Safe enough with fowk. But people don't realize the dogs go chasing mad and then old instincts take over. These fowk don't know animals, not like in my young days.'

'He'd better join the rest,' Mara said. There were already three lambs in the barn, bottle fed, and becoming too tame for her liking. The others were ewe lambs. This was a ram.

'Time you took a day off,' Hennessey said. 'No point in driving yourself up the wall, lass.'

'There's nothing else to do,' Mara said drearily. 'I went to see Steve's doctor yesterday. I'd always hoped he might be able to have an operation to restore his sight, but when I heard what's wrong...'

'Glass in his eyes,' Hennessey said.

'It's more than that. There's inflammation deep down in the eye. They daren't meddle. That's why he has to keep having drop treatments still. Anna mentioned them in her letter. If the inflammation ever clears they could perhaps do something, but Dr Richards is afraid it will be long-standing and do further damage, and they won't be able to do a thing about it, ever. Steve's blind for life now, and that's it.'

'There's been blind farmers before,' Hennessey said. 'With you and me, we could build a team and he'd be needed. He might'a known you'd never change.'

'I don't think he knows me very well,' Mara said. She watched Hennessey put the lamb in the barn, and be greeted by the others, coming inquisitively to nose the newcomer. He was bleating for his mother, too newly orphaned to settle.

'Damn good job the dogs didn't get at him. He's a good little ram. Make a show ram, and then sell him for double what you'd get wi'out the prize card.'

'D'you think he'd get a First?' Mara asked. She had begun to show the best of her stock and already had won first prizes with three ewes and a second with her best ram to date.

'Could be. He's a nice shape. He'll do.'

It was high praise from Hennessey who never enthused. He whistled to Lig, who had been lying by the wall, waiting for his command. Mara watched them leave the yard, and

for a moment her thoughts betrayed her and as Lig ran
ahead it was Steve who followed. They'd have been married
almost a year.

If only.

But ifs were chancy friends to live with and she had work
to do.

'Letter for you,' the postman called, leaning over the wall
to look at her. Prettier than ever even if she were too thin,
with that cloud of dark hair on her shoulders and eyes like a
young mare's, brown and thick-lashed, and sorrowful. Put
on sorrow like a dress, the postman's wife said, being given
to writing poetry. Not that Donald thought it poetry. Too
fanciful by half but Mara roused poetic fancies even in him
and he as hard-headed a man as maybe.

'How's Steve doing?' he asked.

'Fine,' Mara said. 'He'll be home soon.' She crossed her
fingers. No lie.

The postman nodded and mounted his bike. He had
work to do. Mara looked at the letter. If only Steve could
write, if only he sent a message that mattered. The letter had
been sent to her own home first and been re-addressed. Her
father was busy with lambing too. Both of them out at all
hours watching over the sheep, doing it in the old way, and
benefiting because they rarely lost an animal. She was angry
about the dogs. The owners would pay; but the dogs would
still run wild. People never learned.

She thought suddenly of a poem sent her by a friend who
also farmed, that he had found in an old book published in
the late nineteenth century.

Why should the singing birds
Fall by the fowler's gun?
Why should the young lambs die
When life has just begun?
O all the world I see
Would be free and fresh and fair
Did not men's cruelty
Put a shadow everywhere.

She hated breeding the lambs for the market. It was an
insane occupation, but people had to eat. She felt

151

sometimes like a priestess preparing constant sacrifices to the god Appetite, as she knelt with the small heads butting against her, knowing that of most of these only a few would live to breed. The rest had to be sold to pay her own bills.

She put the letter on the kitchen table, and made coffee for herself and for Hennessey, who would return as soon as he had disposed of the sheep's carcase. She did not want to know what he did with it.

She sat, stirring her coffee, staring at the wall. Steve had chosen the paper. It was chipboard, painted white, to go with the old cottage atmosphere; with the black beams and white between; with the horse brasses on the wall; with the rocking chair and the wicker chair where her stray cat nursed kittens again. Steve would never have tolerated that. She collected cats. There were eight outside now, and another in kitten, as well as the two Cameos.

Hennessey was slow. She waited, and then, reluctantly opened the letter, knowing it would contain nothing new; Steve was well and sent his love.

It was a much longer letter than usual. And Steve had dictated it. She read it slowly, and then re-read it and ran outside to greet Hennessey with a smile on her face. It was the first time he had seen her smile gaily for almost a year. He waited, delighted, his own face creasing into a thousand wrinkles.

'Good news, lass?'

'Steve wants me to tell him who is farming The Nunneries; and what sort of tenancy as he's going to have a Guide Dog and thinks he'll come back and work here himself. He can take farm pupils and teach them about sheep; and he's been helping Anna with her animals; and met a sheep farmer called Gunter . . . he can't be called Gunter! He's learning Braille; Hennessey, we're going to celebrate. I'm having a sherry and so are you; and I must ring Andrew and tell him; and Dad.'

She was suddenly transformed, a whirlwind of energy, laughing as she poured out the sherry, drinking it down as she walked round the kitchen, looking at it, appraising it, seeing things that Steve had started and that she could finish, seeing the little garden he had made for her, that she and Hennessey had not had the incentive to complete; seeing the sheep on the hill and Lig lying patiently in the sunshine, waiting to be needed.

Her enthusiasm infected Andrew, and her father, putting down the receiver, stood looking at it thoughtfully. Steve might come back; but what about Mara? There was no mention of her coming to live at The Nunneries. Where would she fit in?

But he hadn't the heart to depress her.

Her letter reached Steve two days later.

Dear Steve,

I didn't tell you before, but I'm living at The Nunneries and looking after it till you come home. Everything here is fine; Hennessey is helping me. You'd be proud of the flock. Dad gave me one of his rams, and we've bred some good stock this year. I have all the returns from lamb sales and from the shearing; everything, I think, is just the way you kept it. My little garden looks lovely, and I've added lavender and rosemary, parsley and thyme, and we've grown our own potatoes and a lot of salad stuff. Your father has put up a little greenhouse for me, so we had lots of tomatoes last year. He also built me a pigsty and I've a fat sow with fourteen piglets.

I am breeding cats too. I have two Cameos; they are in the house at present, but we can make a shelter for them outside later. I know you don't like cats indoors.

I'm sleeping in your bed. It was easier than buying a new one for the spare room and I feel more at home there anyway. I hope you intend to make an honest woman of me. My wedding dress is waiting, though I don't think the bridesmaid's dress will fit Lorraine; she's grown a lot since last year.

Lig is fine. And so am I.

The Riot Squad decided on your dog long ago. They know all about Gemma and have photographs of her. Crazily, they sent me one; she's beautiful. She'll probably find the hills hard going after Chesire!

Steve listened as Anna read it. Mara living at The

Nunneries, running it for him, waiting for him. He thought she was living a life of her own, forgetting him, writing out of duty. Instead she had taken up where he had left off, had kept the place busy and thriving, had taken over as she might have done if he could still see.

'What are you going to say?' Anna asked, more aware than Steve of the difficulties Mara must have faced, a woman running a busy farm. She had enough problems without Dan, with just her few animals. She could do most things, but not if they needed a man's strength.

Steve's thoughts were whirling. Mara wouldn't be ditched and didn't want his sacrifice; she was making her own. He should have known her better. He was suddenly buoyant, seeing a future where none had been before, making plans again, visualizing The Nunneries, and the sheep on the hills, with a place for him in there, with Mara beside him, not having to pity him or help him, but adding to his capacities, extending his abilities, complementing his skills. And he had skills still. He had a brain and could use it, and he was not a cripple, or likely to be.

'Can you get me her number?' Steve asked.

Anna dared not comment. She dialled the number, and handed the receiver to Steve, who listened anxiously, only half aware of the shutting door as Anna left the room.

'Mara?'

There was a silence and then a disbelieving 'Steve!'

'I'll be home in six months,' Steve said. He couldn't say half what he wanted to, especially on the phone. He was never a man for soft words and sweet talk. 'Hey, Funny face; you can start the wheels rolling. We'll be married as soon as I get back.'

'Shall I come down?' Mara asked. She was busy; very busy, but she'd make time. 'Just for a weekend?'

'No,' Steve said. 'I'd like you here all the time; but I'm ready for my dog, and the sooner I get her the quicker I'll be home; there's a lot to learn. I want to learn it fast. Only phone me, Mara. Whenever you can; and we can talk. In any case, can Dad spare you?'

'Not really,' Mara said regretfully. 'We're pushed to the limit and short of men; one of Dad's men had an accident last week in his car and is out of action, and Andrew had help for six months but Joe was old and he found the work too heavy. The young men don't want farm work. It's too tying. And there's a calf due. I've bought four Jersey cows.'

'Daft, on a hill farm,' Steve said. 'They'll never winter there.'

'I'm a good cowwoman,' Mara said. 'You'd be surprised. Take care, Steve, and learn fast.'

'Can't learn quick enough,' Steve said. His voice was jubilant, the thought of a farming future exciting him as nothing else had done since the crash. And the thought of Mara, waiting for him, after all. He didn't deserve it.

Anna, busy outside with the dogs, was jubilant too. Steve was making progress at last; was thinking positively instead of negatively, was planning, and had hope. Without hope, life had no meaning.

And, for a moment, bleakness overcame her so that she lifted one of the kittens, busy playing with a straw, and held it to her. The kitten wanted to play, and struggled free.

She did not want to go indoors. Her own sudden depression might reach Steve; he was now so sensitive to mood that he knew at once how she felt, without being told; and how Sue felt. Through Steve, she had learned that Sue was by no means as equable as she seemed. She put a brave face on life; but there were days when her mother's tantrums were more than she could bear, and she came to talk to Steve, and he sensed the turmoil inside her.

She had wondered about Sue and Steve, but she knew now that only Dave existed for Sue.

And there seemed little future for them for Sue's loyalty bound her to her mother, and while her mother was alive she had no time for anyone else; and no freedom.

There was food to prepare for the dogs. There was time to kill. Steve was going and she would be alone again, waiting for tomorrow, seeing nothing ahead of her but the need to keep alive. She did not know why. Day after day, with only the animals to care for. A lonely woman whose family were grown and whose use was over.

Dave came in through the gate.

'Steve's engaged again,' Anna said, and for no reason

155

whatever, tears rolled down her cheeks, so that Dave put an arm round her shoulders.

'What's wrong, Anna?'

'Just futility; Steve's going and I feel useless.' She was furious with herself, hating to show her feelings to anyone else, above all to Dave who had enough problems of his own.

'You're doing a great job,' Dave said. 'No one else can do it. We need your experience, Anna. You've an important place in the world, believe me. You helped Steve, far more than any of us. Don't underrate yourself. There'll be others.'

Anna smiled at him, and returned to her work more cheerfully. Dave went indoors.

'So you've come to your senses at last and set yourself a deadline for returning to the farm,' he said, satisfaction in his voice. 'Your dog's all ready for you; or rather, your bitch. You know her already and should take to her fast. We picked Gemma out for you, long ago, hoping you'd see sense at last. You ought to know her quite well.'

'I don't really,' Steve said. He had been too engrossed in his misery to take much notice of the dogs when he arrived. He found pleasure in Sam and Mellie now and played with them, throwing the ball that Sam brought back to his hand, putting it firmly in the palm as if he knew that that was the only way that Steve could possibly find it. Mellie ran too; but Sam never let her have the ball, though she always hoped.

But when he had first arrived he had been aware only of himself and of his limitations; of a depression so dark that it was worse than blindness itself; of constant fear crowding in on him. Gemma had left for her training before he had become conscious of the outside world.

All the same there would be no difficulty, he was sure of that. He had trained so many dogs. A long succession of Collies, all from the same line as Lig. Difficult pups at first, wilful, determined, with minds of their own but he had overcome the stubbornness, had been firm and consistent all the time and shown who was Master. No dog ever got the better of him.

There would be no problems, both he and Dave knew. They couldn't have been more wrong.

Chapter 14

Gemma had proved as good a pupil as Dave had hoped. He took a special interest in her training, remembering all the time that she would be around farm animals. He took her out every day himself, during the learning time, walking her constantly among sheep, among cattle, among horses.

She ran free on the sheep farm, on a long line, that could be tugged at once if she showed chasing tendencies. Luckily, chasing was not one of her vices. Her main hobby, that would annoy a man living alone, but be little problem if Steve were to marry, was that she rolled in muck whenever she found it. She stank to high heaven the day he walked her on the pig farm, forgetting that pig muck, to Gemma, was pure bliss. The piglets ran free, protected only by an electric fence, to keep them within bounds. Gemma jumped the fence, and found more delectable messes than she had ever found before. It took Dave the whole afternoon to remove the smell from her, and even then, Sue, going to play with the dog, had to beg scented talcum powder before she could handle her.

'Niffy little beast,' Dave said, watching the two as they played. 'Think Steve will get on with her?'

'I don't see why not,' Sue said, blithely unaware that a Collie was a breed on its own; a Labrador/Retriever cross was something quite different.

Dave, who sometimes helped teach at a local dog club, knew enough to know that Collies matured much earlier than the gundogs; wise and sober and working by one year old, whereas often a gundog kept its puppy madness to some extent to four or even older. But training worked, and Gemma knew she could only play the fool when she was not wearing her white harness. That was the trigger that switched her brain on.

Dave supervised her final training; walking with a big suitcase at his side through the main streets, under narrow arches, across a building site, where Gemma had to stop and warn him of obstacles ahead and lead him round them.

The bitch had to learn well and she had to learn fast.

Anna had taught her basic kerb drill; to sit at the kerb and wait while vehicles passed her, and not to move until the road was clear, but now she had to learn far more complex manoeuvres. She was taken out to a quiet street, where a van drove up and down, stopping in front of her just as she was about to cross, turning into a gateway as she was walking along the path; going into reverse when she might have expected it to go forwards.

She learned to watch for the almost silent bicycle that might be masked by a vehicle and come swiftly and unexpectedly; she learned to watch speed and distance, to cross fearlessly when all was safe. She learned to use zebra crossings and pelican crossings and to cross at traffic lights.

She went by bus and she went by train, leading Dave along the station, or to the bus stop. She was taken to London, and walked through rush-hour crowds. She was taken to the seaside and walked in a high wind along a promenade with the waves crashing against the wall.

She was taken to high buildings, and travelled up and down in the lifts. She learned to go fearlessly into small shops and large shops. Because of Steve's occupation she was taken to the Beast Sales, walking among the pens,

158

pushed under the bench in the auction tent, or at the ring at the side of pens, lying quiet while beasts of all kinds came under the hammer.

She went into banks, through swing doors and revolving doors, though she did not like either at first, nor did she like automatic doors that swung mysteriously open as she approached. Dave had to spend much of three days going in and out through one of those. At last she went in boldly, not caring at all about the mystery.

'She's a cracker,' he said to Sue.

Sue handled the next stage in the dog's training. She was so used to Guide Dogs now that she tried them out in the grounds of the Centre, their first experience with a non-sighted handler. Gemma passed every test with flying colours.

It was time for her to meet Steve.

It was time for Steve to leave Anna. This was a full-time course, and there was more to learn than he realized. He had to find his own way about a strange place; he had too to contend with seven other blind people; live more closely with them than he had lived with a large group since he had left school; and he had to be taught about the dog. He knew about dogs; the initial lessons would, he was sure, be a waste of time, a courtesy on his part to attend; he had trained dogs since he was seven years old when he had been the best child handler of the year with his father's Collie.

There was nothing he could learn about dogs. He knew every Collie trait in the book; and all dogs were dogs. He had never lived closely with any other breed, and had never done more with Sam than play with him. Sam was Anna's dog, and Steve would never try to command another man's animal.

Anna dropped him off at the Centre.

'I'll miss you,' she said. 'Good luck.'

'Thanks for putting up with me,' Steve said, holding her hand, wishing he could see her, wondering if she were plain or pretty, if her looks matched her voice. Unable to ask any of those questions. She had mothered him without fussing him; had endured his black moods and helped to make him independent. He felt bereft as he heard the car drive away.

Then Dave was beside him, familiar, welcoming him, showing him to his room, guiding him to the stairs. He was the first arrival as everyone else had a long journey to make. There were to be three men and five women on the course. 'Three of them are elderly, and have gone blind through various disorders that can come with age,' Dave said. 'There's a boy who has been blind all his life; he's only just able to have a dog now. There's a woman who has been waiting for two years, who is tiny, under five feet high; we needed a small dog for her, but have only just found one good enough. There's a fair wastage. We have a small Labrador bitch and crossed her with a small working sheepdog; the pups were a bit of a disaster except for this one. There's you; and there's a young racing driver, blinded in a crash during a race; and the last of them is a headmistress; I think she is going to be a bit of a problem as she struck me when I interviewed her as one of those people who always knows more than everyone else and she tends to treat everyone as a school child.'

Steve, drinking coffee with Dave in his room, felt briefly privileged; part of the place, almost behind the scenes, though he knew that once the others came, Dave would treat him as one of the group, making no favourites.

He had been intrigued to discover that if Gemma had been smaller, she would have had to go to someone else. He was tall, and needed a big dog. Gemma had taken after Sam, and not Mellie in that respect.

'What does she look like? Lab, or Retriever?' Steve asked.

'She has a Retriever coat and head and tail, and in fact to anyone but an expert I think she'd look pure Retriever,' Dave said. 'She's a pretty bitch; we got a lot of attention from strangers when she was being trained. People want to stop and pet her, but that's not allowed while she's working. I expect you'll find the first days a bit dull; not much I can teach you about grooming or feeding; Gemma gets fat easily, and of course she's spayed, so you'll have to watch that. She doesn't need half the amount of food the books say; nor as much as some of the other dogs. One of the other bitches, Lulie, is as thin as a rake, and needs four times the amount you'll have to give your dog. We had all the tests done on her to make sure she's fit; it's just one of those things. Like me, I eat like a pig and am as thin as a drink of water; while Matron only has to look at a biscuit and she puts on five pounds!'

The first evening meal was an edgy event; Steve felt at more of a disadvantage than he had for weeks, among people he had never met, people he would never see, needing guidance as to their characters from their voices, and from their words.

Conversation was uneasy and, as Dave had feared, it was dominated by the headmistress, whose rich, rather fruity accent irritated him beyond measure.

'Of course, once I have mai dog, ai will be able to go back and live among mai gals, without any problems whatever,' she said at one point and a soft voice in Steve's ear said gently, 'Won't that be naice?'

He chuckled.

'I'm Steve Drake,' he said. 'I'm a farmer. Or I was,' he added soberly, overcome by sudden distrust of himself and his future. He had been hoping that a Guide Dog would be the key to the world again, and now he felt he had been telling himself fairy stories. A dog was only a dog.

'I'm Lynn Ferguson. I was a dancer,' the girl beside him said. 'I was at the Ideal Home Exhibition when they let off that bomb.'

She had said it matter-of-factly; she had lived with the knowledge for two long years, waiting for her dog to release her to some kind of world again, yet her voice held laughter. She had laughed at the woman who had been irritating Steve so much. She laughed now.

'Damn, what did they give us peas for? I've got a lap full. One thing, my dog will probably turn into a dustbin. I won't need to feed it. I don't know why I always make a mess of eating fiddly food, but I do. Don't you think they ought to give us all dog plates and let us get down and lap? I'd do much better.'

Steve's laugh rang out across the table, and Dave turned his head to look. He had never heard Steve laugh so joyously before.

'Share the joke,' he said.

'Lynn's dropping peas all over the place. She thinks we ought to be fed on the floor like the dogs.'

There was laughter round the table, except for the rich plummy voice.

'What a disgusting idea,' she said.

But the ice had been broken and the voice was ignored as one of the men went on to explore Lynn's idea further.

'Maybe we could have specially designed drinking troughs too,' he said.

'Personally, I always drink water out of the teapot,' one of the older men said. 'You can't dribble it down your chin then.'

'I put on a bathtowel before I drink,' another voice said.

Later that evening, talking to Lynn, Steve realized why she had made a constant joke of her blindness.

'My mother was devastated,' Lynn said. 'I had to be the brave one and lead her back to sanity. She'd planned so much for me. If I have children I won't make any plans at all for them. It puts too much responsibility on their heads.'

'Will you marry?' Steve asked.

'Oh yes, I'm engaged. Larry was with me at the Exhibition. He's lost his leg. We don't know yet whether the halt will lead the blind, or vice versa. He's got an artificial leg now and he's learning to walk and run again, and says he'll go back to playing football with his bionic leg. I can do most things now; the dog will mean I can go places by myself, do all the shopping. I used to see two blind people when I went up to Town every day; a husband and wife. Later the wife used to come to the station with her Guide Dog to see her husband on to the train, with a baby strapped to her back. The baby could see. She said it gave the dog exercise to come out each day. I never thought then that I'd need a dog myself one day.'

Lying that night in a strange room, trying to orientate himself, wondering whether he was facing the window or the wall, feeling suddenly enclosed and trapped, Steve forced his thoughts on to Lynn. She was twenty-two; and her blindness was even more senseless than his. He had at least the knowledge that he had saved five children and a woman

162

from death; she only knew that the criminally insane had planted a bomb to kill people.

'I was lucky,' she said to someone else in Steve's hearing. 'Some bomb victims have died, and some have had much worse injuries. I can listen to music, and walk in the sunshine; I can marry and have children. And I've always wanted a dog, but never before been at home to look after it, so I went without.'

The first lessons were not news to Steve. Grooming and feeding; exercise and care; and the use of the voice on the dog; praise or blame, having to remember that the dog was only aware of the precise instant; not the future and not the past, only a forty second memory of any event, so scolding had to coincide with the fault and praise follow immediately, or the dog associated the scolding with the wrong action.

'Never scold a dog when it returns to you, even if it's covered in mud, or stinking with pig dung,' Dave said, thinking of Gemma. 'The dog will have forgotten everything that happened; all it knows is that it has rushed to greet you, and you have scolded it for COMING to you; fuss it, tell it it's a great dog, and that you adore it even if it does smother you in muck and stink to high heaven, but never, ever rebuff it. Or next time it won't come. Would you come to me if I greeted you by boxing you on the ear?'

The third day came.

Everyone was sent to his or her own room, to wait for the dogs. Steve sat, knowing that Gemma would not be his dog for a long time yet; Anna had been her first love; and Dave would have taken over. Dave had done most of her training; Dave had her respect. It was not like taking on a pup, that came to the first human it had ever known. This was a dog with a past; and no dog transferred its allegiance instantaneously to a new owner. Some never transferred at all; Gemma might not, and if that happened then Steve was back to the beginning again, and sat wondering if he could breed a Collie pup, could have Mara walk it, and then have it trained to guide him, if this failed. But it would mean a long time waiting and life was flying by. He had already wasted more than a year. He was becoming impatient.

Steve had only been with Gemma at Anna's for a few

weeks before she went for her training. She had come in and played with the other dogs; but most of her time had been spent outside. He wondered if the bitch would remember him.

He sat, keyed up, and extremely anxious, listening to sounds from the other rooms; a dog barked. The wind was howling outside the building, hurtling itself against his windows. He hated wind; the constant keening made him as edgy as the cattle in the field and he remembered how the sheep always ran on a windy day and how the lambs indulged in their madder antics. One had leaped to the top of a briar hedge. Lig found it and Steve had struggled against the thorns caught in its thick fleece to free it, while it fought him in panic. There was nothing quite as stupid as a frightened young animal.

He was consciously filling his mind with other thoughts; as edgy as a lad on his first date with a girl. If he and Gemma failed to match one another; if he had to wait for another year.

He heard Lynn's voice in the room next door.

'She's licking my face. She's sweet. Oh, you darling.'

He could never enthuse like that to any dog. A dog was a dog, to be kept in its place.

And then there were clicking claws outside his door, and the door opened, and Dave said, 'Here she is. Make a fuss of her, Steve,' and the door shut, and he was alone with his new dog.

'Gemma,' he said, and knew at once that she had remembered him. She came to him cautiously, and her cold nose sniffed at his clothes; sniffed at his hand. Anna had handled his clothes; Sam had leaned against his legs; and so had Mellie. He smelled of Sukie. He missed Sukie. Andrew was to drive down to fetch him and bring a basket with him for the cat. Steve wondered what Mara would say when he told her he had been sleeping with a cat curled against him every night; carrying her around on his shoulders, eager for her to come to him, and feeling cheated if she chose Anna instead. He wondered how Sukie would settle down with Mara's Cameos.

Gemma was still sniffing him and then recognition came.

She chased her tail, ran at him, putting her paws on his shoulders. She leaned against him as he stroked her, thinking how odd it was to have a dog full-grown and full-trained, and not to have to start with a puddly pup, and teach from the very beginning.

It was easy enough to stroke the bitch and fondle her, to sit with her lying against his legs, with the radio turned on softly, real music coming from it for once. 'Desert Island Dics', with a conductor of one of the best orchestras in the world choosing music that he loved.

Steve lay back against the chair, his head pillowed comfortably, his new dog close against him, and let the sound wash over him. For the moment, he was free; totally relaxed and at peace, forgetting all he had lost.

A new phase was beginning. They had finished the treatment of his eyes; no more drops; no more hospital visits. Only now the acceptance that this was for ever; and a new way of life had to begin.

He thought of Lynn, joking about her blindness, knowing she could never dance again, but planning for the future.

'We've a lot to learn, girl,' he said, and Gemma's tail beat hard against the floor. Steve smelled of her mother, and she accepted him at once.

Chapter 15

It was easy enough to get on with his dog when they were off duty. On duty, Steve soon found, was a very different matter. Gemma was playful when she was groomed, teasing at the brush, annoying him, so that he used his sharp voice on her, the voice that brought Lig to order.

Within seconds, he had lost her.

He felt around the tiny grooming cubicle, on the bench, in the corners, and Dave, hearing him call, 'Here, Gemma, here,' came at once.

'She's dodging you,' he said. 'What did you do?'

'She was playing the fool. I only told her off,' Steve said. 'She bolted.'

'She's a very sensitive bitch,' Dave said. 'She needs only a slight difference in tone to correct her. Listen. "Here, Gemma. Good girl then, that's a very good girl".'

'I'm not used to sensitive dogs,' Steve said irritably, seeing hurdles ahead. 'I've always been boss, and I can't change now.'

'You don't have to change. Just remember this isn't Lig. And she isn't a Collie. This is a bitch, not a dog; she's keen, eager to please, and very submissive in some ways; but she'll also take the initiative if anything crops up that entails her using her brains. You have to learn all over again, Steve. You aren't the trainer now. She'll have to train you. I thought you'd find it easy with your background. But thinking over what you've told me about Lig and your other dogs, I'm not sure Gemma is the right dog for you; she can't take hard handling. She maybe needs someone very gentle. But she's too big for Lynn. Lynn's got a slightly tougher-tempered dog, and she's going to have to learn to exert her authority or Meggie will play her up and get spoilt.'

'Do you always have these problems?' Steve asked. He was dispirited and irritable, having thought it would be so easy.

'All the time, though yours is different. But that's just a challenge to both of us; I've got somehow to re-train you; and you've got to accept that all breeds are very different. Lots of people expect all dogs to behave the same way. They don't. The Collie's one on its own. And Lig was a genius. Gemma isn't; she's a bright little bitch and she'll do you proud if you let her. Now watch that voice; and don't get ratty with her. She can't bear it. Her head and tail droop, and her whole body looks defeated. She's a very ebullient little animal; don't knock it out of her.'

Steve, sitting in his room, thought over the morning. It hadn't been a good one at all. He wasn't used to a dog that walked ahead of him all the time; he wanted to snap his fingers and get her back to heel, where Lig had always walked, closer than a shadow, he and the dog aware of one another all the time.

He couldn't see this dog and the harness seemed to remove her completely from him. He was hanging on to it like a child with a hobby horse and it seemed as futile, not like a real animal; he began to wonder if the dog were on the harness or if he still had a trainer instead of a dog, and he began to doubt himself.

Several times when Gemma stopped, he spoke to her more sharply than he had intended. He had never realized how forceful a voice he needed to control Lig. Either that or a shrill whistle.

'It won't do,' Dave said in despair, after Steve had stopped dead, refusing to move at all when Gemma tried to go forward. 'Try using signals for her, not your voice. The tone is too hard. You're confusing her completely. Use a clenched fist for SIT; and a downwards sweep for down; and trust her for heaven's sake to know when the way is clear. It was perfectly safe to cross then.'

They were in the complex of alleyways round the Centre, with the practice vehicles driving slowly to and fro. Steve had not realized how sensitive his ears had become. Also he had not yet learned to judge speed by sound; he was sure there was a vehicle near when in fact it was behind him, some distance away on another road, and he had stopped dead, saying, 'No, Gemma,' sharply, sure that she was leading both of them to death.

It was far more exhausting than anything he had known. He had to re-learn everything. And when they went to his room, Gemma did not come to him. She lay against the wall, watching him anxiously, afraid he might reprimand her again. He sat, helpless, afraid to call her, in case he frightened her even more, knowing that he could never manage this bitch. They would have to find him a tough dog, a male, an animal that he could order as he ordered Lig. An overwhelming longing for Lig took him by surprise and Dave came in to find Steve lying back in the chair, his face set, his fists clenched, struggling with an overpowering sense of total misery.

He looked at Gemma, who had given a half wag of her tail. Her eyes were still on Steve, anxious, afraid of some unpredictable act on his part. Somehow this partnership had to be made to work; somehow Steve had to be brainwashed into handling her properly. She had been handpicked for him. The Riot Squad had wanted her for him; Anna had trained her for him; they had never expected any difficulty of any kind; not with this man or this dog.

How wrong could you be, Dave thought.

The dinner gong interrupted them.

Dinner was a much more silent meal than usual. Nobody

168

was finding it easy. The headmistress had been shocked into discovering a field of knowledge that was totally alien to her. Dave was not at all sure that she could be given a dog at all; she was stubborn and very slow to learn. Everyone had had at least one unnerving experience.

Dave, who had hosted too many groups like this, knew that most of them were no different. Progress was as usual, except that he was bothered about Lynn, whose dog had sensed her nervousness, and was playing on it, concerned about Steve, and slowly finding it difficult to be patient with the headmistress. She had a bitter tongue and used it on both him and the dog.

Even Lynn was subdued.

'I was so sure I was right,' she said, telling Steve how she had fallen down a small flight of steps. 'Meggie stopped dead, and I couldn't feel a thing in front of me. I've learned to sense obstacles and there was just nothing there. So I went on, knowing the way was clear, and wham, down the steps I went. I've got bruises on places I didn't know I had.'

'You were lucky you didn't break a bone,' Dave said. 'There will be worse hazards than that, Lynn. You must trust Meggie. She won't let you get into trouble. And none of you are praising your dogs enough. They need to be told they're right and you're pleased with them, all the time. It's not worth working for someone who never tells you you've done a good job; and dogs will pack it in unless you praise.'

'They're like children,' one of the men said. 'I found when I was teaching that if you took a dim child and praised it extravagantly when it did even one tiny thing well, it tried much harder next time.'

'We must look odd enough to people as it is,' the headmistress said, 'without making ourselves look total fools by going around talking to our dogs.'

'I like talking to my dog,' Lynn said. 'It makes me feel I'm part of the team; only somehow I don't seem able to get the right sort of voice. I need your voice, Steve, and I guess you need mine. Dave, could they do a voice transplant on us, do you think?'

'I'd sound pretty odd with your voice,' Steve said.

'Mm. And I'd sound dead kinky, wouldn't I, with that

honey-brown beery voice of yours.'

'Beery?' Steve said, startled by such a novel description.

'Only because I like beer. Dave, when we've got on a bit could we go out for a drink with the dogs? It's one of the things that Larry enjoys and I want to be sure Meggie and I can behave in pubs and not hurtle around as if we were both tight. Steve, I didn't tell you . . . I found myself careering after Meggie at ninety miles an hour this morning. I just couldn't stop her. She wouldn't listen. There I was saying, "No Meggie, slow Meggie, for goodness sake Meggie, stop it Meggie, don't pull, stop damn you," until suddenly everthing Dave told us had gone clean out of my mind and there I was rushing to God knows where behind this mad dog that had gone clean out of her senses, into a river or something, and I just screamed. Stewart was behind me and Meggie had seen a bally cat, if you please. And forgotten her lessons.'

'No, you'd forgotten yours,' Dave said. 'I'm going to get a tape recorder; I've a little one I can carry around, and I'm taping all of you talking to your dogs. And then you can listen to yourselves; and I hope make vows to do better. I can't do that for you; we've done all we can and now you're all on your own.'

Steve, listening next evening to his tape, suddenly saw why Gemma was afraid of him. There was more than command in his voice; there was a sharpness he had certainly never used on Lig; a venting of his frustration with himself; and a resentment because he was so dependent on this dog; no longer master, to send the dog where he wished.

'Leave me the tape recorder sometime, can you?' he asked Dave. 'I'd like to practise.'

'You can coach Lynn and she can coach you,' Dave said. 'I mean that seriously, Steve. Until that dog has recovered her confidence, you're going to have to work twice as hard. You've got to gain it all over again. She got on well with you till you started working with her.'

It became a daily custom to team up with Lynn and listen to her commands, while she listened to his.

'You sound as mad as a hatter with her, Steve. Soften it,' Lynn said.

'No, more like this; Meggie's got to obey you as well as guide you,' Steve said.

'You can't change dogs; Meggie's too small for Steve and Gemma's too big for Lynn. Also Gemma's had farm training and Meggie's had town training. So you just have to try and get on with it,' Dave said.

Gemma was still hesitant. Dave came up to Steve's room with small pieces of hard-baked liver, cut into fingernail size.

'Play with her; call her and feed her each time she comes,' he said. 'I'll be here to listen. Come on, Steve, you're an intelligent man, not a fool. What's got into you?'

'Self distrust, I suppose,' Steve said. 'I thought I'd find it dead easy. Too cocky by half. It's hard to accept that after a lifetime with dogs you don't know anything about them after all.'

"Nobody knows it all,' Dave said. 'I've brought you a whisky. I'm having one too; we have to get this licked tonight, or not at all. I couldn't even start to train a sheep dog and I don't know a ewe from a tup or are they both the same?'

'A tup's a male lamb,' Steve said, gaining confidence from his own knowledge.

'Drink up, and then start talking to her,' Dave said. 'And try a bit of fun; all work and no play . . . you're far too serious. Life is real, OK, but let's ease up sometimes. Don't get too intense.'

'It's easy for you, damn you,' Steve said furiously.

'Oh no it's not, mate,' Dave said, suddenly angry. 'I agonize over and over again with every fresh lot of people; go through hell with all of them; share their hells, not once *but* for ever, as each one is different; all of you locked inside yourselves, enduring; I can only guess, but I see more than I like at times. Lynn's laughter, but you don't see her red eyes every morning, because she's been crying half the night; and a man who came a year ago who drank himself sodden every night. We couldn't let him have a dog. He jumped out of a train on the way home. How do you think it leaves me? Sometimes so raw I want to give up, go and get a job that doesn't flay me alive. You're one of hundreds, and luckier than most, with a home to go to, a job you can carry on doing, a woman waiting to marry you. She rang me the other night to ask how you were doing; she sounds a great girl. Now get to terms with that dog, and damn you to hell for one of the most awkward bastards I've ever had here.'

Dave went out, and the door shut with a definite thud behind him, as expressive as a slam. He couldn't take any more. He had spent an hour with the headmistress before coming to Steve; she was going to be one of his failures as she took out all her frustrations on her dog, and he couldn't let her take it home. She pulled its ears and tail when she was angry. He couldn't even like the woman and was angry with himself for that.

He was even more annoyed when he left Steve. He had probably undone all the good he had done and said everything he should have kept to himself. But one way and another, it had been one hell of a day.

Behind his door Steve sat thinking. Dave was right and he wasn't trying; he needed to forget Lig; he should have listened harder to the first talks, but he had felt he knew it all and need not bother. Now he was lost, foxed by a cross-bred gentle little bitch of a breed he had never lived with.

'Oh, Gemma,' he said. 'What am I doing to you, girl?'

She crept to his feet, tail wagging. He sensed the servility in her attitude and knew it was something he didn't want. She was female; she was young; and it was six years since he'd trained Lig. He'd been expecting her to behave like an older dog of a totally different breed.

He bent to stroke her.

'Come up,' he said, tapping his leg.

She put her paws on his thighs and he felt her body against his legs. He lifted her onto his knees.

When Dave returned later to apologize there was no answer to his tentative knock at the door. He opened it, afraid Steve might have gone out, or even run off, but Steve was obviously asleep, lying back in his chair, eyes closed, body totally relaxed, while Gemma was curled on his knees, her head against his shoulder. She looked up, but it was only her trainer, signalling her to be silent. Her tail thumped, but Steve did not wake. He was completely exhausted.

That night marked a turning point.

Steve, concentrating on the feelings conveyed to him through the harness handle, concentrated also on his voice. He tried to make it lighter, softer, and to remember all the time to praise his dog. Gemma began to respond again, to enjoy working, and Dave following behind, saw the telltale beat of her tail, as her eagerness returned.

The sessions became more complex.

Crossing roads in busier places, trying to sort out the traffic sounds, learning to know the bleep of the pelican crossings that signified safety; learning to know that when Gemma stopped he must stop, and that the faint signal she gave was a signal to move on.

Learning to trust her.

Once, when she stopped, he was sure it was unnecessary, and tried to make her go on. 'Leave her,' Dave's voice said behind him. 'Someone's left a pram on the pavement outside a shop. There isn't room for you to get by without going into the road, and the traffic's jammed, waiting for the lights to change. If you go into the traffic you may get caught; and if you go on you'll fall over the pram and might hurt the baby.'

He had never realized there were so many possible hazards in a street. Pillar boxes and telephone boxes; children's tricycles, left by their owners, forgotten, children cycling on the pavement, bicycles leaning drunkenly against the kerb, parking meters; lampposts; telegraph poles; workmen's tents and plants in troughs and ladders and vehicles parked half on and half off the pavements where the roads were narrow.

There were steep kerbs and shallow ones, and some roads had an unnerving camber that made him feel as if he were losing his balance. There were steps down into shops and steps up into shops, and always there was the element of total surprise, of discovery, so that life became an endless exploration.

'There are five steps down into the shoemaker's shop,' Lynn said at lunch one day. 'And two up into the chemist's and the sweet shop has a sort of bar across the doorway. My headmistress used to read out on some mornings a lesson from the Bible or somewhere that began, "Life is an adventure, rich and daring." I know now just what it means, except I don't feel very rich. I do feel daring though. I went all round the ground today by myself; well, by myself with

Meggie and we got on like a house on fire.'

They all had progress to report; an exchange of information; comments on their dogs. Steve knew that Gemma was likely to roll in muck; Meggie was liable to chase cats; Lisa, if let off her harness, made for the nearest water, and came out and shook herself all over everybody; Tara was likely to be unable to resist an ice-cream and would lick at it if she saw a child with one; she usually ended up with the whole ice-cream, and her diet would have to be watched more carefully, unless Stan, who owned her, could remember never to go near ice-cream vans. She even knew the sound of the chimes, and was likely to pull hard if she heard them, in quite the wrong direction.

Paddy could not bear to pass the butcher's, and insisted on going in, as he always kept a bone for her. Margaret, who was going back to lecture in the university in which she had once been a student, laughed as she described the battle they had had, which Paddy had won.

'I suppose it doesn't matter as long as she doesn't go into every butcher's,' she said. 'She does pass the others, and when I go home I'll need her to take me to my own butcher.'

They were now becoming partisan. The headmistress, to everyone's relief, had given up all idea of a dog. She hated contact with the fur; she disliked having to groom and feed it, and Dave had been thankful that the decision came from her and not from him. He had had one or two bad experiences with dogs that had to be removed from owners who either neglected them or resented them and it was easier if the blind man or woman recognized early that a dog was not for him or her. Not everyone realized it until he had tried. Dog keeping involved far more work than most people imagined.

Lynn was sure she had the best dog there; Steve was slowly becoming aware that Gemma had skills that would be totally impossible for Lig. Once he had overcome his prejudice against other breeds, and no longer declared with pride that he was a Collie man, he began to find virtues in his new acquisition, and also to be aware that he did not have to battle for supremacy with this bitch as he had to with his dogs. He was accepted as master from the first; she never challenged him; she was totally submissive to his will, obeying him instantly now when he needed her to, never failing him when she was leading him.

'Your dog instinct's come back,' Dave said, after one of their last sessions together. He had felt elation, walking behind Steve, seeing the change in him, watching him step out confidently, allowing the dog to make her own way, stopping when she stopped, praising her when they negotiated a tricky crossing, so that her tail beat happily and she looked back at him adoringly. This partnership was going to be a good one. It would take time yet but the signs were there, and it was for that that Dave lived. That and Sue. But Sue was trapped by her mother.

It made all the struggle worth-while, even if it only happened rarely. But it happened so often. Lynn and Meggie had adapted too, and Lynn was developing quite a personality. He'd miss her when she went; her capacity for laughter, especially at herself, had helped enormously with this group; they all joked with one another now that the alien among them had gone.

Steve was learning all the time. He soon realized that though the dog was his eyes, he, in fact, was still Gemma's brain, as it was he who decided where they would go; and how they would go. By the end of the month he knew that if he wanted to go to the chemist for shaving cream and razor blades, as he had now decided to shave off his beard, he had to remember the left and right turns, as Gemma was not yet sure of the way. She could find him a crossing if he asked her; or a bus stop; and she knew the way back to the Centre from almost anywhere in the town.

He began to enjoy adventuring; going out and about, walking swiftly again, his pace increasing all the time, until he was once more as sure and fast as he had ever been before his accident. It was a relief too to be free from constant pain in his eyes and the tyranny of the sessions at the hospital, having drops put in to allay the inflammation. That had now settled, but the eye tissue was scarred beyond relief.

Oddly, certainty was better than a faint constant hope. He knew where he was going; Dave and he, one session, had thrashed out the ways in which he could be of use at home, and teaching would-be shepherds and vets was only one of them. He could lecture to Young Farmers' Clubs; he could be part of the world again.

He had discovered that if he used a ruler to keep the lines straight he could manage well enough to write readable letters. The words were oddly placed on the page, but he was able to write to Mara and tell her of his progress; he was fired by her letters back to him. Businesslike letters almost, talking of sheep and lamb problems; of the prices she got for the spring lambs; of the plants she was putting in the garden and the wall her father had had one of his men build her as a birthday present.

'It traps the sunshine and I've put peach and pear trees against it and more scented roses; if we ever have time, we can sit there and eat our meals in summer. It's fun getting The Nunneries ready for you. It's been a real nunnery for the past year; maybe we ought to rename it when you come home.'

She sent him a present by one post; two little china dogs; one a Collie, and one a Retriever. He felt the cold hardness of the glaze under his fingers; the shape of each, differing so much in build. He wondered what Lig would make of Gemma; whether Sukie would remember her. She had been there when he bottle fed the kittens. It seemed like a century ago.

Anna came up to see him, and watched him walk confidently down the road, and back again. She had a new litter of pups, and she was having another blind lodger for Sue to teach Braille. A girl this time, who had gradually lost her sight over ten years, due to some accident when she was born. Anna was making plans too.

'I'll miss you all the same,' she said, when she had finished telling Steve. 'But I have a new helper. Gunter's taken to coming over every day. In spite of his age he's a big man and strong as an ox and he does all the heavy lifting for me, as well as doing a lot of repairs that needed doing on the runs and kennels. He'll let me feed him, but he won't take a penny. Says it's a relief to be needed, and now he's out from under his daughter's feet life's much better for all of them. And you can't have Racket. I'm starting my own flock on the big field; Gunter's brought me four ewes that were also bottle fed; they're all too pesky for the farmer he says. Luckily Racket has stopped his bottle, which is just as well, as he will be a father next year and I could just see myself feeding a large ram for ever!'

Lynn, who had been listening, as they sat over tea in the big common room, laughed as she tried to imagine a huge ram sucking like a baby on a bottle. Steve revised his image of Gunter.

'It's fascinating to think of living with animals all the time,' Lynn said. 'Do you think I could manage to breed Siamese cats? I've always wanted to; and now I have to stay at home I'll need something to occupy me till we have a family and I don't want to do that till I've got used to having the dog and to finding my way about again. I hate asking other people to help out.'

'I don't see why not,' said Anna. 'You don't really need eyes to look after them; after all, you look after your dog, so what difference is there with a cat? You'll need to find someone to help you start and give you advice.'

'I could show them,' Lynn said. 'Larry can do all that's necessary in getting us there. He can drive now he has a modified car. Do you think they'd let a Guide Dog into a cat show?'

'You'll have to learn the objectives of all good breeders,' Steve said solemnly, aware that Gemma was leaning hard against his knees.

'What on earth are they when they're at home?' Lynn asked.

'Quantity,' Steve said. 'Mustn't saturate your market. Quality. Mustn't sacrifice that for quantity. And economy, the most important of the lot. Can't bring them up on caviare.'

'I can see that applying to cats,' Lynn said. 'How does it apply to sheep?'

'Big sheep may not be good breeders; or produce a lot of wool; you need to think of the product all the time. With show cats, you'll have to aim for a show specimen; get a good producing queen, and find the best stud you can and make sure you don't muck up the genetics by wrong breeding. Lots to learn,' Steve said.

'It'll be fun,' Lynn was lost in a reverie. She pulled herself out of it. 'Larry will have to buy in books for me and read them to me. It'll be something we can do together. He loves cats.'

'How's Sukie?' Steve asked.

'Missing you. She'll be overjoyed when you come for her,' Anna said. 'She's taken to needing a lot of nursing and fussing.'

They were all making plans. Anna went away with her head full of information about sheep, while Lynn on her side had picked Anna's brains to find out more about breeding kittens. She wished she could take notes. There was far more to remember than she had ever imagined.

'You live in a different world,' she said to Steve that night, as they sat over the last drink of the day. Only two more days and they would go home. There was the concert, and then all would go off to live their own lives in their own way, with their own dogs.

'A different world?' Steve was puzzled.

'With animals. I live in a town. I've never owned a dog before or a cat; I don't know a thing about them. I don't think I even liked dogs much and now I can't imagine living without Meggie. But the day I knew was a nine to five day and then it ended. Just listening to you talking to Dave, I feel I've never really had any responsibility; out on the hills at all hours, looking over the sheep, bringing the lambs, guarding the flock; I never thought about it before.'

'Have I talked about sheep all the time?' Steve asked, wondering if he had bored her beyond measure.

'Only in the last few days; and I led you on. It's fascinating. The Nunneries must be a lovely place to live.'

'It is,' Steve said. 'Wide hills, and heather; and the wind across the mountains, making white caps on the loch. Peace and the sound of sheep and the shadow of the eagle over head. Here, it's shut in. I feel trapped. I'll be glad to go back.'

'I'd be afraid of wide spaces,' Lynn said. 'I like small rooms and winter, and fires; a room to keep me safe.'

'I like a garden,' Stan said, from behind them. 'I had a

178

lovely garden; I have, I suppose. I wonder if I can weed without being able to see?'

'Yes,' Dave said, having overheard them as he came into the room. 'You can do almost anything if you want to. It's wanting that counts. Steve, we need you for rehearsal. Bring Gemma. She needs to get used to that voice of yours. Mara says there's an Operatic Society in your village and when she told them you were singing they invited you to join.'

Life was opening up vistas Steve had never imagined existed. He let his voice rip, enjoying the noise he made, enjoying the feeling of power it gave him to hear himself developing as a singer, knowing that there he could progress.

When he sang he was the equal of any man and he was no longer afraid of the dark.

Chapter 16

Mara wanted to collect Steve and surprise him, so they pretended Andrew was coming. Hennessey could take over, and Andrew was glad not to have to make the long journey. Steve could have come by train, but with the cat as an added complication, everyone felt a car journey would be easier.

Mara had been amused to read that Sukie would come home too; that she had adopted Steve and was fretting for him, and had been part of his life all the time he was with Anna. Steve must have changed a great deal. She wondered how Xoxes would react. Xerxes had a big chalet and run of his own outside. He wasn't a fit house companion as he sprayed whenever he felt like it and the smell remained. Mara made sure that he had plenty of attention and handling and fussing, and he played happily with Xoxes when she was put out with him.

Mara arrived in time for the concert. She was to stay the night with Anna. By now she felt she knew Anna well, and their letters had become frequent. Anna sent news of Steve and of Gemma; and Mara sent the letters she had received from the Riot Squad, to be read to Steve.

All the same, she was uneasy as she drove south. The motorways were busy; lorries occupied both the slow and the middle lane, and she had to concentrate on driving. The radio kept up a soft background chatter, which she ignored. There was little time to worry while she was driving, but there was time when she sat in the service station, eating indifferent food and drinking abominable coffee, wondering why she had forgotten to pack sandwiches and a flask. She bought a flask in the service station shop. Anna could fill it for her, and she would pack food for the journey home.

And then she thought it might be better for Steve to have a break from the car; perhaps she could find somewhere away from the motorway to eat. It was better to keep her brain busy with practicalities. She had something to tell him; and she didn't know how he'd take it. It had seemed so right at the time, but now she was unsure. Two years was a very long time. And Steve had had to grow through unshared experiences that she would never appreciate. She could only imagine them.

Anna had sent her foolproof instructions. She turned into the lane, recognizing Scott's house from Anna's description of it, past the little wood, and then there was Setter's Dene and the noise of dogs, and a horse's head watching her over the hedge. And Anna, just as she had imagined her, kissing her, and taking her indoors, offering her sherry, with a meal waiting.

Knowing the thoughts in Mara's mind, Anna chattered happily, not giving her guest time to think; introducing Sadie, who had followed Steve. The girl had just arrived two days before, and was settling in, uneasily, not yet having come to terms with her total blindness and a future without light. Also Sadie was a town girl and was afraid of the dogs.

Anna had more problems to face.

Mara did not want Steve to know that she had come instead of Andrew till after the concert. Steve had been told his father would be coming late, unavoidably, and would come to his room before bedtime. Mara sat in the audience, her mouth dry, her hands suddenly shaking. She watched each act; the sketch by two blind women, moving as if they could see; the songs, with everybody joining in the choruses, and then Steve, walking on to the stage, Gemma guiding him.

She was a lovely dog, Mara thought, with a surge of elation as she saw how well Steve coped, and how the dog turned her head when she sat, to look up at him.

Steve could sing.

There was no doubt about that. The notes were rich and true, the words clear, and there was expression in his voice, as he sang the drinking song that Gunter so loved. Gunter, on the other side of Anna was beating his hand to the music. He had greeted Mara as if he had known her for ever, and over their meal, which he had shared, they had soon been deep in sheep technicalities. He had taken Mara to see Racket. And the ewes, ready for mating in the autumn.

The whole audience joined in the chorus. There was a burst of clapping and Gemma, startled, jumped to her feet and barked. Steve laughed and put a hand on her head, reassuring her, and she waved her tail, assuming the applause was for her.

There was noise and laughter and congratulations. Drinks in Dave's sitting room and last night farewells and then it was time for everyone to go to his own room, taking friends or relatives with them to prepare for the next stage in the new life; going home, dogs beside them, learning to live in a new environment, without their trainers to boost their confidence, with only their own wits to surmount the problems though, if they were too enormous, someone would come and help sort out the difficulty.

Steve needed no one now to take him to his own room. Mara watched him run up the stairs, Gemma beside him. He knew the staircase as well as he knew his own room and the position of the furniture and how to avoid bangs and bumps and bruises.

She walked behind him, leaving Anna downstairs. She was afraid. He hadn't known she was coming; and maybe she shouldn't have done it this way, but she wanted to be the first from home to greet him, she wanted to know how he had changed, she wanted to know if she had changed. Watching him, listening to him, she knew that for her, nothing was altered. Steve was hers for as long as she lived, as he always had been, and she sat with tears on her face as he sang, knowing he could never see her again. He stared over the head of the audience, looking into a future that had no shape or substance.

She knocked on the door.

'Dad?'

She opened the door and Gemma gave a small bark.

'It's me,' she said.

There was a silence that seemed to last for ever, and then Steve was across the room, holding her as if he would never let her go and she knew she had done the right thing.

'You're thinner,' he said accusingly, at last. 'Like a kitten, all bones, and no flesh on you. What've you been doing?'

'Working,' Mara said. 'And The Nunneries is nearly the way we planned; there's more to do to the garden; I need you for that as I want a rockery by my wall and you'll have to carry the stones for me. Dad's sent you a wedding present; a horse to match my mare and we're going to breed from them one day. And he's sent over the General as Dad's given up riding. So you can ride when I do. The old boy's rock steady and Dad hasn't time to exercise him. He's short-staffed—men cost too much these days.'

'I take it we're setting up an establishment of sin at The Nunneries then?' Steve asked, laughter in his voice.

'I'm going home and you're going to your parents till Saturday. Hennessey's living in the farmhouse temporarily to be near the sheep. The banns have been called, the hall's booked, the guests are asked, the presents have come, and the wedding's arranged. Lorraine's got a new blue dress and your mother is over the moon.'

'A shotgun wedding,' Steve said, but there was amusement in his voice. 'Suppose I say no?'

'You can,' Mara said. 'It won't make the slightest difference as the first thing I'm teaching Gemma is the way to the church.'

'It will be a long way,' Steve said.

'No. Home is The Nunneries. It's your village church. The

183

minister's on my side too; he said he'll come and marry us in the sheepfield if you won't co-operate as it's high time you fulfilled your obligations to me.'

She tried to keep her voice steady, tried to detect rejection on Steve's face, but saw only his amused smile.

'A blind man? Have you thought, Mara?' he asked, some minutes later.

'If Larry can take Lynn, I can take you,' she said.

'What do you mean?' Steve had never thought about Lynn's appearance.

'Steve. A bomb blew up in her face. They've done what they could, but she's terribly scarred. Luckily, she'll never know how terribly, as they had to take her eyes away. She has two glass eyes now.'

Steve thought of Lynn, making them all laugh; he had met Larry that evening and liked him enormously, sensing the protection in his voice, and the pride he had in his girl. Larry joked too, about his bionic leg and going into the spy racket. They were getting married by special licence on the Saturday, too.

Steve sat in his big chair and pulled Mara to him. Gemma lay beside them, watching.

'Tell me about The Nunneries,' Steve said, and savoured the fragrance in her hair as he listened, and knew that the plans she had made for them both were good plans, and that he had a place in the world after all.

The journey next day seemed like a new beginning. A long way from his lonely travelling, months before. Sukie, in a wire cage that Scott had given them as a parting present, complained every time the car went round a bend. Gemma lay at Steve's feet. She was used to curling up in the passenger well and would not move until told. The car was a small safe capsule, with Mara beside him, driving skilfully, taking them home.

Home. He could visualize it clearly; could imagine the improvements she had made. He wondered how Lig would take to Gemma; if Lig would remember him. Lig was now eight, and they would need a new sheepdog soon on the farm, and perhaps he could show Mara how to train the pup. It would take two years to get him ready and reliable and by then Lig would be ten.

Mara had put out Steve's clothes for him before she left, choosing shirt and tie carefully, making sure he looked his best. He had gained some weight, and his face was harder now, the mouth set firm, seldom smiling. He was still a good-looking man, and she was aware, as she followed him into the little inn she had found just off the motorway near Preston, of eyes watching him as he stepped out behind his dog. Gemma was all pride, her face eager, her tail waving.

'What a beautiful dog,' the barman said. 'Can she find you an empty table, sir, or do you need help?'

'She can do it,' Steve said, his voice confident. Gemma led him to the window, and he put out his hand to find the chair, while Mara went to the counter to order a ploughman's lunch for both of them.

'That's Steve Drake,' a voice said from behind her. 'I'll never forget watching him handle that sheepdog of his.'

'Hush,' said a woman's voice and Mara turned her head to see a couple watching Steve, the woman obviously afraid her husband might be overheard.

Gemma had settled herself in the corner, to lie with her nose on her paws, watching every movement Steve made, waiting for him to pick up the handle of the harness again.

Mara was delighted with her choice of eating place. Their lunch of French bread with lettuce and cucumber, onion rings, tomato and enormous hunks of cheese, and good fresh coffee, newly made, cost less than half the price of the meal she had eaten on the way down.

She watched with amusement and slight disbelief as Steve, who would never give any dog a titbit, cut off a small square of cheese and gave it to Gemma.

'It's her one passion. Never leave cheese about when Gemma's not working,' Steve said.

By the end of the meal Gemma had been patted and admired by almost everyone in the room, and Steve had found himself forced to make conversation. It was still not easy, talking to people he could not see. He found himself speculating about them from their voices and found too, when they returned to the car, a new entertainment as he described his own impressions of one woman and Mara started to laugh.

Steve had thought her a tiny woman, as her voice was

soft and very shy. She had been enormous, dressed in heavy tweeds, with a daunting expression that only vanished as she bent to stroke the dog. A man he had thought tall was in fact only five feet high, but with a booming arrogant voice that compensated for his lack of inches.

And then they were home, and his mother was greeting him tearfully, though she was obviously now recovered and out and about again; and Andrew was gripping his shoulders, his voice warm with welcome, and the men he knew were there, coming in to shake hands with him, to make sure they knew who he was speaking to, to make sure he knew they were glad to see him and that nothing had changed.

Over tea, with homemade scones and cakes, with jam and cream and fruit, with Nettie's home-cured ham, her old skills remembered and a meal to do him honour, the talk slipped back into the old sure ways; beasts and beast prices; the new bull that had had to be restrained with pitchforks down at the Mannerings, where it had almost trampled the farmer to death, and had to be shot as soon as they bought it; the village dogs running free on the hills, after the lambs.

The wedding in the morning, and Nettie talking excitedly of the flans and pies she had made; of sausage rolls and vol-au-vents, taking Mara off to help her with the finishing touches, while Steve's father brought out his treasured Glenfiddich and poured it into glasses, making this an occasion to be remembered.

Later, they went out into the farmyard, Gemma taking Steve safely through the cattle, avoiding the messes on the ground, avoiding the ruts and the puddles, picking her way cautiously, stopping at the gate for Andrew to open it, and then they were out on the hill and Steve discovered he could walk as fast as he ever had walked, his dog taking him wherever he wished to go.

He was so elated when he returned to the house that Mara accused him of being drunk, but it wasn't the whisky that had intoxicated him.

It was the knowledge of a new freedom, of being independent, and his own man again.

The elation stayed with him that night and lasted all the

next day, carrying him through the wedding ceremony, where Gemma was part of the group at the altar, through the reception; and the wedding present show, when Mara took him round the tables, telling him who had sent gifts, describing the flowers to him, giving him her bouquet to smell; the roses were from The Nunneries. Alec's Red. It took him back to the early days with Anna, and Sue talking to him, and for a moment he had gone from her, but the touch of her hand brought him back.

'This is from the children in the other car,' Mara said.

It was a shepherd's crook, the head carved like a dog's head.

'It's Lig. They had it done specially.'

Steve held it, not knowing what to say. The wood was smooth and warm to touch; the balance was perfect. He could still use it on the hill, as a walking stick to feel his way, even if he would never again be able to see to catch a sheep.

Mara drove them over to The Nunneries. Sukie was already installed, disapproving of Xoxes, who in her turn swore every time she saw the Siamese, but at least they didn't fight. Sukie would have to stay in until she knew her home. Xoxes was put with Xerxes, and peace restored, but Mara was not sure how long it would last as Lig too lived indoors now. He was out with Hennessey. And what would Gemma make of Lig?

There were Hennessey's footsteps in the kitchen and the patter of paws. Gemma stood, watching the door. Lig came in, and as he came his head went up, scenting Steve. For a moment he stood, disbelieving, and then he was across the room, hurtling into Steve's arms, knocking him backwards into the armchair that was, luckily, just behind him, tail waving furiously, beating against the wall at Steve's side, unable to contain his joy, not knowing how to make his greeting ardent enough, whimpering with excitement, licking Steve's face and hands, trying almost to work his way into Steve's coat, burrowing against him, while Gemma stood watching.

At last the dog settled, as close to Steve as he could get.

'Gemma,' Steve said, knowing she would be waiting, afraid she might be jealous, and she came to him and stood

187

by him and Lig stood, and sniffed her cautiously from head to tail. Her smell was on Steve, and Steve's scent was on her. And she was a bitch. That was fair enough. A dog would have created problems, Mara realized now, but this was going to work.

Hennessey toasted them, and went out to finish the chores. Mara cooked their first meal together, a Cornish pasty that could be eaten by the fire. She fed the two dogs, and then they sat, exhausted by the day's events, while Steve listened to the wood crackling in the hearth and Mara and the dogs watched the flames.

The ticking clock was a friendly sound.

Steve stretched himself and Gemma jumped up, expecting to be needed, but he settled again.

He held out a hand and Mara came to lean against his knees, curled on the hearthrug, with Lig's head on her knee, and Gemma's firm body at her back.

Steve thought of Anna, more alone than he, of Sue coping with her mother.

It was good to be home.

Chapter 17

Home.

He had thought he knew his way round it blindfold; and now he found he didn't know his way at all. He had forgotten the two steps down into the kitchen; had forgotten the four steps down from the front door; and Mara had altered the shape of the garden, making a new path so that she could get to the washing line more easily.

Gemma showed him the way; but he knew better and twice he tried to turn her at a familiar corner, only to find the bitch standing rock still, knowing that here was a hazard. The second time she did obey his command and walked on, but slowly, so that he put out a hand and discovered there was a wall in front of him. He had been so sure. A wooden wall.

'Take me in,' Steve said, and there underfoot was familiarity at last and he knew he was in the stable block that Mara had told him about; a new block, built to take the horses. He heard an animal huff, and reached out confidently, to pat the big hunter.

189

His hand encountered air.

He had been so sure there was an animal there.

A moment later something pushed against him. He felt. A foal; small, its hide soft to his touch. Mara hadn't told him there was a foal. And then it moved and his hands felt the chunky head. A calf, brought in here for some reason unknown to him. He discovered later that it had been unwell and this was isolation; the horses were out at grass.

Irritably, and unreasonably, he began to feel he had no place in this his home. Mara had taken over; had made changes; had never consulted him; had railroaded him into marriage; he should never have consented. He was useless, and all his plans were sour. And all the time, he had to watch himself with Gemma.

He had never had so sensitive a dog. She reacted to his every mood; she could not bear him to speak harshly, even if he weren't speaking to her. At once came that anxious nose in his hand; what have I done wrong this time? Why aren't you pleased with me?

He had to learn to curb his irritation.

She could not understand that it was life that had cheated him, not her. He wanted to see the sheep he was handling; wanted to see the lambs; wanted to assess the light in their eyes, the way they moved; wanted to watch them running; wanted to look at Lig.

And that one talent that is death to hide lodged with me useless.

The words ran increasingly round in his head. He was locked inside himself again, imprisoned in his own body, without the relief of looking at far horizons, without the distant hills to bring him benison, without the ability to look into eyes. He began to suspect people of hiding things from him; and Mara needed all her patience to coax him to go with her into the village; or down to the pub among his old cronies, where he looked for pity, even if they did not offer it.

It was worse back home than it had been at the Centre. There everyone took the blind for granted; here he was one man on his own, an alien in a sighted world, dependent on them to see that his chair was not moved, that his drink was to hand, that he was warned of hazards that Gemma might not see; there were always hazards on every table. A beer glass left by someone sitting there before that he knocked to the ground; an ashtray, too close to his hand; once a cat jumped onto his lap, startling him so that he spilled his drink over it and it clawed him.

Adjustment came slowly; so slowly that neither he nor Mara realized he was adjusting. Andrew and Tom, who saw them rarely now, recognized the change. Gemma was now part of Steve; he trusted her completely; and she was learning to trust him as he no longer let his temper ride him. He was infinitely gentle with her, so that she responded eagerly, wanting beyond anything to please him by showing him how clever she was.

By the end of the year she could take him to the village, without Mara's help. She knew the way to the pub; to the blacksmith; to the chemist; to the bank, and was a familiar sight, greeted by everybody, though now everyone knew she must never be distracted while she was working, or she faltered, and she and Steve went wrong.

He had no desire to go away from the village, into the bigger towns. Here he was his own man, and once more could talk sheep talk, and talk with authority.

He did not need eyes to know about breeding; he remembered pedigree, and could discuss the different breeds; could discuss the prices, listen to the farming programmes, keep up with the news. There was always talk in the evenings, and he began to enjoy it; to enjoy crossing opinions with Hennessey; challenging old McLeod, who had a big sheep farm over the other side of the village; and even took to allowing Jack Farthing to tease him about being no longer a Collie man. He was too proud of Gemma to mind. She was incredible, amazing him daily, preventing him from stepping into a newly dug ditch, from falling over a ladder placed across the street by a window cleaner; preventing him daily from the innumerable hazards on the farm; animals in his way, or buckets, or pitchforks. It was impossible for everything to be stowed safely out of his way.

And Lig had his place too. By the next spring Steve was out on the hills, Gemma leading him, Lig at his side. Lig could bring him the ewes; could bark at a lamb in trouble or a ewe in trouble and Gemma would guide him; his hands became an extension of his brain; he didn't need eyes to lift a lamb from the tangle of a thorn hedge; nor to right a tumbled sheep; nor to feel a leg injury and send Lig to bring Hennessey; nor to deliver a lamb that was awkward to come.

Sometimes, looking inside himself, trying to remember how the world had been, he longed for sight again; stood with the wind on his face, wondering if the hills were cloud covered; and knew when rain drenched the valley that the sky was a dreary grey.

He could now appreciate Sue's world; there was a lightness in the air on a summer day; there was a surge of life in spring, a feeling of remission from that dreadfulness of winter; of grey days and cold days when snow trapped him indoors, as there was too much danger from drifts and pitfalls, even for Gemma.

And autumn was all smells; of leaves underfoot, rustling; of dying vegetation, of bonfires burning. There was the sea scent, down on the beach. He loved to sit and listen to the waves crashing on a wild day; and Gemma could now lead him to the beach, where there was both peace and excitement; the restless tumble of water, driving against the shore; the wind reaching for his hair; straining at his clothes, the cries of the speeding invisible birds, wheeling and diving; and above all he began to love a windy day when he had to fight his way against the tearing force that shook the trees, when out-of-doors came to life, and he had once more a glimpse of the world he had lost.

Windy days were sheep bleating and the gallop of horses; the trees crying; the straining world resisting the mad rush of the gale; the bluster of sound all round him. That was reality.

'Looks like the Lord of the Wind,' Hennessey said one day to Mara, as she watched Steve stride out over the hills, his hair lifting in the gale. His face was turned up to the sky. The dog in front of him hated wind, but she learned to work in it for Steve's sake, and he, recognizing her fear, spoke softly to her, praising her all the time, telling her how brave she was. Lig, who always loved wind, raced ahead, but came back time and again to thrust his nose into Steve's hand, having learned to recognize the fact that his master could no longer see. Their reunions were always joyous.

'It's tough,' Hennessey said.

It was tougher than Mara had realized it would be; she had to tread carefully all the time, so that Steve never knew the things she had to do, or ask Tom over to do; Andrew could no longer lift heavy sacks or work too long and Nettie needed help with some of her work too. The two farms and a blind husband, and child soon to be born, made life far more taxing than even Mara had expected.

But Steve had a place; he could handle the sheep for dipping; he could use his skills at lambing time; he could milk; and he could groom. Sometimes he was caught out, as he had been with the calf, startled to find a cow in the stable, when he had expected a horse; and there was always the hazard of muck; Gemma could show him the way round it, but she could not help him avoid a lapful if he were too close to a cow; there was endless washing, and endless bathing. Steve began to feel he must smell like a cow byre, even after changing all his clothes and drowning himself in after-shave.

Lig was Steve's again; accepting that Gemma was essential, but at night it was Lig who lay by Steve's feet; while Gemma tucked herself behind his chair, and Sukie, always demanding, settled herself firmly on his lap. Sometimes they played chess; but it wasn't easy without eyes. The Riot Squad still wrote and sent cassettes; they knew now he loved ballet music, and often when the curtains were drawn and the fire was lit, they played his music. With music came release. It did not matter that he could not see.

Slowly there came a pattern. Steve learned to type in Braille, teaching himself with difficulty; but he could do the farm accounts; he could take over more of Mara's work; he could write letters. He began to lecture to local groups; he and Gemma were in high demand, and Lig often came too, to show how he too had learned to help his master, bringing him items from the table; his wallet, or his handkerchief; or his pen. Lig was retired from the sheep now, and Hennessey worked a new pup. Mara too was training a dog, so that she could work with the men and ease the load. The flock was growing; and she didn't want to cut back. Students came to the farm to learn. Steve was a good teacher.

Time flew.

Each month saw Steve developing new skills without even knowing he had. He could weed the garden now; kneeling, distinguishing grass from plants; could feel the tiny seedlings and bed them out. Could grow tomatoes in the greenhouse; feeling the plants each day to see how they had grown; staking them; picking the fruit. He could pick apples and pears, no longer needing eyes to feel the fruit on the branches; could lift and fetch and carry; could find his way round the house and yard without Gemma, though she was always near, ready to come at once if he wanted her.

Those about him often forgot he couldn't see. Meals were no longer a problem and he was learning to cook. Mara would be out of action, when the baby was born, for at least two weeks. He stood in the kitchen, sniffing at cannisters, using his fingers to tell him which was salt and which was sugar; tasting ginger and cinnamon, learning to cut bread; learning to cut meat; learning to tell when food was ready, using a timer so that nothing was burnt or overdone. He dared not use the grill. Everything was stewed or casseroled.

He was able to prepare the food for the dogs; to wash the dishes; to put away the plates and cups; everything always in the same place in the same order, both he and Mara meticulous.

The rams were in the field with the ewes again; Christmas passed. Next year there would be a baby in the house. And then it was lambing time, and Mara's son was born on the same day as the first lamb. Young David was christened and Dave was godfather; Sue was godmother by proxy as her mother was slowly dying.

Dave walked with Steve by the loch; knowing that Steve was listening to the sound of the waves on the beach. Gemma was beside him, intent on her work. Steve had learned at last, Dave thought. He had never known such a sensitive bitch. They might have had great problems. Steve commented on the bird noises; having learned to accept that he would never see, and to gain all the benefit he could from sounds and scents, and feelings. It was peaceful down by the shore.

194

His son was just beginning to walk when the doctor came to call.

'Steve,' the familiar voice said. 'Those eyes of yours have settled now and you could have an operation. It might not work; but would you like to try?'

To see again.

But suppose it didn't work? Could he bear the future then? And then he knew that if he still couldn't see nothing would have changed. He had a good life now, and it would stay the same; and he owed it to Mara to take the chance.

The days sped by. It was strange to be away from the dogs. It was strange to lie again in a hospital bed, his eyes bandaged; aware of pain. It brought back memories he would as soon have forgotten. They would only operate on one eye at a time. There would be a second operation later.

He was too far away for Mara to visit. Sue and Dave sent a telegram of good wishes; Dave had sent a letter telling him that Lynn now had a baby girl and she and Larry seemed very happy. He had been to visit her and Meggie.

He did not want the bandages removed. Better to hope than to know.

He lay in a darkened room, shaking, the day they unwrapped his eyes.

'Open them,' the doctor said.

He dared not.

And then he forced himself to find out the truth. He opened his eyes, and glimpsed an edge of light at the window, a glint from a glass on the bedside table; the shape of a face above him.

'I can see,' he whispered.

The bandages were re-wrapped. Steve lay, his heart pounding with excitement. Suppose it were only temporary? Suppose it only lasted a few months . . . a few days or a few hours. He couldn't trust Fate, ever again.

But Fate was kind, and each day revealed more of the world he had lost. He had to be careful; bright lights hurt and using his eye even for ten minutes was a strain. In those minutes he absorbed every impression he could get; the faces of people about him; colour, which was everywhere. Such colours; the curtains in his room were yellow, patterned with blue. He could see the roses in the vase by his bed.

They removed the bandages at night, and he lay like a child, staring at the shape of his hand; at the nails on his fingers, at the pattern on his pyjamas; at the dimly seen shapes on his bedside table.

He would not tell Mara yet, just in case it didn't last. She rang him daily and they brought the trolley to his bed, with the phone upon it. He could talk to young Dave, whose only response was a crow of delight at hearing his father's voice.

The dogs were well. They all missed him. Andrew and Tom Hastings drove down to visit him, but saw his eyes bandaged and he did not tell them. Fortune was too chancy; luck didn't last. He had become edgy and superstitious, looking for omens. If he didn't tell a secret, then it came true. Not otherwise.

If there was a letter for him today then he'd always be able to see.

If they brought him an egg for breakfast, then he would be able to see.

There wasn't a letter and breakfast was bacon and sausages. He realized he was being absurd but it didn't help.

Each day brought a widening of his horizons.

And then came the day when the curtains were drawn, and he stood back from the window, looking at a riot of colours in the garden, dizzying his senses. Bright flowers and trees; people in gay dresses; yellow against green against blue. He couldn't bear it and had to turn away, had to draw the curtains and reduce the light. Had to close his eyes and welcome blindness again for the moment. Shaking, he sat in the chair, staring at the closed curtains, unable to believe his luck, wondering if his eye would ever be able to stand bright sunlight. They brought him dark glasses.

With those, he braved the world, and discovered that he had lost his sense of balance; nothing seemed in the right place; distance had begun to play tricks on him. Steps were steeper or shallower than he thought; tables further away; perspective had vanished. Walking among people, he was constantly terrified at the speed with which they walked towards him, sure they would bump into him, bewildered by their presence. Once more he longed for The Nunneries and to be away from the town.

The days passed.

Anna wrote and he could read her letter for himself. She now had a blind soldier staying with her. Martin had been injured by a bomb in Ireland. He played the piano, and Anna had bought a secondhand one and was wondering if she would take lessons too. Martin thought he might teach music.

Dave wrote. Sue's mother had died, and Sue was now living at the Centre. They were engaged. A happy ending at last. Steve was glad; he had almost been in love with Sue himself. She had done so much for him. He and Mara would be able to go to the wedding. He would see Sue; and Anna; see the places that had been so familiar and yet would now be strange; see Gunter; see Scott and Roz; he would see Sukie; see his baby.

He would see Gemma; and see Lig again. Gemma was as important to him now as Lig had ever been; more important because she had brought him a new way of life; and their partnership was total. He had known nothing like it, even with Lig. It was so different.

And then realization hit him.

He no longer needed the dog. And because it cost so much to train dogs for the blind, she would have to leave him, have to go to a new owner, have to learn to obey someone else. To lead a stranger.

It was worse than losing Lig. This was for ever.

He had been so dependent on her, all this time; she had been the perfect partner; had her own small ways, coming to him last thing at night for a snippet of cheese, pawing him when she felt it time to go out; bringing her harness to him at the right time each day, as he walked the hill with Hennessey and talked sheep.

And the baby adored the dog. Lig was not fond of children and sat aloof, but Gemma allowed herself to be used as a pillow; or to be crawled over, mothering the child.

If he pretended he couldn't see ...

But he couldn't do that.

He didn't mind losing a dog to death, but he couldn't bear

to think of her with someone else, perhaps someone who wouldn't be gentle enough, would frighten her; she hated harsh voices. He had re-taught himself through her to understand a much softer dog than Lig. He had learned so much through her.

Almost he wished that he had not regained his sight. Mara would miss Gemma too; she was so much part of their home; had been now for more than three years. He couldn't imagine life without her.

It wasn't possible to tell anyone else his fears for his dog. Dave would understand; and Sue; but the people in the hospital were not animal minded; he was an alien in a city again, unable to make anyone understand how much his life meant to him; he would be out on the hills with the sheep again; be able to see Lig, but Lig now was older and slower and hadn't worked the sheep for two years. Hennessey was training a new young pup; Ruch hadn't taken over yet; his day was still to come.

It was necessary to rethink the whole of his life; impossible to believe he could take up the thread he had lost four years before; could restart on a different basis; would no longer be dependent on Mara for so much. He sat in the darkened room, but walked to the window, and stared out at the trees bending in the wind; looked up at the sky, at the cloud banks, lined with light. Light. Starlight, and he stood at the window, dazzled even in dark glasses, too fascinated to sleep, seeing the bright pinpoints of distant suns, seeing the slim shape of the slender moon, on edge above him, glittering coldly; starlight and moonlight.

There were other lights; the flowers held reflected light; shimmering through fragile petals. He sat with a rose in front of him, seeing the fine lines on each separate part of the flower; the green shiny stem; the shape of the thorns. He picked up a book and looked at the print, seeing words form, seeing reading as a possibility again; looking at the headlines in the paper; staring bemused at the pattern on the wallpaper in his room, seeing shapes and symbols.

He walked in the gardens, his eyes covered by smoked glass, and sat on a bench, watching birds dart about the grass; seeing a cat slink out of the bushes and sit and wash itself, seeing it newly for the first time, an amazing creature, so supple that it seemed impossible it could move its legs in such a way. It came to rub against him and purr at his caressing hand, and then strolled slowly away. Sunlight bronzed the tortoiseshell fur.

He wanted to sit and look for ever.

Yet behind the excitement was sadness, because Gemma would have to go.

Morning has broken, like the first morning.

The words beat into his head. Poetry had come to mean a great deal to him while he was blind because the words conveyed such vivid images. More so than any prose. Mara had read to him nightly.

He rediscovered shadows. He had forgotten all about shadows; perhaps had been so used to them he rarely noticed them, but now he watched his as it stretched in front of him, or suddenly dwarfed itself, or was thrown against walls.

How could people live amongst such incredible sights and not notice them?

There were patterns on the floor; there were flowers in the corridors; there were textures; he had used his fingers to tell silk from wool; sacking from calico; cotton from nylon. Now he could see the fabrics; see the rich folds of velvet in the curtains in the hospital chapel; see the embroidery on the altar cloth. He walked up to look at it; at silver birds and golden flowers; at the minute stitches that someone with eyes had spent hours making. The chaplain, watching him, wondered how it felt to regain sight.

'I can't believe it,' Steve said, a few minutes later, turning to find the man behind him.

'God does sometimes allow miracles to happen,' the chaplain said.

The miracles continued. He looked at green lawns; at clouds breaking overhead, outlined in brilliance from a hidden sun; at the bare brown newly-dug earth of a flowerbed; at the shapes of trees, and the rough bark, the twisted branches; and then the rich autumn colours he thought he would never see again.

One day he might drive again but not for a long time. Traffic was terrifying.,

And then he was going home, again by train and alone, but this time, only the dark glasses shading the light, seeing the people on the platform, reading the notices, seeing a pretty girl turn and smile at him, seeing the way up the steps and into the carriage; walking along the swaying corridor to eat a meal, this time alone, remembering the woman who had bred Collies.

Seeing the names on the stations. Seeing Mara standing on the platform, waiting for him. She had left the baby with Andrew and Nettie and come alone. She was watching for him, her face anxious, and he could only stand and look at her; see the changes made by four years; she was not so slim now, and there were grey hairs, just a few, and her eyes were tired, but she was smiling up at him, unable to believe the truth.

Driving home, seeing again the places he knew; stopping by the loch, to look up at the mountains; the white clouds soaring, and the waves white-capped; berries on the rowans; he had forgotten those; and forgotten the gulls soaring above the water, skimming over the wave tops, diving for the fish.

Then he was back at High Hollows and Andrew and Nettie were greeting him and he could see the changes in them; he went to find the picture he had given his mother, to look at it, to absorb it, and then went to look at his small son, who, quite unaware of any change in his father, promptly pulled himself up against his leg and swarmed onto his knee.

He was dark-haired like his mother with Andrew's intense blue eyes; he was laughing, wriggling, pushing, wanting to be on the floor with the cats. Steve couldn't eat; he was too engrossed in seeing. It might only last for a few days, or a few months; he wanted to store memories; he felt as if time would not wait for him, that there wasn't enough time to see all the things he had forgotten about. He was mesmerized by a buttered scone.

The old dresser and the willow pattern plates. The kittens, sprawling on the pegged rag hearth rug; there were new cushions and different curtains. There was the cuckoo clock, gay with paint; and the old workbasket that had been part of his childhood, shabby and battered now; and the tin tray with the picture of two Shires pulling a plough.

Mara was dressed in blue and his mother in green. Andrew's tie was heavily patterned in reds and golds; the firelight flickered on the walls and reflected in eyes, tiny fires blazing wherever he looked.

There was a calendar; a grey moth lying among yellow flowers; it was held on the wall by two dark blue drawing pins; above it was a picture of horses drinking; greeny-white horses against a dark blue ground; and beyond that the photos of his family's dogs; old Loo, and little Panda; and the three Collies that had dominated most of his boyhood. And then came again the knowledge that Gemma would have to go.

It was time to go back to The Nunneries; and there all over again was too much to take in; the garden; the wall and the fruit trees; the hills soaring high and his sheep moving on them; Lig running to greet him and thrusting against him and behind him the little bitch that had made his life bearable, and that he had never seen.

She raced to him, flinging herself against him, taking his wrist in her mouth; and then ran off again, to return with her harness.

Steve knelt to look at her; at the golden fur, curling softly over her shoulders; she was more Retriever than Labrador. Her head was beautiful, her ears long and her expression wise. Her tail was plumed. She was obviously not pure bred, but the result of the cross was far prettier than Steve had imagined. Lig butted him, jealous. He stroked the Collie.

'We don't need that any more,' he said, and laid the harness aside, and fetched a lead. She had asked for a walk. He whistled to Lig and walked down to the loch and sat there, staring at the rippling water, at the shadows around him, at the shapes of the leaves on the bushes. He scooped up a handful of sand and looked at it; and then looked at the old donkey that came to regard him solemnly over the wall. He had never known that that was there. The pebbles around him were incredible; gemlike in the evening sun.

There were ferns and the heather was now only a memory of bloom. A bird walked by the water's edge. He released Gemma and she and Lig played a solemn game on the sandy beach. Lig would miss her too, Steve realized. He had come to greet the bitch first thing in the morning; greeting her before he greeted Steve. They went everywhere together.

He turned and looked up the hillside. Mara was standing in the doorway of the farmhouse, waving. Supper was ready. He could be called now from a distance. No need for her to look for him. He waved back, and walked uphill. He should have been elated, but as he watched the bitch running in front of him, he was aware only of misery. He wondered how long they would let him keep her now.

Dave knew that he could see. He had written an enthusiastic letter, but he hadn't mentioned Gemma. They would have to write and tell the Riot Squad. Some of them would remember him though they were probably all in different classes now. Mara had kept up a long and sometimes hilarious correspondence with several of the children.

Perhaps he could pay for another Guide Dog to be trained; but £750 was a lot of money and they needed it for the farm.

The days that followed were all tinged with regret; the day would come, but it hadn't come yet.

And then came Dave's letter.

He and Sue were coming north. Could they stay for a little while. And he was sorry, but he'd have to take Gemma. He was sure Steve knew.

Not even Sukie's new kittens would make up for her loss.

Steve watched her run to Lig, and then come bounding over to him to greet him, bringing a present, as Sam had brought presents; her Retriever blood was uppermost. She had one of the baby's slippers in her mouth.

He took it from her and sat by the fire, watching the leaping flames. The baby was asleep.

'A penny for them,' Mara said, watching him.

He handed her Dave's letter.

'Oh, Steve. Did you know?'

Steve nodded.

'I didn't think of it. Must they take her?'

'They'll have to take her,' Steve said. 'All that money invested in her.'

'They'd have lost her if she died,' Mara said.

'But she isn't dead.'

He didn't want to discuss it any more. He dreaded Dave's visit; he knew Lig would fret.

And then, when Dave and Sue had gone, taking Gemma with them, he found a new hazard. Neither he nor Mara had realized that the baby would fret for the bitch. She had been his companion for over a year; she played with him and guarded him, whereas Lig avoided him. And now the baby had no dog. He cried for Gemma; his first word had been Gemma; and he was desolate.

Steve almost wished he hadn't regained his sight.

But he still had Lig. And Lig missed Gemma too, hunting the house for her, sitting at last with his head on Steve's knee, dismayed by the fact that now the bitch had vanished from his life, just as Steve kept vanishing.

Steve stroked the dog's head, wishing one could explain to a dog—but a dog's world was all unfathomable mystery.

'I miss her too, fella,' he said.

Lig sighed, half wagged his tail, and curled on the rug, staring at the flames as if they could answer him.

Chapter 18

Steve's second operation was successful too. He was still afraid; afraid that this was only temporary; that one day the light would die and he would be in the dark again. So much had changed. He had changed; he had learned patience; learned to wait; and now he was learning to watch.

Mara and Hennessey both knew he could never time a job; he was constantly diverted, pausing to stare, at the daisies starring the grass; he had forgotten daisies; white petals and yellow eyes; there were so many flowers; blossom on the hedges; a lamb skipping in the sun; he stopped to look and was lost, revelling in sight, a man new born.

Oddly, they shared his renewal, both of them seeing the world in a new light, learning from Steve; learning with the baby, who also revelled in sight, finding the world entrancing, especially made for him.

Dave and Sue were getting married; Steve and Mara were invited. They would stay with Anna if they came. Mara's mother wanted to have the baby; Hennessey would mind the farm. There were no problems. They decided to travel by train; it would save Mara the strain of driving and Steve could not bear the motorways and the traffic that surrounded him, or the dazzle at night. Even now distances were sometimes deceptive and the hurtling lorries appeared to be coming straight at them; he could not believe they would miss and sat with clenched hands, holding on to his seat belt, remembering the wall that had suddenly come towards him and blotted out light.

The journey was exciting; all discovery. The drab towns gave way to the moors; the Lakeland mountains soared towards the sky, the sun shining, reminding Steve of days spent with Lig, challenging the other sheep men; Lig was past that now and the urge to compete had vanished. He was content to sit back and watch. Steve could not take his eyes from the window; wishing once again that he could draw and record for ever the perfection of a tree in full leaf; the silver blossom on a pear tree; the sweeping mane of a horse that matched its paces briefly against the train.

He wondered at the people who sat, staring into vacancy, or read their papers or a book while the world unreeled itself outside the window, every moment bringing new breathtaking aspects. Cloud on the hills, the shadows racing, and the trees bowing in the wind. The fields of sheep and lambs, other men's satisfaction, none as good as his.

And then they had arrived and Anna was to meet them and he looked at the people standing by the barrier, wondering which of them would come forward; she was taller than he had imagined and her hair was greyer; her eyes were as kind as he had pictured; and she could not help staring at him or suddenly seizing him and kissing him, saying 'Oh Steve!' in a voice that told him everything.

He remembered that other journey. The car drove through drab suburbs, and left Manchester behind. It was like every other city; glass and supermarkets; nothing memorable anywhere. Through the suburbs where there were more trees than he had expected, and old houses, now turned into flats, and then through a small and ugly town, and into the countryside, down a winding lane, to a comfortable cottage farmhouse.

Here he had lived for almost a year and he knew none of it. He stared at red brick walls and a bay window, looking over a small garden; walked to the gate, to be greeted by the barking dogs. They were leaping at the wire of the kennel compounds, greeting Anna and warning him in the same moment.

The sitting-room was smaller than he had imagined; there was the table which he had bumped against so painfully and often; and the leaping fire, wood burning to greet him; Anna's piano in the corner, music ready for her to play. Her last guest had left and her new one was due next week. Dave had planned his wedding carefully, between courses. They would have a whole week to themselves before starting the new people with their new dogs. Perhaps Gemma would be one of the dogs. She would have had to be re-trained. Steve could not ask about her.

He walked out into the yard; to visit the goat and a new kid; to look at the mare and her foal. It was years since he'd seen a foal. He watched it bolt round the meadow, enjoying the sunshine and then stop by its mother's side, watching him suspiciously. The new-growing mane stood up on end; the tail was a tuft tail; the spindly legs were too long for the body; the sun shone on the chestnut coat, burnishing it to brilliance, and the brown eyes watched him.

Mara and Anna in their turn watched Steve exploring, pausing to take in the shape of the buildings, their relationship to one another; the lie of the land; to stand at the puppy kennel and watch the tumbling black and gold sprawling bodies; the pups were almost ready to sell.

'It must be like being born again,' Anna said.

'Four years of dark. He wakes at night, sometimes, crying out that it's so dark again; that he can't see. I give him a nightlight now,' Mara said. 'I started it when Davey began to wake in the dark and cry; do you think they can inherit thought and fear? I used to try and picture Steve's world; suppose I passed it on?'

'You couldn't,' Anna said. 'It will take time; but perhaps you never lose the excitement; we take it all for granted, and forget to look. Sometimes when Martin was here, I seemed to catch his thoughts; he was much bitterer than Steve;

Steve at least knew he had given his sight to save lives, which may have helped; Martin only knew his had been taken away by idiots, for no reason at all except hate. He, and Steve, and Sue, have all made me look at things. And know how lucky I am.'

Steve explored all morning, finding out things he had never known. He went back to play with the pups and watch them explore in their turn; watched them savour the air for food; watched a tiny bitch find a bone bigger than herself and growl at the rest of the litter as she struggled to chew it; watched the mother stretch, lift her pup nonchalantly and take the bone for herself. He would never tire of looking.

At lunchtime Gunter came in for his meal and Steve gasped as he looked at the old man, and then laughed.

'And what's so funny?' Gunter demanded.

'I thought you were small; about five foot tall; and very thin.'

'Is that what I sound like?' Gunter grinned and tapped his vast stomach; all his chins wobbled as he laughed. 'The thin man inside me trying to get out.'

He rumbled at intervals as he ate; Steve remembered Gunter's curious laugh; a wheezing sound that at first had been very difficult to identify as laughter. Gunter was vast; six foot of him, run to fat, red-faced, bright-eyed, enjoying himself enormously, now that he could help Anna.

Steve walked down the lane, looking at the ruts and potholes, remembering the difficulty he had had, remembering being caught in the brambles; seeing the giant blackberry, and staring at the huge thorns, wondering that he had got off so lightly. They could have seared across his face and torn his skin to ribbons.

He found his way to Scott's house, arriving just as surgery ended. Scott was older than he had thought, grey-haired, and tall and chunkily built; Roz was younger, small and delicately made, her hair cut shorter than most men's today; her movements quicksilver fast as she brought out sherry to toast his new-found sight; and Scott took him on a tour of inspection, watching Steve's face as he discovered places he had known well, yet only known in the dark.

The Flatcot was older now and steadier; she greeted Steve, obviously remembering him, once she had sniffed his fingers.

'Ever used her for shooting?' Steve asked.

'He's never even used a gun; he bought a camera last year; I think he took a few pictures once,' Roz said. 'Now we're thinking of buying a tent and touring the Continent. So far I've stopped him; we'll never go.'

'I might surprise you one day,' Scott said.

'One day the blind might see,' Roz answered, and then caught her lip between her teeth. 'I wasn't thinking. I'm sorry, Steve.'

'Why?' Steve asked. 'This blind man can see; you've no idea what it's like. Nothing will ever be the same again. I can't get used to it; look at your calendar. Flamingoes. I'd forgotten what they looked like; they're so absurd, with those stiltlike legs and swollen knees and flat feet, and the bodies of swans on top of them; and pink; it's an unnatural colour for a bird. And the other day I saw a kestrel hovering; I'd forgotten how extraordinary it is, to see him there, poised on the air, not moving, his tail fanned, and then soaring away. And the owl, with its silent wings, slowly quartering the field. I never get anything done; I can't stop looking.'

'We should all look more,' Scott said, when Steve had gone. 'We take too much for granted, all the time.'

None of them had realized that Steve would bring a new quality into the wedding ceremony; his excitement at colour, at Sue's fragile beauty, at Dave's appearance, was only half hidden; it spilled over in an elation that infected all of them. Dave's mother, introduced to Steve, sat listening to him enthralled as he talked of the things around him, his excitement bubbling out.

Everything had a sharpness to it, reflected by Steve's eyes; his head moved constantly, looking at the restaurant where once before he had eaten; at the food, as if he had never seen food in his life before, almost reluctant to spoil the colours and the shapes; the wine gave his tongue a quick edge, so that he did not mind commenting on his new-found discoveries, holding the glass to the light, eloquent about the colour of the champagne, the world seen through the wine, the shimmer on the surface of the glass.

It was a memorable meal.

Later they went with Dave and Sue back to the Centre.

Dave showed Steve round the place, empty now, except for the dogs in their kennels; some in training; some yet pups, to go to the puppy walkers; newly brought over from Anna's house. It was hard to look at them and remember Gemma. She must have gone to her new owner now.

'Remember this?' Dave asked. 'Your first contact with your Guide Dog. Come into the kennel and see what it's like.'

There was another dog in the kennel now. A dog that reminded him of Gemma, very like her indeed to look at. He stood, watching the sleeping animal. She had not heard them come to the doorway.

'I remember,' Steve said, wishing he could forget.

The dog was electrified. She leaped up and ran at the door, and Dave opened it and she was hurtling herself at Steve, groaning and crying, licking his hand, leaping up at his face.

'It's Gemma. Gemma, Gemma,' Steve said, and knelt to her, holding her.

'I wish you hadn't,' he said, a moment later. 'It isn't fair on either of us.'

'I've a problem,' Dave said. 'I don't know what you did to her, but she's useless to us. No one can handle her. Tell her what to do and she cringes; she can't bear being spoken to in command; and she's traffic shy. Useless in a town. You never took her to town, did you?'

'Not for four years,' Steve said.

'How do you talk to her?' Dave asked. 'What words do you use? Did you change the commands?'

Steve looked down at the bitch; she gazed up at him, waiting.

He flicked a finger and at once she was beside him, sitting, waiting for the harness, her face expectant. He moved his hand, and she went down, lying across his foot so that he knew she had obeyed. He moved his left hand and she sat leaning against his leg, waiting for him. A tiny hiss between his lips and she was walking with him, down the path, to turn again, and at the silent command, to sit, waiting till he was ready for her.

'I couldn't get my voice right,' Steve said. 'So Hennessey helped me work on signals. He said the words and I used the signals and he told me if she obeyed. We worked out a lot of things together.'

'She's no future here. Will you take her back?'

She had been his second self; his eyes and his saving sanity. Without her he still felt lost. He had never had such a close relationship with any other dog. Not even one of his wonderful Collies; not even Lig, who was still his dog—in a totally different way.

'Or are you still a Collie man?' Dave asked.

Steve put his hand on the golden head. Brown eyes looked up at him, knowing he could now see her; they had to build a new relationship.

'Not any more,' Steve said. 'I'm learning. All the time. She can do things that Lig could never have done for me; and he can do things that she would find impossible. And I no longer need to master a dominant dog. Lig's mellowed too.'

He turned to walk back to the car, where Mara was waiting.

'Four years in the dark; it changes a man,' he said.

Dave watched him walk away, Gemma by his side.

Steve turned.

'There's a debt to pay. I can sing now; I'll sing till I've bought you another dog to replace Gemma.'

'The Riot Squad bought her for you; maybe it's as well she goes back,' Dave said.

'They'll be able to see her when they visit us,' Steve said. 'There's going to be a well-worn trail from the States to our farm; Mara's asked all the kids over, one by one. We're going to be busy.'

A few weeks later, he recalled his words as he climbed the hill. One of the children was due that day. Mara had gone to the airport to meet her. His mother had come to look after the baby. Nettie had a new lease of life as a grandmother. It was just what she had needed.

There was a blustery wind blowing and it was good to be

alive. He looked down the hill at the field below him, busy with new lambs; at the clouds above him sweeping across the peaks; at Lig, grey-muzzled now, walking sedately beside him, enjoyment in every muscle, tail waving happily. Beyond him, her eyes always on Steve, was Gemma, her plumed tail waving happily too. She nosed Lig and the two dogs bounded up the hillside, and then Gemma rolled in submission and the Collie licked her face.

Steve sat to eat his midday snack.

He was on top of the world and would not change places with any man.

A sunbeam fingered the cloud and he watched it touch the ground, so that every blade of grass was soaked in light.

He whistled his dogs and they came and stood beside him, waiting till he had looked his fill, knowing without understanding that he spent much of his time watching unseen wonders that did not shadow their horizons, always willing to wait.

He walked down the hill, still whistling, and walked into the house, to be greeted by his son running to meet him. He swung the baby high, laughing, and bent to kiss Nettie and squeeze her shoulders.

'It's a great world,' he said. He paused to look at the tea table, at the mundane food, at bread, and fresh butter, at the yellow sponge of the cake, the red jam between the slices; at the baby's blue bowl, filled with creamy banana and yellow custard.

Nothing would ever look the same again.

For a moment he was back in darkness. He put out his hand, and Gemma nosed it, restoring him to the world.

'Steve?' his mother's voice was anxious.

'I was remembering,' Steve said. 'Dr Johnson said, "We all know what light is; but it's not easy to *tell* what it is." He couldn't have been more right!'

And then the quiet was shattered by the sound of Mara's car stopping and the quick footsteps and excited voice of Wistar, the first of their Riot Squad visitors, and there was no more time to think.

The room was full of noise and laughter and then came

the bark of the dogs, as they raced in to see the visitor.

'Is that Gemma? Isn't she beautiful?'

Mara looked across the room, and answered Steve's smile with her eyes.

CASEY BY JOYCE STRANGER
The touching story of a cat with a difference.

Life at Wayman's Corner could never be dull. Crises lurked around every corner...marital friction, careless city visitors, farmyard accidents, and Casey.

Casey, son of a Siamese tomcat and a black farmcat, was an animal with great determination, strong affections, and a nose for mischief, whose strange friendship with Sultan, the terrifying Jersey bull, becomes a central part of life on the farm...

0 552 10125 7   65p

KYM BY JOYCE STRANGER

Joyce Stranger's novels have become well-loved favourites with all age groups. Her first non-fiction book is sure to take its place among them.

Kym is the autobiography of her Siamese cat who, for thirteen years, adored her, dominated her, and played havoc with her life. A more accident-prone cat never lived. Even on holiday he managed to turn their caravan into an ambulance—or a peep-show. A born eccentric and voluble talker, a cat with the grace of a dancer and the instincts of a prizefighter.

An endearing story of the misadventures of a unique pet, seen through Kym's blue-eyed squint, and his owner's humorous and observant eyes.

0 552 10695 X   70p

A SELECTED LIST OF FINE NOVELS THAT APPEAR IN CORGI

WHILE EVERY EFFORT IS MADE TO KEEP PRICES LOW, IT IS SOMETIMES NECESSARY TO INCREASE PRICES AT SHORT NOTICE. CORGI BOOKS RESERVE THE RIGHT TO SHOW AND CHARGE NEW RETAIL PRICES ON COVERS WHICH MAY DIFFER FROM THOSE ADVERTISED IN THE TEXT OR ELSEWHERE.

THE PRICES SHOWN BELOW WERE CORRECT AT THE TIME OF GOING TO PRESS (JULY, 79)

☐ 09475 7	A Raging Calm	Stan Barstow	60p
☐ 11202 X	The Tide of Life	Catherine Cookson	£1·25
☐ 10450 7	The Gambling Man	Catherine Cookson	95p
☐ 08419 0	The Fifteen Streets	Catherine Cookson	85p
☐ 08444 1	Maggie Rowan	Catherine Cookson	85p
☐ 09035 2	The Invitation	Catherine Cookson	85p
☐ 09074 3	Love and Mary Ann	Catherine Cookson	85p
☐ 09075 1	Life and Mary Ann	Catherine Cookson	85p
☐ 09076 X	Marriage and Mary Ann	Catherine Cookson	70p
☐ 08538 3	Katie Mulholland	Catherine Cookson	£1.25
☐ 08849 8	The Glass Virgin	Catherine Cookson	£1.00
☐ 11203 8	The Dwelling Place	Catherine Cookson	£1.25
☐ 09318 1	Feathers in the Fire	Catherine Cookson	£1.00
☐ 09373 4	Our Kate	Catherine Cookson	95p
☐ 11205 4	The Slow Awakening	Catherine Marchant	£1.00
☐ 09796 0	House of Men	Catherine Marchant	85p
☐ 10074 9	The Fen Tiger	Catherine Marchant	85p
☐ 10375 6	Csardas	Diane Pearson	£1.25
☐ 10249 0	Bride of Tancred	Diane Pearson	70p
☐ 10271 7	The Marigold Field	Diane Pearson	95p
☐ 10414 0	Sarah Whitman	Diane Pearson	£1.25
☐ 09462 5	Lakeland Vet	Joyce Stranger	70p
☐ 09891 4	Chia the Wild Cat	Joyce Stranger	70p
☐ 09893 0	Breed of Giants	Joyce Stranger	85p
☐ 09892 2	Zara	Joyce Stranger	80p

All these books are available at your book shop or newsagent, or can be ordered direct from the publisher. Just tick the titles you want and fill in the form below.

A SELECTED LIST OF CRIME FICTION PUBLISHED BY CORGI

WHILE EVERY EFFORT IS MADE TO KEEP PRICES LOW, IT IS SOMETIMES NECESSARY TO INCREASE PRICES AT SHORT NOTICE. CORGI BOOKS RESERVE THE RIGHT TO SHOW AND CHARGE NEW RETAIL PRICES ON COVERS WHICH MAY DIFFER FROM THOSE ADVERTISED IN THE TEXT OR ELSEWHERE.

THE PRICES SHOWN BELOW WERE CORRECT AT THE TIME OF GOING TO PRESS (JULY '79)

☐	11043 4	Trusted Like The Fox	*James Hadley Chase* 75p
☐	11042 6	Consider Yourself Dead	*James Hadley Chase* 75p
☐	10991 6	The Doll's Bad News	*James Hadley Chase* 75p
☐	10922 3	The Paw in the Bottle	*James Hadley Chase* 65p
☐	10877 4	Why Pick On Me?	*James Hadley Chase* 65p
☐	10876 6	My Laugh Comes Last	*James Hadley Chase* 65p
☐	10817 0	A Plague of Demons	*John Creasey* 65p
☐	10992 4	Executioner 33: Monday's Mob	*Don Pendleton* 75p
☐	10923 1	The Executioner 32: Tennessee Smash	*Don Pendleton* 65p
☐	10830 8	The Executioner 31: Arizona Ambush	*Don Pendleton* 65p
☐	11076 0	The Destroyer 30: Mugger Blood	*Richard Sapir & Warren Murphy* 75p
☐	11025 6	The Destroyer 29: The Final Death	*Richard Sapir & Warren Murphy* 75p
☐	10960 6	The Destroyer 28: Ship of Death	*Richard Sapir & Warren Murphy* 65p
☐	10901 0	The Destroyer 27: The Last Temple	*Richard Sapir & Warren Murphy* 65p
☐	10945 2	Tumbleweed	*Janwillem Van De Wetering* 85p
☐	10947 9	Corpse on the Dike	*Janwillem Van De Wetering* 95p
☐	10948 7	Death of a Hawker	*Janwillem Van De Wetering* 85p

All these books are available at your bookshop or newsagent, or can be ordered direct from the publisher. Just tick the titles you want and fill in the form below.

CORGI BOOKS, Cash Sales Department, P.O. Box 11, Falmouth, Cornwall.

Please send cheque or postal order, no currency.

U.K. send 25p for first book plus 10p per copy for each additional book ordered to a maximum charge of £1.05p to cover the cost of postage and packing.

B.F.P.O. and Eire allow 25p for first book plus 10p per copy for the next 8 books, thereafter 5p per book.

Overseas Customers. Please allow 40p for the first book and 12p per copy for each additional book.

Name (Block letters) . . . .

Address . . . .

. . . .